NEW YORK REVIEW BOOKS
CLASSICS

T0014065

WOMAN RUNNING IN THE MOUNTAINS

YŪKO TSUSHIMA (1947–2016) was born in Mitaka, Tokyo, the youngest daughter of Michiko Tsushima and the novelist Osamu Dazai, who committed suicide when she was only a year old. Until she was twenty-two, Tsushima was educated at the Catholic Shirayuri College, where she earned a bachelor's degree in English. That same year, she briefly attended graduate school at Meiji University and published her first short story in the prestigious literary magazine *Mita Bungaku*. Her debut story collection, *Shaniku-sai* (*Carnival*), appeared two years later, marking the beginning of a prolific literary career, which would eventually comprise more than forty collections and novels, including *Child of Fortune* (1978), *Territory of Light* (1979), *To High Noon* (1988), and *Mountain of Fire* (1998). Much of her fiction draws on the literature and mythology of premodern Japan, as well as on her own experience as a single mother in Tokyo, where she lived for most of her life. Widely considered one of the most important Japanese writers of her generation, Tsushima was awarded the Kawabata Prize, the Yomiuri Prize, and the Tanizaki Prize. Her work has been translated into more than a dozen languages.

GERALDINE HARCOURT (1952–2019) was a translator of modern Japanese literature. Born in Auckland, New Zealand, she lived in Japan for much of her life. There, she developed a close working relationship with Yūko Tsushima and translated five works by her, including *Territory of Light* and *The Shooting Gallery*.

LAUREN GROFF is the author of the novels *Matrix*, *Fates and Furies*, *Arcadia*, and *The Monsters of Templeton*, and two short-story collections, *Florida* and *Delicate Edible Birds*. She is a two-time National Book Award finalist and was a 2018 Guggenheim Fellow. Her books have been translated into more than thirty languages. She lives in Gainesville, Florida.

WOMAN RUNNING IN THE MOUNTAINS

YŪKO TSUSHIMA

Translated from the Japanese by
GERALDINE HARCOURT

Introduction by
LAUREN GROFF

NEW YORK REVIEW BOOKS

New York

THIS IS A NEW YORK REVIEW BOOK
PUBLISHED BY THE NEW YORK REVIEW OF BOOKS
435 Hudson Street, New York, NY 10014
www.nyrb.com

Originally published in Japan as *Yama o hashiru onna* by Kodansha Ltd in 1980.
First published as a New York Review Book Classic in 2022.

Library of Congress Cataloging-in-Publication Data
Names: Tsushima, Yūko, author. | Harcourt, Geraldine, translator.
Title: Woman running in the mountains / by Yūko Tsushima ; translated by
  Geraldine Harcourt ; introduction by Lauren Groff.
Other titles: Yama o hashiru onna. English
Description: New York : New York Review Books, [2022] | Series: New York
  Review Books classics
Identifiers: LCCN 2021029323 (print) | LCCN 2021029324 (ebook) | ISBN
  9781681375977 (paperback) | ISBN 9781681375984 (ebook)
Classification: LCC PL862.S76 Y3613 2022 (print) | LCC PL862.S76 (ebook) |
  DDC 895.63/5—dc23
LC record available at https://lccn.loc.gov/2021029323
LC ebook record available at https://lccn.loc.gov/2021029324

ISBN 978-1-68137-597-7
Available as an electronic book; ISBN 978-1-68137-598-4

Printed in the United States of America on acid-free paper.
10 9 8 7 6 5 4 3 2

CONTENTS

INTRODUCTION

AT DAWN one hot August morning, a young woman in labor walks down a dim alleyway in Tokyo. Her name is Takiko Odaka, and she is unmarried and determined to make her way to the hospital alone. When she stops to let a contraction pass, "The pain made her think of the pressure of ocean depths. She had heard that when a deep-sea fish is hauled rapidly to the surface the change in pressure causes its body to blow up and burst like a balloon. She felt exactly as if such a deep-sea fish were in her belly. It seemed to want to bring all the surrounding pressure to bear on its small body until it hardened and sank, deeper and deeper. She must stay quite still and withstand the pressure or her own body would be sucked down by it too." Takiko waits patiently until the pain leaves her, then she strides on. Within moments, she is repaid for her endurance with great beauty: "As she turned to the right, all of her was bathed in the direct light of the morning sun for the first time that day. It was a dazzling light. The city streets spread out at her feet and the dawn sky spread above, faintly pink... No one was aware of her joy at this instant—not her mother, not her father, not a soul. She didn't think there could be any moment more luxurious than this."

This scene of entangled pain and rapture from the novel *Woman Running in the Mountains* (first published in Japan in 1980 as *Yama o hashiru onna* and translated by Geraldine Harcourt in 1991) could stand as a motif for the larger urgencies that animate Yūko Tsushima's fiction. She wrote again and again of profoundly conflicted maternity and the burden of single motherhood in Japan, during a time when it was rare for women to raise their children alone; she wrote of physical anguish and ecstasy, of troublesome dreams and shimmering, transfiguring light. Her heroines carry their despair around with them, drink too much, sleep with the wrong people, sometimes even deliberately hurt their own children. Still, they always stay afloat, never letting the difficulty of their lives submerge them. In 1989, Tsushima wrote in the *Chicago Tribune* that she loved the work of Tennessee Williams because

> his heroines are dissatisfied with the existing condition and are courageous enough to spring out into a new place no matter how dangerous it may appear from a common-sense judgment. They hate to be self-contained in everyday life. Self-destructive, maybe, but I feel close to their expansionism—going outside to find happiness. Women figures I created in my novels also don't compromise with reality. They may appear stoic, but they are strong enough to search for their own happiness in their own ways.

For many of Tsushima's heroines, this searching seems to emerge out of personality, out of stubbornness and sheer, relentless common sense. In *Woman Running in the Mountains*, Takiko is given something both finer and rarer: a deep sensitivity to beauty and a craving for the kind of freedom she has only ever known indirectly, from her glimpses of other lives, from stories she has been told or has seen in films, from her own wild dreams. Throughout her pregnancy, Takiko has pictured herself "holding a baby lightly to her breast and running at top speed...At school she hadn't actually liked running at all, yet now she couldn't stop seeing this image of herself. It was not that she was running away. She just wanted to be tough and free to move." Takiko's home life is devastating: She is afraid of her physically abusive drunk of a father, of her mother's slow and inexorable illness, of the pain of her baby's hernia, of her debilitating poverty and her inability to get a job while her child is still so young. The only respite she can find is in her own mind.

Because Tsushima frequently wrote what in Japan are called I-novels, otherwise known as *watakushi shōsetsu* or *shishōsetsu*, her biography has often been conflated with her fiction. The I-novel literary genre is a form of autofiction, often told in the first person, arising out of the Meiji period from the late 1860s to the first decades of the twentieth century, when Japan expanded out of feudalism and began opening to global influences. The I-novel emerged from the collision of traditional Japanese diaristic narratives with the Western literary school of naturalism, an extreme mode of realism that sought to extend the nineteenth century's development of the experimental method in science into the "passionate and intellectual life" of literature, as practiced by Émile Zola, who first defined the genre in his essay "The Experimental Novel." Japanese writers and readers were enthralled by intimate access to characters' psychology, and the I-novel became immensely popular.

In Tsushima's work, life and fiction do circle warily, both constantly returning to the same shared places. The primary thread in her work, single motherhood, has a doubled biographical resonance because Tsushima, a single mother, was herself raised by a single mother. She was born in 1947, but never knew her father, the celebrated I-novelist Osamu Dazai, because he committed suicide in 1948; the absent father, or the father who has committed suicide and left his children, is a common refrain in her work. Her fiction is also haunted by the recurrence of a mentally handicapped older brother who dies young, like Tsushima's own beloved brother. Yet a reader should be wary of such conflations, particularly because Tsushima reached for fiction so that she could create an imagined life that would be so vivid and true it would become a new sort of reality. She said, "If I stop writing, I will feel like a kite without a string. I write fiction, but I experience the fiction I write. In that sense, they are not fiction anymore, but reality. That's frightening. Like other novelists, I live a real life and a life as a writer. At times I get confused which is which."

In this light, it feels significant to mention that Yūko Tsushima is in fact a pen name, a way to deliberately delineate the boundaries of her own narrative. She kept her real surname, though it might have been easier for her career as a young novelist to choose Dazai, her father's professional pseudonym; by eschewing it, she turned away from publicly claiming his influence. Though her first name was originally Satoko, Tsushima wrote that "when it came time for me to think of my own pen name, every writer's privilege, I chose Yūko, a simple character, but one which suggests movement toward the outside. And it means happiness." Her pen name is her own small replica of her heroines' stubborn persistence—they who stand outside of society due to their poverty or the choice to bear children out of wedlock, yet who still insist on their own happiness.

Tsushima was only twenty-four and still in college when she published her first short story, and she swiftly became celebrated through her mastery of the form, publishing at least twelve collections before her death in 2016. She also published numerous novels in Japanese, of which four have been translated into English. Like the elegant and recently reissued *Territory of Light*, *Woman Running in the Mountains* began in serialized form, covering a whole year in the life of a struggling mother, a cascade of potentially devastating failures transcended by moments of astonishment. This may seem familiar to anyone who has known the grind and ecstasy of caring for a small child, the way that time folds in on itself, simultaneously a single endless agonizing moment and a span too swift to capture. Yet the two books differ vastly. In *Territory of Light*, the heroine's imagination relentlessly circles back to the difficulty of raising a child as a single mother, turning the text hermetic. Though it is very beautiful, the book's inverted imagination makes it a closed circuit. *Woman Running in the Mountains* has a grandeur to it, a constant flickering outward to the wider world because Takiko, our profoundly unheroic heroine, resolutely holds the space inside herself to dream, to take pleasure in her body, to fall in love, to discover a green place called Misawa Gardens and pursue a job there surrounded by calm and beauty.

It is with great wonder that the reader beholds Takiko, this uneducated and ordinary young woman, who, though exhausted and at her highest pitch of despair, retreats to the cool mountains of her imagination, seeing herself as a girl running "faster, faster. Something in the girl's body echoes like the howl of an animal among the mountains. It sweeps down to the vineyards as a gust of wind. The girl races on and on. When she has run till her body is empty, she stops abruptly and lets her gaze return again to the distant, delicately sparkling world below. Rivers trace silver lines. The sea is in sight. As her eyes follow the coastline, drifting ice appears and expands into a world of white. There's something running freely over that white expanse, its heartbeat reverberating." Over and over, through Takiko's tremendous longing for beauty, through her carefully nurtured imagination, Tsushima in turn gives the reader such astonishing, glittering moments of wonder. *Woman Running in the Mountains* tracks one insignificant person's defiance in the face of the overwhelming darkness of the world. Although its struggles are the drudgery of the domestic, of the kind of maternal pain that is not often taken seriously either in life or in literature, the ferocious truth of this book is that it is out of such smallness that true and daily greatness arises. The result is a book that shines with hope.

—LAUREN GROFF

WOMAN RUNNING IN THE MOUNTAINS

MIDSUMMER

The pain was like a voice calling Takiko's name in her sleep. It was Takiko as a small child who was being called. But soon the voice would go away. This one impression wavered like a pleasant dream inside her sleeping body.

Gradually, though, the voice drew nearer. Her belly began to tremble a little in response. I don't want to wake up.

There's no reason to wake up. With this thought she opened her eyes.

Takiko Odaka was alone in bed in a dark room. One of the floral curtains, the one on the left, was faintly whitened by the street light in the alley. It was night still, as it had been when she'd gone to sleep. Behind the curtains the window was open, as she'd left it, but it gave almost no relief from the heat. Since the end of July the daytime heat had hung stagnant in the air even after nightfall.

Takiko rolled over in bed to escape the stuffy flannel sheet that was clinging to her body. She was suddenly aware that her abdomen was still responding to the voice in her sleep. The pain seemed to be trying to expand. It wasn't like having a full bladder. What was it, then? Dubiously, Takiko laid her hand on her belly. A great heavy belly was there as if it were someone else's. Her whole body emerged all at once from sleep.

She got out of bed and drew back the curtains, then stared at her watch which she kept by the pillow. If this dull pain was really what was known as a contraction she should feel it at regular intervals. So she had been told. It was one week past the date she'd been given at the maternity hospital.

The watch's hands indicated ten minutes to four. Takiko lay with her eyes fixed on them. An hour went by. Outside the window it began to grow light. The pain, though still indistinct, applied a steadily increasing weight on her whole body. It seemed to come at intervals of about ten minutes.

At five-thirty Takiko finally made up her mind and left her bed. She dressed quickly and took from the closet the bag and bundle she'd packed for her stay in the hospital. These she had kept hidden away from her father's sight, and had packed without requiring any assistance at all from her mother. Among other things, they contained a set of clothes to dress the baby in, bought with a sense of uncertainty—would they really be any use?—and yet with the sort of pleasure she might take in buying toys.

Her parents were still asleep in the next room, while in the back room so was her younger brother, who was in high school. As on any other morning, her mother would be the first to rise at six-thirty. She would realize, as soon as she noticed Takiko was gone, that she had set out for the maternity hospital. After phoning the hospital in a near whisper from the room where her parents lay sleeping, Takiko picked up her bags and went outside. It was after six by her watch.

The house faced onto a twisting, narrow alleyway. The neighborhood was one of closely built, old wooden apartments, with alleys ending here and there in culs-de-sac, so that it was difficult for anyone who didn't live there to find a way through. Although Takiko lived in a house, she was actually envious of the apartment tenants, for even in this sunless neighborhood most of the upstairs windows would be bathed in sunlight at some time between morning and evening. After she'd started her job, Takiko had bought a new kerosene heater, a new color TV, and a shower attachment for the bath, but whatever else she might be able to do she couldn't bring the sun's light into the gloomy single-story house.

Takiko walked slowly along the alley. It was in semi-darkness, but overhead the sky was already glowing a brilliant color. The drowsy cry of a lone cicada pulsed in the air nearby. The bag and bundle were quite heavy, as she'd found when she started to walk, and the pain in her belly was growing stronger. Though she wanted to hurry to avoid the neighbors' prying eyes, she had to keep her pace slow. She made her way along the street with her shoulders back and head high. In the three months or more since her size had been noticeable, Takiko had never once walked along the alley with her head down. Even on rainy days, when there were puddles everywhere, she hadn't lowered her eyes. She refused to lower her eyes before "the neighbors"—those people who had made Takiko a sorrow to her mother because her mother cared what they thought. She felt that by holding herself in this way she was directly supporting the fetus inside her.

That same Takiko would not return to the alley, however. The next time she walked down this street, whether or not she was holding a living baby, she certainly wouldn't be the heavy figure she was now. Then, a little while later, she would really leave. With the baby.

For an instant Takiko closed her eyes and pictured herself holding a baby lightly to her breast and running at top speed. This was the way she had gone on imagining herself, while her mother's crying and her father's shouting echoed around her, ever since her mother had found out she was pregnant. At school she hadn't actually liked running at all, yet now she couldn't stop seeing this image of herself. It was not that she was running away. She just wanted to be tough and free to move. A state that knew no emotion. To be allowed to exist without knowing emotion.

She could not yet imagine the feel of a baby against her skin. There was something that moved inside her belly, but it was foreign and unreliable; it could vanish anytime and she wouldn't think it strange. It was Takiko's mother who, in viewing it as such a calamity, had already accepted the baby. Takiko herself had been far more concerned with caring for the growing fetus until the day it emerged naturally from her body, normal in every way. And it looked as if that wish had been granted.

She came out of the alley into a one-way street with a guardrail. There were no cars or people in sight. She turned left. The sky was more brilliant now. Behind the row of houses to her right was this morning's sun. In places the morning light broke dazzlingly across the bluish-tinged asphalt. To reach a main road where she'd be able to find a taxi, she still had to turn right and take the wide street down the hill. Her belly began to hurt again. She put down her bags and stood waiting for it to return to itself. The pain made her think of the pressure of ocean depths. She had heard that when a deep-sea fish is hauled rapidly to the surface the change in pressure causes its body to blow up and burst like a balloon. She felt exactly as if such a deep-sea fish were in her belly. It seemed to want to bring all the surrounding pressure to bear on its small body until it hardened and sank, deeper and deeper. She must stay quite still and withstand the pressure or her own body would be sucked down by it too.

Although it had been her own idea to go alone, she couldn't help feeling a little forlorn. The municipal maternity hospital that she had chosen for the birth was almost an hour away by train. Could she get there in half an hour by taxi? There were private hospitals within walking distance but they were too expensive; and about fifteen minutes by bus from home there was a municipal general hospital which she had tried first of all two months ago, but they told her that they were already fully booked and she couldn't have the baby there. Then she went through the phone book and managed to reserve a place at a maternity hospital in a part of the city where she'd never

been before. The hospital was an old, wooden, two-story building. Behind it there was a dismal park, enclosed like a courtyard
by two-story row houses that were fairly large but even shabbier
than Takiko's own. Wash was hanging in every available space
and there was a clutter of all sorts of junk—a doorless refrigerator, an empty television cabinet, a broken chair, bundles
of newspapers and magazines.

After quitting her job two months ago she had begun having
a checkup at the hospital every two weeks, partly for something
to do. The heat of summer had already come. Once the examination was over she wouldn't feel like going straight home.
Instead she would buy a popsicle or two at a nearby candy
store and take them to enjoy their coldness at leisure in the
park, which never seemed to be in the sun at any time of the
day. There was always an old man, who appeared to be dis-
abled, dozing on a piece of cardboard spread under a tree. No
one paid any attention to Takiko.

Her belly was light again, and her body freed. Picking up
the bag and bundle, she strode ahead. From the one-way street
she came out onto the broad slope. As she turned to the right,
all of her was bathed in the direct light of the morning sun
for the first time that day. It was a dazzling light. The city
streets spread out at her feet and the dawn sky spread above,
faintly pink. The color of a midsummer morning.

Squinting at its brightness, Takiko descended the slope. The
sun was shining directly before her, full onto her body. She
smiled. No one was aware of her joy at this instant—not her
mother, not her father, not a soul. She didn't think there could
be any moment more luxurious than this. The sunlight felt
good on her body. A hot midsummer's day was about to begin.

Lately her mother had taken to saying, with a sigh, whenever she saw her, "I'll go with you. What else can I do, now that it's come to this?" Takiko would turn her face away without answering. She felt no need to argue. She had decided to leave the house alone when the time came to have the baby, and should this turn out to be impossible, she would just have to accept her mother's help. She could no longer shout back, as she had until now, "You've got to be joking—who was it that kept harping about an abortion?" The closer the day approached, the harder she too had found it to stay firm. In case she was forced to seek her mother's help after all, she mustn't give her any reason to say, "There, what'd I tell you? If I wasn't here you'd be stuck, wouldn't you?"

All the same, she did want to set out alone when the time came. Every night she'd gone to bed half praying to something or someone: Please let it happen that way. I want to go without my father or mother knowing. She would go to sleep thinking that tonight would be the night, and wake each morning to yet another disappointment.

What was in Takiko's belly continued to grow without being a joy to anyone. To Takiko it was simply her pregnancy. It seemed entirely natural to her. But this also meant that she didn't want any offers of help.

At one point she'd been ready to leave home sooner than she originally planned—after her father had attacked her once too often with his fists, yelling at her to get out. Her brother, too, had said wearily, "Go on, it'd be better if you did." Her mother, though, had cried aloud and held her back.

"You can't go, not in that condition. Where do you think you would go? You've already brought enough shame on us all. Don't listen to your father, he's as big a fool as you."

When she reached the bottom of the slope her belly tightened and grew heavy again. She put down her bags and, still hunched forward, raised her hand to hail a taxi that happened to be stopped at a traffic light.

The cab drew up in front of her and its automatic door opened. But she couldn't get in. She opened her mouth to speak to the driver but she'd lost her voice. There was nothing to do but smile as best she could.

"Are you all right?"

One look at Takiko, with her bags, and the driver must have summed up the situation. He opened his door and stuck his head out to speak to her. She nodded repeatedly, still smiling. Cautiously, so as not to let the strong pressure that was acting inside her belly overcome her, she attempted to move. She managed to pick up one bag.

"Careful, now." Before she knew it, the taxi driver was behind her, lifting the cloth-wrapped bundle and placing a guiding hand on Takiko's back.

She was barely able to climb into the taxi. The pain was in no hurry to go away. At least there wasn't any more need to move by her own efforts. The taxi would carry her to the maternity hospital and the maternity hospital would handle her according to its established procedures. That dazzling time alone was over. Now that it was gone it seemed all too short.

"Are you sure you're all right? I'm going to start now. I'll drive as gently as I can. But please don't suffer in silence—let me know right away if anything's wrong. If you don't speak up till it's too late, we'll both be in trouble."

Still smiling politely, Takiko nodded to the driver's eyes in the rearview mirror and in a small voice told him the name of the hospital. Then she shut her eyes and sank back without reserve into the soft seat. Her heavy belly seemed to be slowly returning to its original weight. There was nothing to worry about now. She wished she could share her own sense of relief with the taxi driver, who didn't seem at all happy at having landed himself with this one.

"All right back there? It's not affecting you?"

Apart from repeating the same inquiries every so often, he said nothing.

"I'm just fine," Takiko assured him brightly each time.

The streets were empty. The taxi sailed along and they reached the hospital in half the time she'd anticipated without having to speed.

"Thanks for taking so much trouble. That was very quick," Takiko said to the driver as she handed over the fare.

He smiled for the first time. "In another half hour the traffic would've been too heavy. We couldn't have made it so fast. . . . Can you manage your bags?"

"Yes, I'm all right. Thank you, really."

The labor pains would be returning at any moment. Takiko climbed out of the car, clutching her bag and bundle against her chest. As the automatic door swung shut she got her first good look at the driver's face. His small features were those of a man nearing sixty, like her father.

After watching the taxi drive off she turned toward the hospital entrance. The building seemed deserted. No one came out to the street through the glass swinging doors, and there wasn't the usual line of pregnant women waiting inside to present their consultation cards to the receptionist. The old building was completely hushed. The glass doors mirrored the bright morning sky and the houses opposite.

The doors didn't appear to be locked, but was it all right just to go in, on her own? She was uncertain. If only the taxi driver were still there. Remembering, however, that she had telephoned the hospital before leaving home, she timidly pushed open the doors. On the phone a nurselike voice had simply said, "Well, in that case you should come at once. The entrance is unlocked, so go directly upstairs to the nurses' station and give your name. And don't forget to bring your outdoor shoes upstairs with you."

Feeling as if she were sneaking into a stranger's house, Takiko took off her sandals in the deserted entrance and put on a pair of hospital slippers, then, carrying her sandals in her right hand along with the bundle, she headed down the corridor that also served as an outpatients' waiting room. The examination rooms were along the right-hand side, consultation rooms on the left. The corridor was usually lively with expectant mothers and the children that some of them brought along. There was an air conditioner, but it made so little difference that it was far cooler to open both the emergency exits and let a breeze through the corridor. Takiko wasn't the only one who thought so; others too were constantly being scolded by the nurses for leaving the two doors open.

Passing through the quiet, dim corridor, she started up the stairs to the right. She was familiar with the building only as far as this point.

The scene that met her eyes at the top—in striking contrast to the silence downstairs—was the inpatients' bustling early morning. A couple of women in nightgowns were brushing their teeth at the washstand opposite the stairs. Along the corridor, women in cotton bathrobes sat chatting and smoking on benches. In the middle of the corridor stood a large stainless-steel meal wagon to which other women were returning their breakfast trays.

Instantly feeling relaxed and even lighthearted, Takiko went to the nurses' station and gave her name to the little nurse there.

"Let's see . . . Odaka-san, is it?"

After checking Takiko's name in her file of cards the nurse reeled off a list of instructions. Then she went busily away.

Not having taken in very much, Takiko stood outside the office waiting hopefully for the same nurse to come back.

"What are you doing there? Move out of the way, will you?" An older nurse spoke irritably as her wagonload of instruments bumped into Takiko.

"I'm sorry." Startled, she stepped aside and then asked, "Um, what do I do to get admitted?"

The nurse glowered at her. "You're being admitted? Why are you standing around, then? There must be someone at the desk."

"There was, but I didn't understand what I was supposed to do," Takiko replied very apologetically.

"You really should try to pay attention at a time like this. . . . Where are your bags?"

"They're here."

"That's all?"

"Well, yes."

"Didn't someone come with you?"

"No, there's only me."

"Oh. . . . Well, I suppose it can't be helped, then."

She called sharply to another nurse who happened to be going by and placed her in charge of Takiko.

The bed assigned to her was one in a large room at the end of the second-floor corridor. The room had the high ceiling of a lecture hall and nearly thirty beds. Babies' voices echoed, one over another. At the foot of every adult's bed stood a small crib. The curtains surrounding each bed were pulled back and the windows on both sides of the room were open. A cool breeze was blowing across it. Women lying in bed, women breastfeeding their babies, women reading comic books: a great many women were relaxing, each in her own way, while the breeze blew over them.

Takiko hurriedly changed into a new cotton bathrobe and settled into bed. She was evidently going to be called at any moment for an examination, but having come this far by herself she was beginning to feel extremely sleepy. I'll get some sleep first, she thought, and closed her eyes.

Noon came, then night, while Takiko slept on in the same bed.

Late at night, on the doctor's instructions, she received a drip of a labor-inducing drug.

Toward daybreak Takiko heard her own baby's first cry. It was a healthy baby boy.

THE WOOD

From the window of the ward a single large tree could be seen. A poplar. Early every afternoon the tree began to shine. A glittering white light danced and scattered as its leaves stirred in the wind. The view bordered by the square window frame gave a deceptive impression of nearness, like a mirage. In the evening the tree would bask in the setting sun, reaching the height of its brilliance.

The fine midsummer days seemed to be continuing.

Takiko first noticed the tree outside the window on her second evening in the hospital. While she lay sleeping, as she'd done since returning to her bed from the delivery room very early that morning, the peaceful sound of women's voices in the ward reached her.

". . . the doctor's in terrific shape, isn't he?"

"He's young, that's why. But really, you wouldn't think he had it in him, would you?"

"Ah, there's another smash. Great shot."

"The guy he's playing against is not too bad either."

"Who is he?"

"I don't know. A friend of the doctor's, I guess."

"Uh-oh, he sees us."

"He's laughing. *Doctor!* You look great!"

The women burst into peals of laughter. Takiko opened her eyes and dreamily turned her face toward the sound. There was a wide-open window, the shapes of three women appearing as bluish shadows, and behind them a flood of light. For a moment she wondered where she was.

The women were leaning out the window, still laughing. An off-duty doctor must be playing tennis in the hospital yard below. She couldn't make out the sound of the ball, though, no matter how closely she listened.

Takiko shifted her head to look around the ward from where she lay on her back. The large room was quiet and dark. Or so it seemed to her—in fact two or three babies were crying, many conversations were going on from one bed to the next, and the room was brightly lit by fluorescent ceiling lights. The bed on her left was unoccupied. On the one beyond it a woman was nursing a baby. She smiled when she noticed Takiko's gaze, and said, "Yours'll be along any minute. You had a hard time, didn't you? This is my third, so he didn't take long at all, even though I came in after you. I hope we didn't disturb you last night when the other two were here with their dad?"

"I didn't hear a thing. I was asleep," Takiko answered, watching the child's head.

The small bed by Takiko's feet was occupied by the bundle of baby clothes and diaper covers. She remembered the baby's first cry that she'd heard toward daybreak. Several minutes after the pain had suddenly faded away, the sound had echoed through the delivery room and she had asked herself if it was the cry of the living thing she'd given birth to. The nurses had seemed to be attending busily to the baby near her feet. Soon it was taken from the room. Takiko was shown its face for a brief moment. It was bright red, but at the same time familiar somehow. She hadn't seen the baby since.

Was it still alive somewhere, and looking like the others in the ward?

Takiko stared at the ceiling while she explored her stomach with both hands. It was wrapped in something thick and bandage-like, yet the sensation was unpleasantly like wetting her hands in a shallow puddle. Yes, the fetus that had been growing there until last night was gone. But she was still far from confident in the notion that she had a baby.

When they'd told her at dawn, "It's a healthy baby boy," they must have been talking about her child. But she could also have dreamed those words. She was in no hurry to find out. Whether what she'd given birth to was alive or dead, and what it might be like if it was alive, need not concern her right now. Takiko couldn't help being profoundly relieved to find that her own body seemed to have come through safely. As long as she, at least, could live that would be enough. She couldn't let anything happen to her because of this, not when it had turned out to be such a simple thing.

Her eyes returned to the window. The women who had been looking into the yard had moved away, and a large tree shone dazzlingly outside. The evening sun was striking its countless leaves and shivering into tiny pieces which scattered as they flew into the ward so that she couldn't make out the outline of the tree itself. Takiko gazed in surprise at the tree shining in the setting sun.

A hot day was drawing to a close out there. When was it that she'd walked in the morning light? For the first time since waking, Takiko felt an exquisite joy.

Over to her right she heard a woman shriek.

A neatly made-up woman in a nightgown was standing by her bed while a nurse massaged her breast. She shrank tearfully from the nurse's touch like a child squirming away from an injection. Laughter swelled from the surrounding beds.

"Now just keep this up and you'll have plenty of milk." The nurse too was laughing at the woman's childish protests. "You can't tell me the milk won't come, not with your breasts this full. Here, let's give it another try."

"No more! Please! I'll do it myself, I really will."

"Ah, yes, but you go easy on yourself when it hurts, don't you? That's no good at all. You won't keep it up when you leave here anyway, so just let me provide this free service one last time."

On the woman's bed lay a half-packed small suitcase and a shopping bag.

Takiko turned her face once again to the window on her left. She tried to roll over in bed, but there was a dull ache which she couldn't quite identify pooled in her lower abdomen and extending into her legs, and to shift even one leg sent such intense pain through her whole body that she couldn't move. She tried feeling her own breasts under the futon. They were her familiar breasts, their usual size and not at all sore.

Suddenly she noticed a parcel that she hadn't brought with her on the nightstand by the head of her bed. The creased wrapping paper had a red and blue pattern that she remembered having seen before. Wondering if her mother had been in, Takiko called to her nearest neighbor on the left, the woman who'd told her that this was her third child. She had returned the baby to the crib after its feed and was changing its diaper, clucking soothingly.

"Excuse me, um, is this mine?"

Takiko picked up the parcel in one hand and dangled it over her head. It was heavier than it looked.

"Oh, that, yes. Your mother must've left it, she was in around lunchtime. Said she wouldn't wake you because you were sound asleep. She took a peek at mine here before she left. Said her grandson was handsome, and this little fellow was very nice-looking too. She seemed terribly pleased—her first grandchild, I think she said?"

"Uh-huh . . ." After giving the woman a smile, Takiko raised herself a little, propping herself on one elbow, and opened the parcel right away. There were two big peaches inside. They looked expensive. Peaches were a great favorite of hers. With some reluctance Takiko said to the woman, "It's a couple of peaches—would you like one?"

"Oh no, thanks, dear. Your mother gave me one. It was delicious."

Relieved, Takiko nodded in reply.

She hadn't in fact eaten anything all day. The realization made her suddenly hungry. She took out one of the peaches and peeled it with her fingers. It was very ripe and the skin slipped off easily. Opening her mouth wide, she sucked at the sweet, soft flesh.

As she ate she glanced at the tree outside the window. Already the splendor of the evening sun was beginning to fade, yet the soft flesh of the peach held before her eyes the dazzling shining tree that she had witnessed just now. She went on sucking the peach, spellbound.

A scene started to take shape around the shining tree. A dry, white plain uninterrupted in any direction. There was no green in sight, but boulders jutted out here and there, each suggesting the shape of a living thing. Swept ceaselessly by the wind, the dry ground appeared covered in a yellow haze. The sun itself was dimmed by dust clouds even as its light and heat cut off the earth's surface from moisture.

Where could she have seen such a sight? Takiko was both puzzled and fascinated by the scene unfolding in her memory.

A woman was walking alone on the plain—an American Indian woman. Behind her there was an Indian village. She made her way without expression over the inhospitable plain. Her belly was big.

Takiko smiled in sudden recognition: it was a scene from a movie. She'd seen it one New Year, her second year in high school, with the senior boy who'd been her boyfriend then. She couldn't remember anything else about the film, its title or plot or even the face of the actor in the main role, but she was sure she'd watched this one scene in acute suspense. At the time she wouldn't have been able to connect childbirth with herself. She'd regarded even pregnancy simply as something that mustn't happen to her. Rumors that another girl at her school had had an abortion always irritated her because she couldn't understand the situation. Although it was mere luck that had enabled her to get by until now, she had taken that luck for granted all along.

She could still recall the boyfriend's face, though not, of course, what they'd had to say about the movie. She wondered if he ever remembered that scene. If he did, whenever that might be, did he also think of Takiko Odaka now that they'd lost touch? And would he look back on those teenage years as nostalgically as she did?

The Indian woman, feeling the time of birth approaching, was leaving the village alone, carrying as much food as she thought she would need. Takiko couldn't be sure that this part had been in the actual movie, though she had a strong feeling it had. The scene that she distinctly remembered watching began once the woman reached the shade of a rock and began softly moaning.

First she walks slowly across the white prairie which shimmers in the heat of the sun. She has to travel out of earshot of the village. Sound carries far on the prairie. She walks until she arrives at last at a certain rock. Seating herself in its shade, she awaits the time of her baby's birth. She may wait three days or a week, eking out her food supply. She will not move from there, it seems, until the baby comes. And if the baby should refuse to be born alive, she might perhaps go on waiting a year, or ten years.

However, in the movie scene the onset of strong labor pains comes quickly. Clinging to the rock with both hands, the woman gives all the strength of her body to the baby trying to be born. Her sweating face suddenly takes on a wide-eyed look of surprise. A stranger, the hero of the film, is staring at her from the shelter of the rock. Returning the man's gaze with wide eyes, the woman clings to the rock and groans again and again. There is no fear in her face as she stares at him with large eyes. The man, too, watches the woman's labor steadily, his mouth a little open.

The newborn baby's cry suddenly rings out. The sound drifts over the white prairie.

The woman takes her eyes from the man for the first time and bends over the baby she has just given birth to. The man continues his watchful gaze.

Some time later the woman lifts the baby, wrapped in a cloth, and stands by the rock. Again she and the man exchange looks. Then without a word or a flicker of expression she walks away at the same pace over the prairie.

She would have been younger than Takiko's own age of twenty-one, just a girl, really, with the face of a child.

Takiko found it strange that she remembered this scene only now. Why hadn't it come back to her when she was packing for the hospital, or having an examination, or maybe on the day she'd quit her job? Although she had heard of labor pains when she saw that movie at sixteen, she hadn't known how far she was from being able to imagine the pain as she stared at the screen with the same eyes as the young Indian woman's.

Instead, during her pregnancy Takiko had often remembered an old childhood dream.

Over a frozen sea as endless as the prairie where the Indians lived, people were speeding this way and that on dog sleds while she looked down as if from a great height, seeing every detail of the tiny figures with sharp clarity. The dream consisted of just this, and although they seemed to be chasing something, they never stopped the sleds or started any other action. It was a quiet dream in which no voices or sounds could be heard. The thick sheet of frozen sea was a world of white tinged with blue.

Perhaps she had made up this scene after hearing how people lived in places like that in her social studies class, and then it had begun to haunt her dreams. It had been an eerie, frightening dream for young Takiko. The frozen sea was too quiet, too white, and too vast. She couldn't help fearing she might have to go there herself someday.

By some chance, it had been this dream that came to mind on the day she'd left her job two months ago. And she'd realized then that, far from being afraid, she was able to gaze with a kind of admiration at the frozen sea and the people speeding over it.

Whenever she'd thought about it since, Takiko had felt an increasing attraction to the people on the ice. They were men clad in the pelts of sea animals they had shot. She hoped the baby would be a boy. Her hopes swelled: if it was a boy, he might grow into a young man who'd be allowed to join the men speeding over the ice, and then Takiko could join them too. For all she knew, this might not be so utterly fantastic.

She started to think that she'd been right to quit her job. It hadn't occurred to her at first to quit, even when the bulge began to show, since she didn't expect trouble as long as she kept quiet about the name of the man involved. She could still see no reason to quit when her boss asked indirectly whether she would be leaving and the other women in the office began to keep a shocked distance.

The fetus had already grown quite big when it dawned on her that the changes in her body added up to pregnancy.

Experiencing these changes for the first time, Takiko became so preoccupied with them that, while time slipped by, she couldn't bring herself to think at all practically about an abortion. She did feel she'd been in a dilemma in her own way, but when asked later by her mother why she hadn't gotten an abortion, all she could say was that she hadn't been able to think that far.

She was a full six months pregnant by the time her mother noticed. Her mother at once launched into an endless stream of angry questions, demanding to know why hadn't she gotten an abortion, how had it happened, who was the man, did she want his child because she loved him, was he a married man, did he know, did she plan to bring it up herself, did she think she knew how, was she doing this to get back at her parents, did she have such a grudge against her father, did she realize what this would do to her life, and just what was the big idea?

The questions were unanswerable, every one. In fact, Takiko was surprised to hear such questions in real life, asked in all seriousness by someone close to her. Her mother's use of phrases like "a married man" struck her as comical. Her mother seemed convinced that everyone had to have a reason or "idea" before they could give birth. She even brought up the Christian Sunday school that Takiko had attended a few times as a child, wondering if she'd taken it into her head that it was wrong to kill the baby, when it wasn't really a baby, it wasn't anything before it was born.

Takiko had finally burst out laughing. "Of course I don't think like that!"

"Then what's got into you, you stupid fool! It's nothing to laugh about!" her mother had shouted and slapped Takiko's cheek as hard as she could. Then she'd started to cry. "Oh,

what a nightmare. I won't be able to go out of the house.
. . . There's a clinic down by the station, isn't there? That'll
do, go tomorrow. You must. Please . . ."

Takiko muttered in confusion, "Look, I'm almost seven
months. Even if I went to a clinic now, they wouldn't do
anything."

Her mother grew paler.

"Seven? Then it's due in two months? Why didn't you tell
me sooner?"

"I wasn't hiding anything, you just didn't notice, that's all."

Her mother covered her face with her hands and groaned,
"What am I going to tell your father? And Atchan is still in
high school. This'll be hard on him."

"What's it got to do with Atchan? Mom, calm down a bit,
will you?"

But her mother had burst into tears again.

It seemed odd, no matter how busy her mother might have
been with her dressmaking, that she could live in the same
house, see Takiko every day and yet fail to notice she was six
months pregnant. And now that she knew, it didn't make sense
to Takiko to be blamed for not having a good reason. Her belly
had grown bigger while she hadn't done anything. It was as
simple as that. Takiko had had no "idea" in mind beyond
thinking: Ah, so I'm going to have a baby. I've looked after
my little brother, I like children, it might not be such a bad
thing after all. She had no special hopes for her own future.
She wanted to get away from her family. That was the one
vague plan she'd had since high school. The baby would at
least give her an opportunity to leave home.

From that day on her mother complained that all she could
see when she went out were clinic signboards. She held on to

Takiko and tried to steer her, if only a little, in their direction, but Takiko, who was bigger than her mother, was not to be steered. When Takiko couldn't stand it any longer she would shove her mother aside easily and cry, "Is that all you can think about? Killing it?" and her mother would weep and curse, tremble and grieve. Until Takiko quit her job a month later, her mother was obsessed by the clinic signs. Even in her dreams, it seemed she roamed among shifting masses of many-shaped signboards that floated in the air.

Her father didn't look the other way either, of course. In fact the discovery may have made it easier for him to take out his true feelings on Takiko. About the time his daughter's body had matured and she started to go out with boys, his discontent had turned from his wife, who had always borne the brunt of his rages, to her. It was not uncommon for Takiko to fight violently with her small father when he was drunk.

When she came home late at night in her teens, he would have had more than enough to drink and would bawl her out in a thick voice, as if he'd waited eagerly for this moment. "So you've been at it again, have you? I didn't raise my daughter to be a whore!"

"Oh sure, we all know what a wonderful father you've been," Takiko would snap back.

"What? You sex-crazed little—" And to start with, he would fling his glass or ashtray onto the tatami.

"Oh, great, here we go again," Takiko would retort. "You're the one who's crazy."

By this time her mother would be shouting, "Stop it, you two!" But already her father would have hit Takiko with all his strength, and Takiko would have leaped at him sobbing with fury. Small as he was, he was still more than a match for her, and she had never won yet.

After learning that she was pregnant, her father tried more bluntly than ever to show her who was stronger. During the three years since she'd left high school, with Takiko bringing home a paycheck bigger than his disability pension, he often had a frustrating sense that he was picking on her unfairly. Certainly, since she'd started working, life had become a great deal easier for all four members of the family. Her brother, Atsushi, had probably benefited most: he now planned to take the entrance exams for college. As he wasn't especially bright, he was evidently looking at a number of private universities. Their father didn't tangle with Atsushi, who had overtaken him in size and strength a year or two earlier. And anyway, Atsushi's presence had never been the irritant to their father that Takiko's was; she had always seemed to be aligned with her mother against her father, but Atsushi was a boy, and wasn't born yet when his parents had separated years ago—he was the child they'd had after their reconciliation.

Atsushi had been the first at home to notice the signs of Takiko's pregnancy, or so she concluded when he began to avoid her rather nervously. Always a taciturn boy, he had ceased to look any of the family in the face. Most of the time he kept himself shut away in his tiny two-mat room, where as far as his parents knew he was studying for exams. It was Atsushi, however, who came to the rescue when Takiko and her father began to brawl, and who pried her free from the grip which her father wouldn't relax even when she wept in pain and frustration. Her mother would fuss about and merely provoke the two of them still further with her noise.

Her father noticed Takiko's pregnancy himself, three days after her mother did, but before she had told him.

At the moment when he realized, his face, flushed from the neck up with drink as usual, took on an expression that seemed almost to beg Takiko's forgiveness as she stood before him. It was an expression that seemed quietly sad about something else. Taking advantage of her father's silence, Takiko attempted to slip away into the next room.

"Where do you think you're going, Takiko?"

Although she heard him, she went into the other room anyway and started to close the sliding doors.

"Takiko, you come back here, you little sneak. What the hell have you been up to? I said come here, damn it. You hear me?"

Takiko looked around at her father and saw the familiar drunkard's face. Hurriedly she closed the doors. His voice boomed, one of the heavy paper doors fell inward, and her father rushed at her. She screamed, then wept aloud under his fists.

She had known that the baby would inevitably come as a shock to her parents, but since she intended to leave home as soon as it was born, and to keep on sending them a share of her earnings, they would surely come around and see the change as no more than a temporary clouding of their sky. She went on believing this even after her parents realized she was pregnant and became unable to think of anything else. Since it was only until the baby was born, she would go on as if she hadn't seen how they looked at her or heard what they said. She mustn't face her parents.

Yet every night her mother's tearful voice swamped her like waves swelling without pause, whispering like a curse in her ear, "You've got to have an abortion, do it tomorrow," while her father picked quarrels at the slightest excuse, ordering her to stay out of his sight, to keep quiet in his house, not to watch TV. Unlike the sessions with her mother, this reduced Takiko to sheer fury every time, almost as if she was just waiting for the chance, and she'd let fly with some retort—"Bitch, bitch, bitch, like a woman, is that all you can do?"—which enraged him even more and always drove him to punch and kick and pin her down on the tatami, while she pulled his hair and bit his shoulder and scratched his face and neck and screeched, "You idiot, I'll call the police, are you trying to kill me?" and her father roared back, "You think you're smart enough to die? You just go right ahead and try it," and the tears streamed from her eyes. Neither of them could stop themselves in this state. They would go on saturating each other's bodies with pain until Atsushi came running to the rescue.

When Takiko quit her job and started buying things for the baby with her severance pay, her mother ceased to stare at clinic signs wherever she went and instead brought home a huge armful of work from the factory, surely enough for three seamstresses. She seldom got up from her machine, and when she did, her tired, pale face was often dazed and preoccupied. From time to time she remarked to Takiko, in a bewildered tone, "I suppose if you're going to give the baby up, it's better to do it quickly."

Takiko kept to her routine of leaving the house in the morning and coming back at night, since being at home all day would have meant constantly seeing her mother and her father (who hadn't worked for several years because of an accident on the job that had lamed his right leg, and because, he said, he was too old). She spent the day at the zoo a half-hour's walk from home, or took the bus downtown and watched the summer vacation entertainment for children on the rooftop playgrounds of department stores. She went to the movies a lot, and also strolled around the art exhibits, which she used to visit now and then while in high school.

When she was in third grade her painting of houses on fire had won a poster competition for Fire Prevention Week. She had announced gravely to her friends that she was going to be an artist. Once she reached junior high, though, the fact that there were any number of people with more talent came to her notice, and she never thought of herself as an artist again.

Her winning entry had been a painting of a hillside at dusk, dark rows of houses spreading out at the foot of the slope, and red flames blazing up from about a third of them. In the darkening sky she had written in matchstick letters, HANDLE FIRE WITH CARE. She'd never actually seen such a fire, but at the sound of sirens she would always dash outside and head for the road on the hill, which had the best view, to try to spot the flames among the rows of houses below. She never managed to see anything but smoke, though. Her mother explained that the color of the flames would be very hard to make out in daylight. This hadn't helped, and she'd always been convinced that the reason was her own bad luck.

Takiko remembered this on her way through an exhibit when she stood with her big belly in front of a large abstract canvas covered in an intense red. Yes, she thought, I do like red. She'd once given red as her favorite color and afterwards had been ashamed of how childish she'd sounded—she would have been ten or eleven at the time. She had wished she'd had the sense to say blue, or maybe white. Ever since, she'd been claiming blue as her favorite color.

Even though she had no business to attend to, it wasn't difficult to stay out all day. In fact there was never enough time. If the weight of her belly made her tired she would go to a jazz coffeehouse and bar that she had known since her high school days. There would always be several familiar faces there, high school acquaintances who were now in college. She also knew the student who worked part-time behind the bar. When she dropped in like this she always ended up drinking more whiskey than she'd meant to and leaving just in time to catch the last train home. There, before she knew what was happening, she would be caught up in a noisy struggle with her father who had gotten drunk at home, and next morning she would find her lip swollen or her cheek bruised.

As she studied her face in the mirror and remembered the previous night's fight with her father as a surprising yet dreamlike event, she began to find a powerful consolation in the repeated sight of her bruised face, which she accepted as the event's inevitable aftermath. She might have a vivid welt right in the middle of her cheek, where it was most obvious, or blood still dripping from her nose, but she wouldn't stay in the house even if she had to stuff tissue paper in her nostrils. She went out as usual, and if passersby noticed her face she returned their stares.

From the end of June, when the heat set in, until the day before she entered the hospital, on August 27, Takiko continued to walk the streets perspiring heavily. At her back were her mother's eyes, reddened by the sleeplessness she had begun to complain of. Atsushi's eyes, with the same coolly expressionless light they'd always had. Her father's nose, beaded with sweat from his drinking and his rages. Her mother's weeping came echoing after her in low, swelling waves. And her father's shouts and her own high-pitched cries echoed too.

She couldn't turn to look, she mustn't pay any attention to what went on behind her. She seldom spoke, even outside the house. The unseen fetus in her belly continued to grow quietly, without a word or a thought. Takiko spent her time in the same way. Hiroshi Maeda, the only person besides herself who meant anything to the fetus, was too far away by now, and without having deliberately decided to keep her pregnancy a secret she had simply ceased to think of the connection they'd once had.

All the same, before she had left her job, there had been sometimes strong and sometimes faint reminders of Hiroshi Maeda's existence, signs which aroused something close to fear in her. They seemed unlikely to meet again, even by chance, as Maeda had moved away with his wife and children to the town he originally came from in the Tohoku area where he was apparently setting up some kind of business, a coffee bar or restaurant or some such thing. So he'd announced in the polite printed postcard she'd received at the office before she knew she was pregnant. Only her work address on the other side was written by hand. Maeda didn't have Takiko's home address; nor did she have his—in fact she learned where Maeda had lived in Tokyo only from this announcement of his change of address. Their relationship being what it was, they'd never had much of a conversation.

Maeda had worked in a government department to which Takiko's job frequently took her. During lunch hour they had often run into each other at a nearby noodle restaurant. He was a skinny, quiet man of thirty-two. He had a strong northern accent, and more than once Takiko had missed what he'd said across his office counter from behind his little window, and had unintentionally embarrassed him by asking him to repeat it. Blushing, he would pronounce the words again with great care.

The previous autumn, Takiko had shared a table with Maeda at the usual noodle shop. It had seemed odd to go on taking separate tables when they knew each other by sight. Takiko had said hello, Maeda had smiled. Not being able to think of anything to talk about, Takiko had eaten in silence, and Maeda remained silent too. As they left the restaurant together and were about to go their different ways, Maeda suddenly asked her her age.

Takiko had burst out laughing rather too loudly. It had simply struck her as an absurd question. When she finished laughing she asked Maeda his age, and laughed again. Maeda answered her seriously.

"And at a guess," he continued, "I'd say you weren't twenty yet. Or perhaps just twenty. You laugh a lot, don't you?"

That night, she had another meal with Maeda. Takiko was bored. She'd hoped at least for a fancy restaurant, but the Chinese place they went to was in the same class as their lunchtime noodle shop. Still, Takiko made sure she didn't go hungry. Neither of them could find anything to talk about. They drank beer. On the way out of the restaurant, Maeda placed his arm around Takiko's shoulders. She didn't push him away. She matched her pace to his and they went into a hotel without further talk. She wanted to part quickly from him. Maeda's desire must be released with no resistance. Though she couldn't really have said why, Takiko responded to a man's desire with sympathy. She could think of it only as pitiful, and thus not for her to violate. Maeda's desire seemed somehow not to belong to Maeda himself.

After that she met Maeda away from the office just twice. She continued to be bored, with nothing to talk about. Most likely Takiko was a puzzle or embarrassment to him too. Before long he ceased to have anything personal to say when they happened to face each other at his window.

Winter came, and by the beginning of the new year Maeda was no longer working there. Belatedly Takiko received the announcement that he'd changed jobs. It was another month before the word "pregnant" first entered her mind. She tried to find Maeda's postcard, but she could hardly expect it to turn up however carefully she searched since she'd thrown it away herself, just after it came, thinking it of no further use once she knew what it said. It wouldn't have occurred to her to make a note of Maeda's new address. She could perhaps have inquired at the government office, but it didn't seem necessary to go to such lengths to trace him. She preferred to think she'd had no connection with Maeda in the first place.

She was beginning to feel herself lucky not even to know his address. Especially since he was hundreds of miles away now. He'd probably already decided to leave Tokyo when he became involved with her—that was probably why he'd been interested. If she'd had his address, most likely she would have wanted to contact him when she knew she was pregnant, and then of course she'd have had to take his situation into account. As it was, it looked like she wouldn't have to go to all that effort. And she couldn't help seeing this as a very lucky break— strangely enough, for she couldn't work out why, as she was definitely in a lot of trouble. Yet she was able to accept that

the baby would be born into an atmosphere of good fortune.
Just as Maeda's desire had seemed not to belong to him, Takiko's pregnancy seemed not to be hers. She was being told
something through her body. She wanted to listen.

Nevertheless she was still having second thoughts when
spring came. In a corner of her mind she was still aware that
if she was going to have an abortion it would have to be soon.
She considered what clinic she would choose if she were to
go to one and how much it would cost. But she had the distinct
feeling that she was aping somebody else when she thought
about these things. All this drama and seriousness was a pose,
and it embarrassed her.

Am I really going to go ahead and have a baby just as I am?
If she could have had just one question answered, that would
have been the one.

By May, Takiko's belly was becoming obvious, and she had
ceased to go through the motions of thinking about an abortion.
The answer she wanted wouldn't be given, it seemed, until
the fetus came to term.

She was planning to take maternity leave in July and return
in October. Two of the married women she worked with in
accounts had taken maternity leave while Takiko had been
with the company.

The rainy season made little impression that year, hanging
back as if to make a fast retreat before the impending hot
weather. A light rainfall would be followed by three or four
days of midsummer sun. Takiko's pregnancy was noticed at
home and at work, and now neither home nor work was the
same. While looking with wide eyes at the scene around her,
Takiko went on waiting for the fetus to come to term.

One summery lunchtime in June, she went down to a

boathouse not far from her office, on a stretch of water that had once been part of the outer moat of the palace. Just standing in the sun made sweat trickle down her thickening thighs and neck, the sides of her belly, her face.

In the glare from above, the water's surface had a fine sheen too bright to look at directly. Takiko stood at the water's edge and felt herself take in its sparkle. Shutting her eyes made the world a solid red. There were few boats on the water, which was overrun with pondweed and had turned a heavy muddy color. In view of the danger to boaters and the steady decline in business, the boathouse was due to be closed down.

Takiko stood still at the water's edge. Receiving that dazzling sparkle gave her a sense that something was rapidly melting away from around her body. The opposite bank was emerald green. The cherry trees along the top were also mantled in translucent green.

There was no one else about by now, perhaps because the lunch hour was over. She didn't want to move. She was sure the eight-month fetus must be as enraptured as she was. She wanted to drench it in the light from the water's surface and the green of the grass and trees, as if she were watering a plant. As a life that was due to arrive in the middle of summer, wouldn't it need more light than babies due at other times of the year? Wouldn't it be wanting the smell of greenery? Takiko was convinced that it must. For the first time, she thought of quitting her job, though she mightn't have done so if the baby had been due in the spring. Again she wanted to hear an answer: I'm doing all right, aren't I? Otherwise this won't turn out right, will it?

But she would just have to wait the full nine months before she could expect an answer.

July brought the end of the rainy season, such as it was, and the beginning of summer. The streets were all but deserted by day in the intense heat they reflected back under a cloudless blue sky. Asphalt melted, greenery wilted and lost its green smell. Only trickles ran from the taps. The temperature barely went down at night. There wasn't even a brief evening shower. Into such a summer, Takiko's baby was about to be born.

One day, she picked up the phone book. She had suddenly thought of a place she would be needing later on. Finding three listed nearby, she phoned each one. The answering voices were not encouraging: "Please come and see us," they all said, "but we have a long waiting list and can't promise to take you."

She set out for one of them at once, taking the bus. She got off at the fourth stop and started down an alley. The alleys here were as complicated as those of her own neighborhood, and it was impossible not to lose her way. She wandered around for a good half hour.

It turned out to be a small, old house very like her own. There wasn't even a sign to identify it. She couldn't see anyone inside through the glass door which was open to the alley, though three child-sized red futons with flower patterns were sunning in the scorching heat on the upstairs windowsills. Takiko ducked into the dim hallway anyway, to get out of the strong sun that had been steadily beating down on her. Sitting on the step in the narrow entranceway lined with cardboard boxes and plastic buckets, she set about wiping away a fresh burst of sweat with the handkerchief she'd been using along the way to mop her face and neck. She wiped her throat, patted her face, and reached down the front of her dress to dab her chest. The handkerchief, like her underwear, was already soaked. She was flushed and almost dizzy from the long walk in the midday heat. After she'd been sitting on the step for a while, her legs began to tremble.

Relieved that no one had come out yet from inside, Takiko waited for her body to slowly recover sensation. Sweat seemed to pour from her endlessly. It felt good on her skin.

Eventually, she stood and called down the passageway. She couldn't make out what was back there from the entrance. There was no sound of voices or movement. On the wall beside her hung a blackboard, and around it pieces of paper of many sizes were tacked up. She could see headings like "A Request from the Treasurer" and "Report from the Steering Committee." So she wasn't in the wrong house; and there had to be someone inside. She tried to attract attention again, calling repeatedly at the top of her voice.

At last there was a drawn-out "Ye-es" from above. It was followed by footsteps clattering down the stairs, and a young woman with a white apron around her waist emerged into the hall.

Takiko tensed and bowed her head. To her own astonishment she was suddenly afraid. As far as this pleasantly smiling young woman now gazing at her was concerned, Takiko was already simply the mother of a child. That she quite naturally regarded her as such frightened Takiko.

Choosing her words so that the woman wouldn't think her odd, she told her the purpose of her call. The woman replied without taking her eyes off Takiko's bulging belly, a slightly troubled look on her face.

"Ah, you've come to enroll? I'm afraid the person you need to talk to isn't here just now . . . but we already have ten reservations for babies due this summer. Our usual intake is six, and we can't possibly squeeze in more than seven. If only you'd come earlier. You must be due next month, aren't you?"

Takiko answered that her due date was in the third week of August.

"Then you have less than a month to go and you haven't looked for a day-care center yet?"

"No, I just started looking today. Actually I thought I could apply after the baby was born."

The young woman stepped back inside for a moment and returned holding a sheet of paper. Babies could now be faintly heard beginning to cry. It seemed the children were upstairs. The woman noticed the crying also and glanced up at the ceiling, her mouth slightly open. Then she commented with a wry laugh, "When one starts, it gets all the others going. So much for their nap. Now where was I? Well, anyway, please fill in this application form before you go, but you must understand we're not likely to be able to help. You'd better try a few more places. The other mothers get in early, you know. Some of them come here straight from the doctor's office to sign up as soon as they know they're pregnant."

The paper she'd been handed was a roughly mimeographed form. The first space was headed "Name," and Takiko had begun to write hers in it when she noticed that the next section, headed "Family," had spaces for both parents' names: "Father," "Mother," and then "Applicant's Name" once again. She gave the woman a doubtful look, and the woman glanced over the form in her hands.

"Leave the name blank for now. Once you've safely had the baby, please phone us as soon as you can. The name can come later, as long as you notify us of the birth. Then if we find we're going to have a vacancy we'll call you. Otherwise you can assume you're still on the waiting list. At this stage, I wouldn't count on anything happening until, say, January at the earliest."

Nodding obediently, Takiko filled in her own name under "Mother" and put "Between jobs" under "Occupation." She gave her address and phone number as indicated in the "Applicant" box with its blanks for name and sex. The baby itself might not have entered the world yet, but Takiko was certainly being treated here as its mother. The woman looked at the form without suspicion as Takiko handed it back, merely bowing her head lightly and thanking her for coming. She didn't ask "Why are you having it?" like the other people did. Takiko left the house wondering if perhaps she hadn't noticed the blank space under "Father." It was a bit of a letdown.

She set off walking in the sun again, and again lost her way. There was no one around to ask for directions. She walked for a long time looking for the bus stop. The sun's rays on her body were too strong, making her feel as though she were walking in darkness. She couldn't see clearly enough to know where she was. She had never cared for hot weather, yet now, with the birth only a month away, it was a pleasure to be in the heat of the light. The more she wished that she could be napping in an air-conditioned room, the more satisfying it was to keep on panting down the hot road. She wouldn't even have minded if she had collapsed on the street and been reduced to ashes by the sun, and the fetus with her. Perhaps a baby like a blazing fire would appear before she knew it. Whatever happened, it would be right.

Wiping her streaming face and the back of her neck, she looked up at the sky. The summer light that filled it should have been brighter than anything on the ground, and yet to

Takiko's eyes it appeared that tangled black shadows like crooked tree branches were running this way and that across it as fast as they could multiply.

The path she took on those days seemed to go around in circles in a wood. It seemed as if she wouldn't be able to get out until some future date, but even knowing this, she couldn't allow herself to stop walking in circles. It was necessary to keep walking.

She was making her way up a hill one day. On the right was a university hospital, and on the left the largest shrine in the district. As usual there was no one else out on the street and few passing cars. The steep road was glaring white between borders of azaleas. A row of two or three coffeehouses had their glass doors shut tight, their air conditioners making a low hum that was barely a noise. Hot air blasted Takiko's body as she passed by.

She'd been here often as a child. Her mother had been taken to that hospital with appendicitis. She had an idea that it had been during the winter. Takiko and Atsushi used to visit her room every day with their schoolbags on their backs— Takiko was in fifth grade and Atsushi in first grade at the same school—and when their mother told them between exaggerated groans to go away and not make so much noise, they would kill time in the hospital yard. The yard was a gloomy, empty place, and the children were worried that they might get into trouble for playing there. Takiko had memories of huddling in the corner by the concrete wall, making themselves small. By the time they got home, after dark, their father would have started drinking, alone and sour-faced.

They used to go every spring to the festival at the shrine across the road from the hospital, either with their mother or on their own. Takiko had lost interest in these outings, however, in her early teens.

There had been a balloon vendor who came every year to the festival, when the shrine compound was turned into a fairground. "The gorilla man," they called him. If children ventured too near as he was blowing up the balloons, the man's face would suddenly turn into a gorilla's and he would come lumbering after them with a fearful roar, sending them screaming in every direction. The gorilla man would growl and roam around his stand for a while until he'd established who was boss, then return to his lair where dozens of balloons were floating.

There weren't many things she remembered having truly terrified her, but she could clearly recall the tension she'd felt staring at this gorilla man from a little distance. She just couldn't understand how much of a real gorilla he was, or why a gorilla man like him was selling balloons, and not understanding had frightened her.

Walking through the hushed and apparently deserted grounds, Takiko concluded that he hadn't been putting on an act, he must have believed he was a gorilla set down amid the swirl of humanity without others of his kind. Otherwise why would he have had such an effect on her as a child?

The trees in the shrine compound were all very old, their dense foliage thickening the surrounding silence. Staying within their shade, Takiko made her way to the back of the compound. Cicadas' cries were ringing in the air in many layers of sound. There was no wind, but the shadows cast by the trees had a dampness that felt good after exposure to the strong sun. As she made her way to the back the shade of the increasing number of trees deepened. The stillness, too, seemed to take on a clarity that was not to be disturbed lightly. Treading carefully to soften the sound of her steps, Takiko carried herself with her back straight. The leaves of the canopy overhead had a glassy transparency, each glinting a small green light.

Although she thought of the shrine grounds as familiar territory she had never set foot in the wooded area at the very back, a dark recess which had a disquietingly deserted air. The house to which she'd been directed over the phone was supposed to be at the end of the path. Until the blue-roofed prefab came into view between the trees, however, Takiko half forgot where she was headed, so that it felt strange to find herself standing in front of the house with its porch overgrown by a large red oleander. Babies' crying could be heard from inside. Looking around she could see two old three-story concrete buildings through a grove of trees. They must be the dormitories for hospital nurses that had been mentioned on the phone. At this hour of the day they would be almost unoccupied. The washing at the windows lent a few splashes of color.

Takiko pushed aside the hanging oleander branches with one hand and stepped into the entranceway of the small house. She called in the general direction of the babies' cries. The entranceway was roomier than she'd expected. Two baby carriages were lined up on the concrete floor.

By dialing the numbers under "Day Care" in the Yellow Pages, she had learned that this center was for the use of hospital employees but also accepted a small number of babies from outside. Here too, though, there was no prospect of a vacancy, and Takiko had been warned that it was scarcely worth putting her name down. Still, she made up her mind to apply just in case. Since being advised to try a number of places, she had already applied at three other centers. One was on a very large scale, a company offering nighttime as well as daytime services for a hundred babies at a time; another consisted of one aging woman minding several babies in a room of her apartment.

The glass door to the room beyond opened and a woman of about her own age appeared. When Takiko explained her business, the woman invited her to come in. Takiko took off her shoes and followed her inside.

It was a light, air-conditioned room. One corner of the big space served as a kitchen. A low fence penned off the infants' area. Green carpeting covered the floor. There were babies sleeping wrapped in bath towels, others crying, and one, a few months older, clinging smilingly to the wooden fence. Beyond closed French windows the trees could be seen, tipped with gleaming light.

After telling Takiko to find herself somewhere to sit, the woman picked up one of the crying babies and began to change it. A plump woman who had been washing dishes in the kitchen swooped up the baby at the fence and seated herself in front of Takiko. Studying the child's face, Takiko explained again that she hoped they could take her baby, which was due next month, starting around October. As she spoke she couldn't suppress a rush of excitement at the thought of her baby becoming a part of all this. Takiko believed in her luck. But would she be lucky enough to succeed in butting in here, when she was a complete outsider?

The plump woman replied, after first giving the baby on her lap a clothespin from her apron pocket, "I ought to make it clear that I really don't think you stand a chance. Certainly not in October, anyway."

Over in the corner another of the babies started wailing.

"But," Takiko insisted eagerly, "I'd really like to try." It was the first house that had captured her imagination as a place for her baby. The light that filtered into the room was soft and green. She could have been in a cabin in the mountains. Cicadas echoed in the distance.

The plump woman was laughing as she took a closer look at Takiko's face. "Of course, you never can tell. . . . Why don't you make yourself comfortable? Stretch out your legs. It must be hard to sit so formally when you're this far along. Looks like you're having a big baby. This little one's eight months old. His name's Ken—isn't it, honey?" She rubbed cheeks with the baby on her lap.

"Eight months, and they're as big as this already. The vocal ones over there, they're about four months old. Then the baby who's fooling with a bottle, he's just about six months. What an appetite! The one who's tugging at that towel is about six months old too. She has a thing about towels, just give her a towel and she's happy. We have to watch her or she helps herself to them all."

Now that the younger woman had finished changing the baby (one of the four-month-olds), she glanced over at Takiko and laughed, which made the plump woman turn around.

"It'll be time for his bottle soon. What a grouch he is today."

"He's covered in heat rash. It's these hot nights."

"How about bathing him again later on, after his feed?"

"Okay. Aren't *you* the lucky one? You get to have two baths."

The plump woman's smiling face turned back to Takiko. "Babies are all so different. If you like, why don't you stay here where it's cool and do some sightseeing before you go?"

"All right." Takiko nodded very earnestly.

"There's just the two of us in charge, and as you see, we've got more than we can cope with as it is. Next month we take on another two. Everyone's so anxious to get them in, it's hard to refuse. How we're going to manage from next month on I really can't imagine." She looked Takiko in the face. "That's the situation, then. We'd really like to have you with us, but we can't do the impossible, I'm afraid."

"Ah." It was as much a sigh as an answer. The plump woman turned toward the French windows; after a moment's silence in which she seemed to be noting the cicadas' shrill whir among the trees outside, she began again.

"Unless . . . Our annual rummage sale is in December, run by the fathers and mothers, and if this year's is a good one we're considering hiring another staff member. We simply can't go on like this. We're paid out of the monthly fees, but our bonuses have to come from the proceeds of the sale. You see, the center was set up by several of the hospital staff—so you couldn't ask for a safer place when it comes to illnesses— but with no subsidy of any sort, so it's always been a struggle. And people can't afford higher fees. So you see, we're counting on the winter sale. It's generally brought in three or four hundred thousand yen in the past, but this year the organizers say they're aiming for over five hundred thousand. That would allow us an extra helper and a slight increase in our enroll-ments. So there you are: if it works out, we'll be able to take your baby. Wish us luck, won't you? And of course, we'd be delighted if you could help out in any way. But otherwise, I wonder if you'd mind waiting till after the rummage sale?"

Takiko nodded with a smile.

The plump woman handed her a well-worn exercise book in which they kept reservations and asked her to take the page after the last entry and write down her name, address, occupation, due date, and any comment she might wish to add. Takiko borrowed her ballpoint and opened the notebook. There were only two blank pages left.

"Now if you decide to enroll your baby somewhere else, you'll let us know right away, won't you? If we haven't heard from you, we'll call you once the winter sale is over and we know the outcome—that'll be after the New Year, I expect. Well, I'll leave you alone. Take your time and write anything you like."

Lowering the child on her lap to the floor, she stood up. The baby started to cry, watching Takiko's face. The woman went over to the younger infants without looking back.

Since Takiko had no idea what expression to turn to the howling child in front of her, she kept her eyes on her notebook entry. Apparently frightened by her unfamiliar presence, the baby screamed so hard Takiko was afraid he'd have a fit.

After she'd filled in the due date, she thought a while but couldn't come up with a single thing to write, so she closed the book and got up as if driven away by the baby's cries. She returned the book to the plump woman, who was applying white ointment to the smallest infant's bottom.

"I'm sorry to have bothered you when you're so busy."

"Not at all. Oh, the notebook—leave it on the kitchen bench, will you? You're welcome to stay longer, you know. You could get in some practice at changing diapers. It's bound to be hot out there still."

The plump woman's laughter was echoed by the other helper, who was feeding a baby off to the right. Takiko laughed out loud too.

"Does it take practice? I guess it does."

"Oh yes, believe me, it's quite tricky."

"Yes, so I see. But, um, I'll be going now. Thank you." Takiko bowed her head politely.

"Oh no, don't thank us. Drop in any time you feel like practicing. Oh, that reminds me," the plump woman added, still laughing, "I forgot to ask you—does your husband work at the hospital?"

"No . . . I'm not connected with the hospital at all. I was told over the phone that it would be all right—"

"Yes, it is. Then you're an outside applicant."

"Yes." Takiko paused and waited for the woman to go on, but she didn't seem to have anything further to say. Takiko bowed once more and left the room.

It looks like I won't be coming back—while she still felt attached to the cool room filled with the trees' greenness, that was her impression. She remembered the maternal and child health handbook, designed for keeping records, which she'd received at her local ward office in June. She had foreseen items that would be awkward for someone in her position to fill in, but they hadn't been there. The word "father" didn't occur, and she found just one reference to "husband," a yes-or-no question under "Cohabitants." The only other relevant item was "Age at Marriage."

The cicadas' cries shrilling overhead seemed to have grown in number. Takiko set off, walking rapidly between the trees.

CRIES

The hospital corridor was brightly lit all night long. Even after lights-out in the ward, the glare continued to shine in through the windows in the double doors.

As the head of Takiko's bed faced the doors, she had to sleep every night with the corridor lights in her face. She remained aware of all kinds of activity around her inert self, from bedtime until the morning temperature reading, like one long dream, night after night. During the day, she would fall into a deep sleep without a moment's dreaming—a sleep like her baby's. Five days after being born into the world, the baby slept quietly during the daytime and cried at night with his eyes closed.

Through her drowsiness the babies' crying sounded like a chorus of cicadas. Shrill cries, low cries, short cries, long cries. No two were the same. How many voices were there? One, two—she would start counting as if unraveling strings from around her body. Soft, transparent strings. Three, four, five. A sudden anxiety arose. What could it be? The crying was calling for something, seeking something. Takiko shifted where she lay and the pain that had been tensed and waiting hit her. It was the soreness of her breasts, grown heavier two days ago.

She got up and looked into the crib at the foot of her bed, where a small human-shaped creature was holding up trembling fists and letting out a yell. The sight of it held her there gazing for a while. It was just too tiny to reach out to. But this was the size that newborn babies were. She carefully lifted the baby and placed him on her bed. There was something familiar about the weight in her arms: until last week she'd felt the same weight in her belly. She tucked up the baby's garment and unhurriedly changed his diaper.

The first time the baby was handed over to her, the nurse had given her quick lessons on diapering and breast-feeding and how to prepare formula if she didn't have enough breast milk. After that, it was the women from nearby beds who demonstrated for a flustered and fumbling Takiko. She got used to the diapers in no time. Takiko's baby was a boy. He had male genitals between his thighs. She enjoyed seeing the little penis there. She also seemed to feel love welling up for this infant she'd produced. Asking herself if she was really its mother brought on a ticklish sort of embarrassment. No one yet had said, "Whatever gave you that idea? You're nothing to the baby." No one had tried to pull her away. Even her mother spent her visits watching with a smile as Takiko held the baby.

The new diaper hadn't stopped him from crying. When she tried holding her finger close to his mouth he pursed his lips and turned his face rapidly from side to side, seeking the nipple. The action reminded her of a nestling. She undid her night-dress and put the baby to her breast. The pull of his sucking was so painful that she let out an involuntary moan. Though her breasts were full, the milk was hardly coming at all. The nurses and her mother had assured her that the baby's suckling would naturally let it down, that she must keep nursing even if it hurt. Apparently the baby was the only thing that could save her from the pain of her engorged breasts. Feeling as though she were sticking a hypodermic needle into her own flesh each time she gave the baby her breast, Takiko tried to accept a little more of the pain.

She was woken frequently again that night by the baby's crying. She changed him and nursed him, but the milk didn't come and his hungry yells only grew louder, until she reluctantly took the can of powdered milk provided by the hospital, ran out into the corridor and prepared a bottle in the pantry. Satisfied at last, the baby would drop off to sleep. But a while later he would cry again, Takiko would get up, take him out of the crib, and change him. Still he wouldn't stop. She'd offer her breast. The baby would latch onto her nipple with uninhibited energy. More than once she caught herself dozing off with him there.

"Doesn't that baby have a funny cry. Kind of like a buzzer," she heard someone remark as she was nursing. Then she heard laughter.

"It really carries, doesn't it?"

The women's voices seemed to be coming from a corner of the ward that the light from the corridor didn't reach. Takiko wasn't sure what time of night it was. She had already nursed the baby five or six times since the lights went out.

She became aware of the baby they were talking about, who had been crying incessantly for some time now. Other cries could be heard here and there in the big ward, but this one's voice was distinctly lower and had a mechanical timbre. She smiled. At that moment someone burst into sobs in the semi-darkness, as if giving up a long struggle.

"Why do you cry so much? I can't stand it. Why won't you stop!"

The sobs seemed to be coming from the mother of the baby who was crying like a buzzer. Takiko turned toward the voice. She could see the vague shadow of a woman also sitting on a bed. As far as she could tell, it was a young wife who had entered the hospital the day after her.

Once she had given way to her tears the woman sobbed and cursed the baby as if swept along helplessly by their force. That evening she'd had a visit from her husband and another young man, a friend of his perhaps, and there'd been peals of laughter from the same bed. She was a fair-skinned woman with charming features who must be partial to cake, as she'd been devouring a slice of strawberry-topped sponge cake while her visitors watched.

The other women's voices, still tinged with laughter, could be heard around the weeping woman.

"What's wrong? Don't let it upset you so. What's the use in both of you crying?"

"You've been breastfeeding all the time, but maybe he isn't getting enough milk."

"You can't be expected to have enough milk yet. Give him a bottle. He's hungry, that's what it is."

"There's nothing wrong with formula. It can't be helped at first, really."

"I cried a lot too with my first. It's so hard to know what to do."

"So did I, come to think of it . . ."

Takiko herself had been told emphatically by the nurse who handed her the powdered formula: "This is for emergency use, you understand—make it your absolute last resort." And when she did open the can, she felt she was doing something very wrong. Since her milk hadn't come in at all then, although she went through the motions of nursing, she had no choice. All the same, as she went out to prepare a bottle, she found herself trying to act like she was on her way to the bathroom.

That was three nights ago. Her breasts were heavy now, but still the milk would not satisfy the baby's hunger. If all went well they were scheduled to leave in the morning. It was their fifth and last night in the maternity hospital.

Takiko put the baby down beside her, having discovered him sleeping attached to her nipple, and lay down herself. The ward doors opened and somebody went into the corridor. Most likely one of the women had gone to make up a bottle for the sake of the crying baby and his mother. After tomorrow she would probably never run into these women and their babies again. Each would spend a few days in the hospital and return home. Takiko was no exception, for tomorrow she must go back to the house where her family lived. There was nothing else she could do. Her days in the hospital had been utterly peaceful. As long as both were doing well, Takiko and the baby remained a very ordinary mother and child. Just a mother and child whose names didn't even matter.

Takiko's baby was sleeping with a querulous expression that put her in mind of an old man. He was a big, dark baby with large ears and a large mouth. She fancied she saw a resemblance to her brother Atsushi. She supposed he must resemble his father Maeda in some way, though she couldn't have said how. The baby was floating comfortably in a place far from Takiko and her parents and everyone on earth, dreaming dreams that she had no way of peering into. As yet he didn't even have the name he needed in this world.

If only they could be like this forever. She stroked the baby's head with its thin hair. Its warmth passed directly to the palm of her hand. A sweaty palm. Though the air conditioning was on, it was hot and sticky in the ward. Every time someone who had trouble sleeping tried turning the flow of air up, someone else would promptly turn it back down to the lowest setting. Most of the women in the ward had stripped off their blankets and were sleeping bare-legged. In the time Takiko had been there the curtains around individual beds had never been closed except during the doctors' rounds. Nor did the women worry about their appearance, even in visiting hours. While they were in the maternity hospital it seemed they were entitled to laze around with their nightgowns falling open. Those who had many visitors were as casual and sloppy as Takiko, whose mother came on alternate days.

She picked up a towel she had tossed beside the pillow and used it to wipe her perspiring hands, forehead, and chest.

Tomorrow morning her mother was to come for her and the baby. They had quarreled over this, keeping their voices low so the other women wouldn't hear, and in the end her mother had argued her down.

"It's not like when you came here. There's the baby to think of now. How on earth are you going to manage him *and* your bags? And how will it look leaving that way? What will people think of me? I've had enough of this stubbornness. You've got the baby to think of now, you know, you can't carry on the way you used to. The baby's more important than your stubborn pride."

I don't want to go anywhere. Takiko pressed the sweaty-smelling towel to her face. Her eyes were swollen with tears.

While having the last examination of her stay the day before, she'd been hoping they'd find something wrong with her. She'd wished that something would go wrong with the baby. But everything was going smoothly, and to her disappointment she was given permission to leave. She thought these five days had been the most restful of her life.

When her mother had come visiting that evening, bringing her favorite peaches and arrowroot jellies, Takiko told her at once that she'd be leaving the next day, and then, as if it had just occurred to her, asked after her father and Atsushi. The first time she held the baby and tried to feed him, it was her father's smiling face that had come to mind. Perhaps it was the way he'd smiled dandling Atsushi when he was little. She'd been startled—did she want that for the baby?—and felt tears come to her eyes. She hadn't been going to expect anything, ever, from any father. She thought she knew better than that.

They were both the same as usual, her mother had answered offhandedly.

"Dad's behaving himself, with you away. He just lies around the house. I only hope this'll encourage him to do a bit of work for a change. Don't you worry—even your dad won't be able to ignore this lively little fellow. Who'd have thought he'd turn out to be such a beautiful child?"

"You were counting on him being deformed, or something, weren't you?" Takiko muttered, almost under her breath. "Well, you're out of luck."

"I don't know what gets into the girl—saying things like that. I won't say another word. We'll just take good care of him. You can forget about everything except looking after the baby. I know you're really very happy he's arrived safely."

"Of course I am," Takiko snapped. It annoyed her to feel drawn to her mother's smiling face; the more she wanted to depend on her the more impatient she grew with herself. She would rather her mother stayed sad, even if she had to slap her cheek.

"I had him, right? And I'm not letting anyone who was so set on an abortion touch him now. When he's bigger I'll tell him who was planning to kill him. I mean it. So you'd better keep your hands off him from now on. . . . I'm sorry you'll have to put up with us for a bit, but I'll be paying you the equivalent of rent, so please let us stay till I'm able to work. It shouldn't take more than a month. Please explain this to Dad, too, if you wouldn't mind."

Her mother tried to laugh off this statement as an invalid's peevishness. "I'll come and meet you tomorrow," she said. Taut with anger, Takiko had insisted that she would leave the hospital on her own and her mother shouldn't interfere. But her mother hadn't even looked her in the face.

During Takiko's six-day stay, at least a third of the patients in the ward had changed.

The empty bed on her left had gone the next day to a woman with a face as chubby as her belly was round. She was wheeled in in the middle of the night, with her bag on her knees in the wheelchair. As soon as she was lying down she began to groan mightily. Takiko went off to sleep, and when she opened her eyes the woman was back from the delivery room. She slept quietly all that day, but by next morning she was up and doing her washing. The baby was brought in to her that day, and in the evening her four other children arrived with their father. These four, and the baby, all looked very much alike. Their father was a small, mild man. The children were all boys. All except the oldest climbed onto their mother's bed and began poking their chewing gum into the baby's mouth and nuzzling their mother's large breasts.

"Well, here we go again. I was so sure it'd be a nice quiet girl this time around," the woman laughed to Takiko after visiting hours were over, and offered her a share of the rice dumplings in bean jam that her husband had brought. She liked to talk. Takiko learned where they lived—over their fish shop—that the woman's husband was, thankfully, a hard worker, and that they'd let her have some great bargains if she'd like to come by sometime.

The woman in the next bed over noted that this was very near her own vegetable stand. Oh, they both laughed, so *that's* where I've seen you before.

Other women also lived in the neighborhood of the hospital. As she listened to them merrily telling each other where, a map of the area took shape in Takiko's head. The florist's. The candy store. The coffee shop. The small home-style restaurant.

The woman from the restaurant, who'd been in for two days, had daily visits from a party of women with children, whether relatives or friends, Takiko couldn't tell. She had come upon the woman in labor in the middle of the night, sitting on a bench in the corridor smoking a cigarette. On her way to prepare a bottle, Takiko had sat down beside her. No, the woman said when she inquired, she wasn't feeling too bad. "But I get bored just lying in bed, moaning and groaning with nothing to do. It's depressing. I wish it'd come quickly."

"I hope it does. I could use a cigarette myself. Mind if I have one of yours?"

She and the woman sat smoking, side by side, hardly talking at all.

On another night, a woman was rushed onto a cot set up next to the door. Her belly was not bulging. The next day she left and the cot was folded away. An old woman who must have been her mother accompanied her when she arrived and again when she left.

The bed on Takiko's right, vacated the day she came back from the delivery room, was filled again two days later. A quiet woman who looked nearly twenty years older than Takiko lay there on her back, hardly moving. She had one visit from a man who seemed to be her husband, and even then there was no laughter.

After asking Takiko how to take her medicine, however, the woman had started to confide in her. Takiko had to lean closer to hear her near-whisper.

"I've been here before, you know, ten years ago." As if she'd only just thought of it, the woman brought this up not long after Takiko had quarreled with her mother over leaving the hospital. "To have a baby, of course. The place hasn't changed a bit, it was just as run-down and dirty then. Still, it's been ten years, so this time I had my doubts. And my husband says we don't need another child now. But I've ended up having it, after dithering for so long. Hm, it must have been the bed you're in, because mine was down there, if I remember rightly. Yes, there was a junior high school girl in the one you're in. I suppose now she'd be about your age. She was just a child. Such a sweet girl. What I wanted to know was how did she get in here? Well, it seems the man was a teacher at her school. And it wasn't the first time, either. Twice with the same teacher—it makes you wonder, doesn't it? He knew they were used to handling these things here, so he sent his pupil along quite calmly. The hospital people were furious, they gave him a hard time, and I don't blame them. And she was in your bed, you see. She wouldn't answer when I spoke to her. She had this blank look, not what you'd call sad—maybe she wasn't very bright, if you know what I mean? Not a talker at all."

Takiko was nodding with her eyes fixed on the ceiling. The three large blades of a fan were rigidly motionless against the high plaster ceiling which she was told hadn't changed a bit in ten years.

She knew nothing at all about the hospital in which she was staying. Yet as she inspected the aging white plaster studded with Western-style decorations, she could almost see the women who must have lain under this same ceiling decades ago. Hundreds, no, thousands, maybe even tens of thousands of women had lain here staring up at the same ceiling. And one of them was her. Takiko felt a sense of sufficiency she'd never known before, a contentment that took her by surprise.

Her last night passed quietly enough, like the others. The

baby with the mechanical cry eventually settled down, apparently satisfied by the bottle, and his mother must have gone to sleep as well. Takiko lost count of how many times she woke to her baby's crying, put him to her breast, then ran into the corridor to prepare formula. There were plenty of others doing this. When she came across the same face twice in the pantry they would both break into smiles. That night again, there seemed to be someone lying in pain in the delivery room, not far from the pantry.

In the morning Takiko slept through the taking of temperatures and woke only when tapped on the shoulder by her neighbor on the left, who had carried in her breakfast tray. The baby was crying against her breast. She must have fallen asleep when she'd meant to put him back in the crib. She scrambled up, thanking her neighbor, and changed his diaper. Then, after a token attempt at breastfeeding, though she had as little milk as ever, she made up some formula in the pantry, sat on the bed and fed it to him. The level in the bottle steadily descended.

With a light sigh she lifted her head and glanced at the window. The poplar tree was a mass of finely burnished leaves, as it had been yesterday and the day before. Behind it there was another expanse of solid blue sky which made her feel momentarily cool whenever she looked out.

During her six days in the hospital, the sky hadn't been cloudy once. The tree outside the window had kept the midsummer glare before her eyes every day. The brighter it shimmered, the more deliciously cool she felt in the dimness of the ward. As the window faced north and never admitted the heat, it acted like a water surface, allowing her to enjoy the sunlight's sparkle as if from under the water. Takiko had grown more fond of this window than anything else during her stay.

The women patients in the dark ward thought almost nostalgically each day of the heat. They could sense it glowing from the bodies of the people who came to see them. Every visitor entered the ward panting and flushed. Even Takiko's mother carried the sunlight and the smell of sweat to her bedside. As she took a peek at the baby's face, she would always exclaim as if noticing for the first time, "It's so cool in here. You wouldn't believe how hot it is outside. They say it hasn't been this hot in thirty years. And on top of everything else they've started restricting the water supply in our area, you know. It really is lovely in here. Won't he be surprised when he leaves? Especially in our house. If only we had some thunder showers to break the heat in the evenings. . . ."

She arrived streaming with sweat and very upset one day, protesting that she never did such things—she'd gone and lost the arrowroot jellies she bought especially on her way to the hospital. It was true, such carelessness wasn't like her. Takiko took little notice. "What if it had been your purse," she pointed out, "instead of a box of jellies?" But her mother went on bemoaning and excusing the loss. "It's the heat, it's too much for me. I can't sleep at night. It would never have happened otherwise, I'm sure. But I'm a bit run down, and in this heat what can you expect?"

Several hours from now Takiko herself, with the baby, would have to venture into that heat. Her eyes dwelled on the gleaming tree at the window.

It was around seven in the morning.

When he'd drunk the formula the baby shut his mouth and went to sleep. She put him to bed and started hurriedly on her breakfast. She was the only one in the ward still eating.

The others were lying on their beds, browsing through the ward's accumulation of comic books and women's magazines, or neatly folding the diapers provided by the hospital, or tidying their night tables, or feeding their babies. There was no conversation to be heard and few babies crying. It was the lull before morning rounds, as quiet as a typical hospital ward.

Takiko would not need to be seen on rounds this morning. She had had her last examination the previous day in the doctor's office downstairs and been given permission to go home. The waiting outpatients had stared at her in her nightgown, reminding her of how she hadn't been able to keep from staring at the inpatients herself. She'd found it hard to believe that such a time would come for her too. Now it was embarrassing to have to walk under the gaze of the pregnant women, with her shape announcing that she had given birth. It was not unpleasant, though. Already she couldn't remember except in a dreamlike way what it was like to be pregnant.

When she'd finished breakfast she returned her tray to the trolley in the corridor, carefully washed her chopsticks and teacup in the water-heater room, and then, returning to pick up her towel and toiletries, headed for the washstand. Beyond it were the stairs and another room the same size as the one that Takiko's bed was in. Three young women came out of this room, laughing, to the washstand.

"I hope mine'll come for us soon. Wonder what time he'll get here."

"Lucky you, having a husband who does things. I'll bet he's got everything taken care of at home."

"Yes, but he's so finicky. He insists that I wash the diapers by hand, and he's got this idea I shouldn't watch TV any more. I don't see what difference it can make—either the baby's bright or he isn't, what's TV got to do with it? He's already worrying about the poor kid's grades. It's depressing."

Takiko moved down to the end of the stand and quickly finished washing her face. She glanced resentfully over at the three, who had cut short the extra-thorough wash she'd been planning for her last time in the hospital. The three young women, not much older than her, were bubbling over with high spirits.

Of course Takiko was not the only one due to leave the hospital that day. Two others were evidently leaving from her own ward, for when she got back two women on the far side with whom she'd never spoken were already organizing their belongings into suitcases and cloth wrappers laid out on their beds. The sight of them made Takiko suddenly want to hurry too. She hadn't finished checking out yet, much less packing. And her mother was to come for her by twelve.

Taking out her purse, which she had wrapped in a gauze handkerchief and tucked into a corner of the baby's crib, she went this time to the office downstairs. There she paid the hospital fee, for which she had saved part of her severance pay, and in return was handed her maternity handbook with the doctor's observations recorded in it and a paper to register the birth.

"Be sure not to lose this, it's very important for your baby. And don't forget you have another examination in one month—you and the baby. That's all for now."

"Yes. Thank you."

Bowing politely, Takiko hastened back to her room. She was happy to find that the charge had come to only a little more than she'd estimated. She had just a few ten-thousand-yen bills left.

Since his early morning feed the baby had conveniently stayed quietly asleep. As soon as she returned to her bed she unfolded her cloth wrapper and began arranging her things. The doctor had begun his rounds over by the window. At this hour every patient was supposed to be in bed, and the other women who had been packing were now lying down. The only sounds echoing in the ward were several babies crying and the doctor's and nurses' voices. Takiko went on with her preparations in spite of the hush.

She folded her two towels, which were beginning to show the dirt, along with the blue bath towel she'd been sleeping on, and neatly packed away the nightgown she'd worn for the first three days. Then she opened the night-table drawer and took out her teacup and chopstick case, a bag of cookies her mother had left, her fruit knife, toiletries, and other odds and ends.

"Odaka-san here is due to leave today."

As the nurse explained apologetically, Takiko turned around. The young, athletic doctor who was so popular with the patients was studying the name card by her bed. With a smile she said, "Yes, thank you very much, I'm being discharged today."

After consulting the records in his hand, the doctor looked at her face and smiled. He had a good tan from the tennis practice he kept up daily, even in the hospital yard. When he smiled, deep wrinkles gathered at the corners of his eyes.

"Yes, it's your sixth day, isn't it, Odaka-san? And everything looks satisfactory."

"That's right," Takiko answered brightly.

The doctor laughed. "She's raring to go, isn't she? Good, but be careful you don't wear yourself out."

"No, I'll be fine," she assured him cheerfully.

Laughing again, the doctor moved on to the next bed. The two nurses accompanying him pulled the curtains and he withdrew inside. Unlike Takiko, the woman on her right didn't seem to be doing well after the delivery.

She went on with her task. Since she hadn't brought much to the hospital in the first place, it didn't take long to finish packing. Having decided to dress herself and the baby later, after her mother arrived, she lay down. With the slight rearranging she'd done, the bed showed so little trace of her presence that it might have been awaiting the next occupant already. While she was gazing idly at the window and its view of the tree, she slipped off to sleep.

She slept almost until noon. In the crib by her feet the baby had started to cry. A nurse, speaking to each infant in a piping voice, was loading them all onto a long trolley. It was time for their bath. A woman handed over the baby she'd been changing in a flurry, another woke from a nap and sat up to see where hers was going, a third rushed over to her bed as the nurse prepared to whisk her baby away. The big ward was suddenly bustling.

It was only after she'd looked around, rubbing her eyes, and spotted one of the women in the far corner dressed in street clothes, her baby in her arms and her family there to escort her home, that Takiko remembered her own departure and sprang out of bed. Her mother hadn't come yet. It would be time for lunch next, once the babies were out of the ward.

Takiko picked up hers, who was crying hungrily.

"Thank you, everybody. We're off now. Take care, all right?" The woman who was dressed to leave in a sleeveless white blouse made her way down the ward bowing in friendly fashion toward this bed and that, while her husband and her mother followed, bags in hand. She came to where the trolley for the babies was standing a short distance from Takiko's bed. As their eyes met the woman beamed at Takiko.

"You're off too, aren't you? Take care."

"Congratulations."

"Thank you."

The woman then turned to the nurse with bows and thanks, her husband and mother joining in by turns, and then left the ward. No one watched them go. There was no link between the inside of the ward and the outside.

"Yours is also leaving today, isn't he? What do you want to do?" The nurse approached Takiko. "How about a bath so he'll be all fresh and clean? Then you won't have to worry when you get home."

"But someone's coming any minute now—"

The nurse carried away the crying baby all the same. "Won't take a moment," she laughed.

Takiko's mother hadn't shown up by the time the babies began coming back from the bath. When she'd eaten lunch, Takiko started to change. The dress she'd brought from home was the first regular, nonmaternity garment she had pulled on that summer. Once she'd put away her nightgown there was nothing left to do. She sat on the edge of the bed and gazed at the light outside the window.

"Here we are! Nice and clean!" The first detail of babies was back. They were being handed, one by one, to their mothers, ready to be fed, but Takiko's was not among them.

"Yours not back yet either?"

The plump woman in the bed on the left had been to check

the trolley and returned empty-handed. Takiko nodded, making a slight frown. The woman sat down opposite her on the edge of her bed.

"You must be happy. I wish I was going home. The kids are driving their dad up the wall. Poor man—I can just imagine it. My younger sister is there to help out, but I can't expect her to do everything. I'm glad of the chance just to lie in bed—if only I could relax. Well, let's keep in touch. Like to give me your address? Here, I'll write mine down. It'd be nice to see your boy again some time."

"Yes, that would be nice, but I live a long way from here . . ."

After a moment's hesitation Takiko took the hurriedly offered piece of paper and wrote out the address of the house where she'd grown up, the house to which she was due to return that day. The address the woman handed her in exchange was on the same block as the hospital.

"Heavens, that *is* a long way. I don't know that area at all. I've heard it's quite elegant."

"Oh, no. Some parts, yes, but where I live it's a mess. It's much nicer around here." Despite Takiko's amusement, the woman looked unconvinced.

Just then Takiko happened to notice the second departing woman on her way out of the ward; she was following her husband, who carried the bags, and held the baby in a white blanket in her arms. From behind, it looked as though she were sneaking out. Enough of this waiting; Takiko suddenly made up her mind. As soon as the baby came back she would get going. She stood up.

Her mother came in at that moment.

She bustled past Takiko to the crib, looking flushed and damp, explaining that she'd meant to be there sooner but thought she'd just get her work out of the way first, and the next thing she knew it was already past twelve. When she realized that the baby wasn't there, she turned her flushed face to Takiko for the first time.

"He'll be back in a moment. He's having a bath," Takiko said flatly.

Her mother sighed, with relief perhaps, and began mopping her face with a handkerchief while she smiled and bowed to the woman in the next bed and the one beyond.

Once she'd greeted the occupants of all the beds around Takiko's, her mother whispered, "Well, can you go when the baby gets back? Is the money all taken care of?"

"We can go," Takiko whispered back testily. "But what about your work, did you get it done?" Her mother shook her head with a shamefaced look.

"I've been trying since last night, but it was too much for me. I've got till tonight, though."

"You shouldn't take on so much at once. You know you can't manage it. What about Dad?"

"He's been out all day. I have no idea where. . . . I did tell him you'd be coming back from the hospital."

"Oh."

They both fell silent. The woman in the bed on the left began talking to Takiko's mother in a polite tone.

"How very nice to have your daughter home with you at last. One really can't settle down in a place like this, can one? Living in such a quiet area, you must find it especially trying? I expect this is all very different from your, er, accustomed surroundings?"

Mystified, her mother was drawn into conversation.

Takiko's baby arrived back soon afterwards, with a number of others. He had on the brand-new clothes and diaper cover that she had sent with him. There was an aura of the hot bath about him as she took him in her arms, and a sweet soapy smell.

Dressed up for the first time in Takiko's own choice of clothes, the baby struck her as novel, even comical. Half laughing and half wanting to cry, she thought, "So this baby, just a baby who doesn't even have a name yet, has been placed in my hands." There was nothing more to wait for. At her mother's prompting, Takiko rose from the bed, the comical baby in her arms.

He lay quietly sleeping, his face pink from the bath.

Takiko and her mother left the ward, bowing repeatedly to no one in particular. When she paused for a quick look back on reaching the corridor, the woman in the bed on the left was waving regretfully. The bed on the right had been curtained off since morning rounds. Takiko and her mother bowed to each nurse or patient they passed in the corridor. One of the nurses—not a very familiar one—greeted Takiko.

"You're leaving? A lot of people going home today, aren't there? Congratulations."

"Thank you."

Her mother bowed her head deeply once more.

They went down the stairs and along the corridor to the lobby. There were only a few outpatients to be seen, and the entrance was deserted. Takiko slipped her stockingless feet into the white sandals her mother set out ready for her. They were the ones she'd been walking in all summer long. Now that her feet were no longer swollen from her pregnancy, the sandals were stretched too wide.

In front of the glass doors Takiko drew a deep breath. She was afraid to go out. What lay beyond them was glittering too brightly in the midday sun.

Her mother was waiting outside for her, holding the door. Takiko took a look at the baby's face: he was asleep, his mouth slightly open. His lips were an entrancing, transparent pink. Having first shielded his face with the edge of the white blanket in which he was wrapped, Takiko bit her lower lip and stepped firmly out.

"Now, then, we don't want to waste time standing around. We need to find a taxi, quick." Her mother hurried off toward the street. Takiko quickened her pace as if clinging to her mother's back.

Everything around her was giving off too strong a light. She was afraid that if she stood still, she and the baby would drown together in the glare. The asphalt beneath her feet was whitened by snowlike drifts of light. Although she knew it was the midsummer heat that was beating against her, the brightness all around her made her think of snow, of ice. She mustn't let the baby disappear in the glare. She held him tightly in her arms and repeated this warning to herself until they were safely settled in the taxi that her mother had flagged down.

It was cool inside. Once she had checked the baby's sleeping face, Takiko relaxed at last and smiled to herself. The taxi was speeding through quiet early-afternoon streets. Rows of houses flashed by outside the window.

"Ah . . ."

She let out a gasp as the taxi began to travel down some very familiar streets.

"Huh? What's wrong?"

Her mother's question made Takiko burst out laughing. Her mother, beside her, grinned in spite of herself.

"What is it?"

"It's just good to be back. I wish we could drive around forever."

"You do talk nonsense sometimes." Her mother laughed too, then glanced down at the baby in Takiko's arms as if suddenly reminded he was there. "He's sound asleep. You should go straight to bed yourself as soon as we're home. There won't be anyone around all afternoon."

Takiko nodded, only half listening. That these awfully familiar streets should strike her now as beautiful could only mean she'd been missing them, she was glad to be back. They were lined with tightly crowded old houses which of course she'd never thought beautiful before. Many contained furniture makers' shops; there were also a noticeable number of shoemakers and luggage makers. The occasional modern building would turn out to house not offices but a funeral parlor or trucking firm or a long-established herbal pharmacy. It was certainly a gloomy neighborhood.

Yet in Takiko's eyes the streets shone with a strange bright clarity, clean and limpid in the summer sun. She couldn't take her eyes off them. She remembered the shining tree that she'd watched each day from her hospital room. Although she didn't expect to see that tree from that window ever again, now she had the view from the taxi window, a view she hadn't known on her way to the hospital.

Her lap was growing hot under the sleeping baby. It was as if she were staring out at the shining tree, the shining streets, with a six-day-old infant's eyes.

"Atsushi should be home at the usual time, I suppose, but I don't know about Dad. . . . Now listen, no more of your cheek to Dad, please. He's a grandfather now, remember. He's the nearest thing to a father that this child's got."

Her mother's words jolted Takiko as if waking her from sleep, and she had just rounded on her with wide eyes when the taxi stopped. She let out a deep breath and rearranged the baby in her arms. He quivered a little.

They alighted at their street corner and Takiko, not waiting while her mother paid the cabdriver, walked on down the alley carrying the baby in a firm embrace.

Both the alley and the house where Takiko grew up were things the baby was seeing—or should have been seeing—for the first time. His eyes remained closed as he puckered his mouth, showed a glimpse of his tongue, and started to yawn. But as Takiko stood in front of her house and waited for her mother to unlock the front door, a feeling that she had something to tell him came over her.

Have a good look. Make sure you don't forget. This is the house you came to first of all. You may be going somewhere else very soon, but you should remember this house. This is where I grew up, and it's the first place you came to after you were born. . . .

Indoors, the house was stuffy with trapped heat. Her mother dropped Takiko's bags in the middle of the room and went around opening all the windows, but even then the hot air was slow to stir. The house was both sunless and poorly ventilated, hotter inside than out during the summer, and cold in the winter.

Still holding the baby, Takiko looked vaguely around. She

was stunned: had the place always been so tiny and such a complete shambles? Her eye fell on a blob of egg yolk and rice grains—probably the remains of Atsushi's breakfast—congealing on the tabletop, three cups with tea left in them, the newspaper and its wad of advertising inserts refolded any old way and left lying where they'd been thrown. In the enclosed veranda where her mother kept her sewing machine, a heap of navy and green striped woolen cloth hulked like some mysterious beast, partly collapsed into the main room. An unpleasant odor arose from the kitchen.

So this was the house she'd grown up knowing, thought Takiko. The bathroom addition. Redoing the kitchen. The neighbors putting up a two-story apartment wing in their garden so that it loomed over them. Atsushi falling off the veranda—would he have been two at the time? And the time Takiko, then about four, tried to tie a ribbon on the cat they used to have and was scratched from her eyelid to her cheek. As if on the point of leaving, she couldn't resist summoning up these memories of her old home.

"Well, anyway, why don't you lie down? Your bed's made up." Her mother appeared from the storeroom—Atsushi's room—at the back of the house. "Are you hungry? I could make some ramen."

"No, I'm not hungry. . . ."

Beads of perspiration were dripping from her mother's chin. Takiko's body broke into a sweat also. Swathed in the blanket, the baby was red in the face until she took him out.

Her mother sat down beside Takiko and gazed at him in the baby clothes. "He's so good and quiet, isn't he? Well now . . . since there's nothing we can do about the heat wherever we put you, I'm going to let you two have Atchan's room. He's moved into your old one. It should be a bit quieter for you that way, and . . ."

"Uh-huh . . . okay, we'll go in there."

Takiko picked the baby up again and carried him to the storeroom, next to the bathroom. Her mother called after her apologetically, "I know it's cramped, but there's your father to think of too."

Not answering, Takiko seated herself on the futons that took up the whole of the two-mat space and set the baby down beside her. He immediately started to cry. She looked around: the things she had prepared herself, the diapers, sets of clothing, formula bottles, were stacked against the wall. The baby's small futon was in place alongside her own. While her mother sat looking in from the doorway, she changed the baby's diaper, took off her blouse, and nursed him. The sweat ran from her neck down her breasts.

Her mother seemed to be inquiring about her milk.

Takiko was beginning to feel weary. She couldn't wait to get herself and the baby to bed. Her breasts were as sore as ever. Her skin, normally quite dark, had turned transparently pale revealing prominent blue veins as they swelled. She didn't like her breasts this way. She remembered her pride when, ten years earlier, they had first filled out. The baby went on unconcernedly sucking at her nipple.

After shifting him from right to left, she surveyed the room once again. There was a bee on the low grating where dust was swept outside, and dusty holly branches were pressing against the grate. The holly bush was the neighbor's. And in the storeroom, futons and diapers. But no supply of powdered formula. She would have to ask her mother to go out for some.

"Mom . . ."

She was just about to bring it up, tentatively, when they heard a man's voice from the front entrance.

"Anyone at home?"

"Oh dear, who could that be?" her mother muttered, and went to see. The man's voice was followed by her mother's, shrill with surprise. The man's laugh boomed. Takiko couldn't see them from where she sat, but in any case the visitor didn't seem to be asking for her. With the baby still at her breast she slid the storeroom door shut, leaving a slit of a couple of inches. She could hear her mother's voice and footsteps.

Reclining on the futon, she continued to feed the baby. Sweat trickled from her breast onto his nose.

"Takiko." Her mother's flustered face peered in to whisper, "Don't worry, I won't let him stay long."

Takiko nodded without raising herself.

Her mother ran back to the front door and continued talking with the visitor. His accent struck Takiko as familiar: could it be someone her mother had known before she came to Tokyo?

Takiko closed her eyes. The baby's mouth was still fastened to her breast, and her back was clammy with sweat. The bee was motionless on the grating. Though naked from the waist up, she hesitated to move and cover herself in case the baby cried while the visitor was there. She didn't want the noise to further upset her mother, who wouldn't yet have worked out how to explain the baby's presence to outsiders.

Before she knew it, she was almost asleep. As she drifted off, she watched a scene unfold in her mother's part of the country.

It was a mountainside. Beyond was another mountain, and above its black crest she could make out a distant ridge of pale blue on the point of dissolving into the sky. If you crossed one mountain in this region, another rose up ahead.

When Takiko was a child, her mother had spoken about the place where she grew up. Not often—it may have been only two or three times—and even then she'd had little to say. No one directly connected with her mother lived there any more. She had never been back, or taken her family even briefly to see the place when they'd been traveling. Takiko, however, had pictured it for herself from her words. She had a feeling that her mother was there still, and this unknown mother had always appealed to her. When she tried to imagine a young girl looking out from a mountain at more distant mountains, for some reason the figure would always turn into herself.

At a certain spot among the pale blue mountains the snow lasted all summer, glinting so sharply it might have been a mirror. The patch was shaped like a white horse. It varied from year to year, and when the figure of the horse flared out in a powerful gallop the local people would be assured of a good harvest in the fall.

From a slight rise deep in the mountain country, Takiko gazed at the white, beautiful horse galloping across the blue peak. Vineyards ascended a long way up the slope below her, the white backs of the leaves rippling into view. From where she stood, the fields were a wild, foaming sea of green. Or a giant creature which seethed with loathing for the mountain.

Beyond the miles of vineyards, in the far distance she could see a village in the misty valley, and a silver river.

"Get up now, Takiko, or you'll catch cold."

When her mother's voice roused her, she didn't know where

she was for a moment. Was this the hospital ward? Or her room?

"The visitor's gone now, sorry. My, you are in a sweat. It's hot enough, isn't it, without shutting the door? Here, let me wipe your back."

There were still traces of what Takiko thought of as her brother's smell in the room, mingled now with the milky smell of the baby. She sat up quickly, feeling chilled. The baby's yell almost bit into her. He was there on her lap. The sheet was wet with her sweat.

"Dear, dear, did you get a fright? Poor little thing, you were sound asleep, weren't you?" Her mother sat down on the futon and, with a glance at Takiko's drowsy face, picked up the baby. "There, there," she purred, "go to sleep now. That's a good boy." The yelling didn't let up. She checked his diaper with a probing finger.

"He isn't wet. What's wrong, then? You've been such a good boy till now. . . . Really, what a time for a surprise visit! But goodness, it must be ten years—no, more like fifteen. We'd even stopped sending New Year's cards. And then he tells me he just happened to be in this part of Tokyo on business and thought he'd look us up! You don't know him, Takiko. I've told you about your uncle who died before you were born, haven't I? Well, this was the brother of the woman who was married to your uncle, though since she remarried after he died he's no relation to us now, but in the country, you know, these connections go on and on. And people are forever dropping in like that without warning. He used to live nearby, you see. He was in the quartz business, up in the mountains. Seems he's quite well off these days. . . . Well, anyway, it's nothing to do with us. There, there. What a lot of crying! Looks to me like he wants another feed. That's one thing your grandma can't do for you, I'm afraid."

"Grandma?" Takiko murmured—and was overtaken by a rage so sudden it caught even her unprepared. "What do you mean, 'grandma'? He's not your grandchild, he's not your anything! Get your hands off him!" And she roughly grabbed the baby back from her mother's arms.

His yells grew decidedly louder. Her mother stared at her face, dumbfounded. Beside herself with excitement now, Takiko went on, "Understand? How many times do I have to tell you? A hundred? Two hundred? That's how often you told me to kill this child. *Grandma.* Don't make me laugh. You were scared sick he was going to be some kind of monster. He . . . he's . . . he's starving, that's what. I don't have enough milk, he has to have formula, and here's you—you still can't believe there's nothing wrong with him, can you? What are you so afraid of?"

"Takiko, be quiet a moment. If he needs formula, then I'll just have to go and buy some, won't I? And don't sit around naked, put your nightie on, there's no sense in catching cold. Well, then, I'll be right back."

When her mother had left, Takiko shed feeble tears while watching the baby, whose face remained tearless however hard he cried.

Atsushi came home shortly before dinnertime. Takiko was at work in the kitchen as their mother was dealing with the last of her sewing.

"Hi, Atchan."

Takiko gave Atsushi a beaming smile; it was a long time

since she'd seen him. His face reddened as he struggled not to smile. She observed his expression and laughed gaily.

"What a face! And how have you been all this time?"

"What's got into you?" Atsushi mumbled, throwing his schoolbag down on the tatami.

"No, no, it's your turn to ask me."

"Huh. I only have to look at you to know."

"Oh. Then why don't you have a look at what's-his-face? He takes after you."

Her mother laughed over the noise of the machine.

The baby was fast asleep in the storeroom. He slept on even when Atsushi prodded his cheek.

When they'd finished dinner, Takiko sponged herself down in the bathroom and washed her hair. Her mother had returned to her sewing and Atsushi had started on his homework in Takiko's old room next door. Back in the storeroom she lay down, but immediately sat up again, opened the front of her nightgown and, screwing up her face for the pain, began to massage her breasts which felt fresh after the wash. Unless she was imagining it, they seemed to be less full. Her father hadn't come home yet.

The baby eventually began to cry after nine o'clock. Her mother went out carrying the finished batch of garments.

Takiko made a very brief attempt at breastfeeding and then gave him a bottle. Atsushi came to the door to watch the baby drink, bringing the electric fan he'd been using. He set it up in the corridor so that a faint breeze reached Takiko and the baby. Takiko merely smiled at her brother; he too was silent as he sat in the corridor.

Their mother came home at about eleven. Takiko had already turned out the light and was lying with the baby in the dark. He was sound asleep, and she herself had lost all sensation in a thick drowsiness. She should have been able to drop off at any moment, yet she couldn't close her eyes.

Her father still wasn't back. These days he always got home by eleven at the very latest.

Her mother looked in on Takiko and the baby. Perhaps thinking they were both fast asleep, she returned to the main room without a word, and soon that light went out also. Atsushi was the only one in the house still up.

In the dark, Takiko pictured her mother's home.

The acres of vineyards that covered the flank of the mountain. As she contemplated what should have been a scene of perfect tranquillity, it was gradually stirred by wild emotion. Surging leaves and purple spray. As if animated by hatred for the mountain, they tried to isolate it from the world below. Then there were the surrounding mountains. Still more distant, blue peaks.

The quartz that her mother had mentioned that day also formed images in her mind.

Her mother had a black necklace of smoky quartz, an obi fastener and prayer beads of amethyst, and a clear uncut block of hexagonal rock crystal. These she had treasured since she was a girl. Though she seldom spoke of home, her mother had shown Takiko these pieces with unconcealed pride. She kept her precious smoky quartz necklace for formal wear, but as Takiko had grown up seeing it often (since it wasn't as if she had any other real jewelry), she had lost her childhood fascination and ceased to speculate about when her mother would give it to her. In the last few years she'd only seen the prayer beads, which her mother took to funerals, and the uncut stone, which had a permanent place as an ornament on the china cabinet. Before that it had been a plaything for the children.

Feeling as though she'd regained that childhood self, Takiko looked on entranced as quartz crystals floated into view over the mountain scene. Smoky quartz and amethysts drifted and sparkled in the sky, against the mountains blue with distance and the vineyards, in untold number and variety. How beautiful it all is, she thought wonderingly. And how remote from the human world.

The imaginary crystals dance and spin through the air, giving off a clear, hard light as they are steadily drawn down to the breast of the girl who stands on the mountain. Takiko's mother. She couldn't have imagined anyone else as part of the scene.

As the girl looks down to the vineyards from a little height above, her neck is hung with heavy strands of the purple and black gems. She has all the grapes, all the quartz, all the sky she could want. They are beautiful things, but they trap the girl in her solitude among the mountains. She lacks even the words to express her longings.

As always when she thought of her mother's home, Takiko could no longer distinguish her mother from herself.

The girl gazes eagerly out at the world below, day after day. She can't go down there. It is a distant, other world, more remote than the blue mountains. Yet she can see it, all too clearly, tiny but visible in every detail. She grows sad amid the grapes and the crystal sky. There are houses, roads, and fields down there. Adults and children. A world in miniature, like a toy. She grows sadder.

That looks like fun. . . .

The village in the valley below isn't all she can see. Beyond the far ridge lies a plain where she can trace a river, and then the sea, like a great liquid amethyst. The coastline stretches away to the north, sometimes straight, then curving, then rugged, until finally the sea ices over and glitters whitely. The girl likes that glittering whiteness best of all. Although it is the farthest thing she can see from the mountain, she feels drawn to the frozen sea. The swift figures of men on dog sleds haven't escaped her notice either. The merest black dots, they glide freely through the white expanse. An apparently endless sea of ice.

The girl senses the sleds' speed. She senses the wind against her body. She senses the men's laughter.

But they can't see me. . . .

A pounding on the front door echoed through the house. Then she heard her father's voice. Her mother got up to open the door.

Takiko didn't move from her bed.

But this was how her mother had ended up, she thought: the wife of a man from a small town, a stranger to both the glitter of ice and the rolling green. Maybe her mother had settled for what she'd got, but Takiko didn't want to give up. She couldn't do it.

Her father came inside. He must have been quite drunk, as he seemed to go to sleep almost at once, in his clothes, without another word.

The name came to her: Akira. There were many different characters that could be used to write this popular boy's name, but the one she'd decided on was "crystal," part of the word "quartz." As if in reply to her thoughts, the baby burst out crying. They were intense cries.

THE ROAD

From late September on, the weather was unsettled. A number of storm warnings were issued as typhoons passed nearby. Rather than fading gradually, the long fine summer had lingered on unbroken until the last possible moment, then vanished abruptly with only a week of September to go, leaving behind a chilly wind and rain.

As the wet spell extended into October—normally a

month of crisp blue skies and welcome coolness—the gloom was enough to make people miss the fierce cloudless blue of summer.

Takiko found herself having to struggle with diapers that wouldn't dry. Although she knew it would irritate her father, who, mercifully, had been ignoring her as she coped with Akira, she had no choice but to hang laundry throughout the cluttered house. Even then the diapers stayed damp and had to be ironed one by one. She was also having to prepare a bottle for every feeding, as her breasts had lost their fullness two or three days after she came home. Akira still woke frequently in the night, and she was chronically short of sleep and beginning to lose weight noticeably.

Akira had been accepted from mid-October at a private day-care cooperative called Midori Nursery. The notice arrived in September. Midori Nursery was the only one of the places she'd tried, going the rounds with her big belly, that let her know of a vacancy. This in itself was evidently a stroke of luck. For some reason two prior enrollments had been withdrawn, allowing Akira to squeeze in at the last minute. Takiko didn't hesitate to take up the offer. The place had made little impression on her one way or the other when she'd gone there to apply, and she could barely remember what it was like until she went back for the enrollment formalities. As for the nursery that had made the best impression, in the wood beside the shrine, even if she could afford to wait there was so little prospect of getting Akira accepted there that she had to conclude the place was not for them.

On the appointed day in October, Takiko went to Midori Nursery, carrying Akira. It was the first time she'd taken him farther than walking distance from home. It had been raining heavily since the early morning, and even if it wasn't a full-blown storm, it wasn't the kind of day she'd have chosen to go out into, with or without a baby. Nevertheless, she bundled Akira up in a blanket and got ready to leave without delay.

Her father was the only one at home. He wouldn't even move about the house, except to go to the toilet, as his withered leg ached in rainy weather. This complaint dated back some time. While no one could understand his pain, they couldn't ignore the foul mood it put him in on wet days. He seemed to grow newly embittered by his bad luck each time.

Once the cool, wet weather set in, Takiko had begun to want to look for a job as soon as possible. She and her father hadn't clashed outright since Akira's birth, but they avoided meeting face to face, and she seldom brought Akira out of the storeroom.

Her mother was convinced that her father would come around sooner or later, that even now he'd like to hold Akira in his arms, but that being a clumsy man by nature he would take twice as long as most people to admit it.

"Besides, there aren't many fathers who'd be pleased by what you've done. I hope you feel a little bit ashamed of yourself. In his own way I'm sure Dad's thinking of you."

Takiko could neither accept nor rebuff her mother's words. She could see that it was because he was her father that he got angry enough to slap her, but she didn't really see why she had to be treated that way. He might be a small man but it hurt when he hit her, and though she tried, she couldn't forget the pain.

For now, her father was, as her mother said, showing un-expected restraint. But the strain would surely begin to tell before much longer. With diapers dangling about his head one rainy day after another, and Akira's crying echoing day and night through the house, her father's patience must be near breaking point. She caught herself starting at sudden sounds. As she was giving Akira his bottle, or bathing him, or hanging out the diapers, or washing the dishes, any loud noise would take her breath away and send a chill through her. Yet her father's fist was never there behind her when she turned.

She longed to be able to take Akira outdoors. This wet weather was beginning to wear her down too. She counted the days eagerly once it was decided that he would start at Midori Nursery at the regulation six weeks of age. She would have liked to have a new job at least lined up by that time, but she couldn't leave Akira, and in the end everything had to wait until he was started at the nursery.

Takiko was so set on enrolling him that a typhoon wouldn't have deterred her.

Her father had been lying around all morning on the futon he'd left down in the living room, glancing up at the television from time to time while he pored over pamphlets and advertising inserts on property deals. He had amassed enough material of this kind to more than fill a large shopping bag. For the past year he had been very taken with the idea of selling their own small house, buying a block of land back home, and building apartments on it. If they played their cards right, he said, they'd be able to live a damn sight better than they did now, but he hadn't succeeded in interesting even Atsushi, let alone their mother, in this scheme. Their present house had been bought soon after the war by Takiko's grandfather on her mother's side, as a gift for the newlyweds.

Before the property scheme, her father had taken up one of the new religious sects. If he could just get onto the executive board he stood to make a small fortune, or so he'd heard. However, he had failed to bring in a single convert.

Takiko would have liked to stay with sleeping Akira in the storeroom until they were due to leave for the nursery, but she didn't have time. There were the breakfast dishes to be washed, the diapers to be laundered and hung up in the bathroom.

It was hot and muggy indoors. Even the tatami and the wooden pillars seemed to exude a greasy sweat. Opening the windows just an inch or two let in large drops of rain which instantly formed pools. With its windows and doors shut tight, the house was stifling.

Her father had only to lift a finger and something was bound to give. Takiko prayed that the situation would hold until they were out of the house. She avoided the room where he was.

At midday she put together a simple lunch and carried it in to the table. She hurried away to the storeroom without a word and began to get ready. She hadn't needed to look in her father's direction to be well aware of his hard stare.

When she crossed the room wearing her raincoat and carrying Akira, again she couldn't help feeling his eyes glaring at her.

She didn't say where she was going or what time she'd be back. The appointment was for one-thirty.

The rain had turned heavier since the morning. The ground at her feet was awash with fast-flowing streams, and her bare legs were wet at once. Balancing her umbrella in the hand that supported Akira, very soon she was completely soaked.

She pressed on to the bus stop, drenched with rain and perspiration, telling herself all the way that she must keep Akira dry. Walking through the rain, she still felt much as she had indoors with her father. She could only be amazed that she'd escaped a fight so far.

"It's all right," she told Akira silently, "I won't get you wet."

When they'd ridden the bus for five stops, then doubled back a short distance and turned the corner by a coffee shop, Midori Nursery came into sight: a small, old two-story building at the end of a narrow side street. A smaller prefab adjoining it was also part of the nursery.

The unpaved alley was a river of mud.

So this was where she'd have to come every day now. She would have liked to take a good look at the alley and the two buildings, but in the downpour they were only a shadowy blur, and, anyway, she couldn't stand around surveying the scene.

Opening the glass door, she threw down her umbrella and rushed into the entrance hall along with the driving rain.

"Wow!" a woman exclaimed from the adjacent kitchen. "It's really pouring!"

Another woman stuck her head out from the room beyond.

"Hey, keep it down, will you? I've just about got all the children off to sleep."

"Yes, but . . ." The woman in the kitchen pointed to Takiko. Now that she'd had time to close her umbrella, get a better hold on Akira, and catch her breath, Takiko bowed and smiled.

"Oh, who is it?"

"I don't know. But just look, she's soaked to the skin."

"*Please*, keep your voice down, will you?"

"Excuse me," Takiko got in at last. "Um . . . he's been accepted here. It's very good of you." The two women nodded with a distinct lack of enthusiasm. "And I was told to come today to complete the enrollment."

The women exchanged a look. Takiko was becoming a little apprehensive, but the second woman answered brusquely, "In that case, it's the prefab next door that you want. We're not using it for the children today because the roof leaks so badly."

"That's right," the woman in the kitchen agreed.

"Oh, I'll try there, then. Sorry to bother you."

As she spoke, Takiko glanced around the entrance hall. It had a time clock, for the staff, she supposed; a large blackboard carrying the month's schedule; a small one for messages; and on the floor, heaped sacks of onions, potatoes, and other vegetables.

In the prefab, there was a group already seated in the middle of the single large room—a father, mother, and baby. Takiko recalled being told on the phone that both parents should come for the enrollment if at all possible. She had asked, sounding more apologetic than necessary, "Is it all right if only the mother comes? His father isn't here. . . ."

"Of course, that's quite all right. Father or mother, it doesn't matter as long as you're prepared to be involved in running the nursery. We don't accept applicants who just want to leave their children here and be done with it. That's why we're anxious to have both parents come at the start. If you're on your own, it's quite all right as long as you come in to see us."

The voice on the telephone then changed the subject. Apparently Takiko's domestic situation was of no further interest.

Takiko put Akira down in his blanket on the floorboards. She had fed him before they came and he was sound asleep. There were only two or three raindrops on his face. She wiped them off with her handkerchief, then wiped down her own face, hands, and hair. From the right-hand corner and the middle of the ceiling, drips were splashing steadily into buckets on the floor. From the larger of the two leaks, the one in the middle of the room, the water streamed down in a column.

"Oh, what a big baby."

The mother who'd arrived first peeked at Akira's face. Takiko gave an answering smile.

"See, I told you ours was small." The mother nudged the father's arm as he sat holding their baby and smoking a cigarette. He wore a cream polo shirt. After gazing down at Akira, he smiled at Takiko.

"What month was yours born?"

"August," Takiko answered, no longer bothering to smile.

"Same as ours." The father turned to his wife with another smile. "And look, not a peep out of him when he's put down on the floor like that. We'll have to toughen this kid up a bit."

"That's easy enough to say," the mother was just beginning when two women, one about sixty, the other young, entered the room carrying files of papers.

"So sorry to keep you waiting."

The two staffers seated themselves before Takiko and the young couple and made polite bows. Then the older woman began:

"We've been unlucky with the weather today. As you see, when it rains there's quite a rumpus in here. The children love it, but I'm afraid we can't share their enthusiasm. They're upstairs now in the other building, taking their nap, though normally that's the infants' room. This room is for the two-year-olds, who we call the Rose Group. They're the oldest, and there are nine of them at present. Downstairs over there we have the one-year-olds, thirteen of them—they're our largest group. Upstairs we have the Violets, seven infants between six months and a year, and the Dandelions, who range from six weeks to six months. Your, um, Akira Odaka-kun and Kazuya Yoshikawa-kun will be joining the Dandelions . . ."

The mother of Kazuya Yoshikawa began to giggle at her baby's being referred to as "Master." The older helper glanced with a smile at Kazuya Yoshikawa in his father's arms and at Akira Odaka asleep on the floor.

". . . and we're the helpers who'll be in charge."

"I'm sorry, I can't help it, it sounds so funny—*kun*! And the Dandelions!" Kazuya Yoshikawa's mother spluttered. Takiko was just as distracted, but she was too tense to laugh.

Akira Odaka . . .

She stared at her baby and tried saying it over to herself a few times. The name still sounded unfamiliar.

After handing both mothers copies of the "Enrollment Guide," the older woman resumed her talk. She explained that for an initial period they would prefer to take the babies for mornings only, until they were used to the routine, then she ran through the schedule and the items that the parents would need to provide, filled them in on the history of the Midori Nursery, and requested their help with the organizing, emphasizing the importance of this. In principle they would be expected to attend general parents' meetings, group parents' meetings, committee meetings if elected, the summer and winter bazaars, and a number of other gatherings. "First," she asked, "how about Odaka-san?"

Flustered, Takiko replied, "I'll attend all I possibly can."

"And the Yoshikawas?"

"Yes, certainly, we'll do all we can to help." Kazuya Yoshikawa's mother answered gravely, but with none of her former confidence.

"And from the Yoshikawas, we'll be able to get lots of work out of Dad as well, won't we?" the younger helper said archly. Kazuya Yoshikawa's father laughed, scratching his head. Had she met this young man anywhere else, without the baby, Takiko might easily have taken him for a student. And the kind of student least likely to be a father, at that.

Takiko felt a sudden affection for the fatherly young man she saw there. It was a side of himself he probably never showed elsewhere. This youth, and Hiroshi Maeda, who was the father of two other children and now Akira, and Takiko's own father: each of these men had a child and was thus a father. She could think of nothing else that they had in common.

Takiko had gone to report Akira's birth at the ward office on the very last day allowed. At the same time, she had her own records transferred to a new family register with herself as the head of the household. She didn't tell her parents. Several days later she went out for a walk with Akira and called in at the nearest branch of the ward office, where she applied for a copy of her family register. Although she had no need of this document as yet, she wanted to see it with her own eyes.

It took several more days, but at last she held a copy of the new register. Her own name was entered where her father's had always been, and it was followed by Akira's name as a member of her family. The space for Akira's father was blank. Her name was entered again as his mother, and the address of the maternity hospital as his place of birth. It was also noted that the birth had been registered by the mother, Takiko Odaka. Her own section of the records stated that Takiko's father had registered her birth. Where Takiko was listed as "first daughter," Akira was not "first son" but "male."*

Stealing a few moments away from prying eyes, she would study her copy, reading the simple entries over and over again. Then she tore the paper up and threw it away. It wasn't all that interesting once she was used to it. But she couldn't forget it either. It was as if the very things to which she wanted answers were all there on one sheet of paper. What was this baby, Akira Odaka, to her? The child she'd borne. She couldn't help feeling there was more to it than that, that he was someone she hadn't known. There was something to it, but she didn't understand what it meant.

It was agreed that Akira and Kazuya Yoshikawa would start at the nursery on the Monday after next, and the interview came to an end. It had taken less than an hour. With a final reminder about having their checkups at a specified pediatric clinic before then, the two helpers left the room. Kazuya Yoshikawa had started crying hungrily. Akira slept on, straining now and then till he was red in the face.

Kazuya Yoshikawa had to be fed before going home. His mother turned her back and began unbuttoning her blouse.

"Well, then, if you'll excuse me . . ." Takiko murmured, gathering up Akira and getting to her feet. Her legs were cramped from the formal position she'd been sitting in. She stood there foolishly, unable to take a step. The young father

---

*This status distinguishes illegitimate from legitimate children in the family register, copies of which are required for school enrollments, job applications, etc. Largely as a result, Japan has a very low illegitimacy rate. (In 1980, when this novel was written, it was 0.8 percent, compared to 18.4 percent in the United States.)

looked up inquiringly from rocking his howling child and she burst out laughing in embarrassment.

"My legs, they've gone to sleep."

"Have they?" The young father laughed also.

"I never sit so formally."

"I *thought* you were being awfully polite." Kazuya Yoshi-kawa's mother looked around, laughing too, then reached out for the crying baby.

"Looks like they're going to work us hard, doesn't it?" the father said, lighting up another cigarette. "Can't be helped, I guess."

"He must've been starving, the way he's sucking."

"He'll be bottle-fed in the daytime after this, won't he?"

"Of course."

"Won't he reject the taste?"

"That's why we're supposed to start him on a little formula from today, so he can get used to it. They just told us the brand, remember?"

"Ah, I was wondering what that was about."

Takiko tested her legs. The numbness hadn't gone completely, but she could walk well enough.

"Well, I'll be seeing you." With a slight bow to the parents of Kazuya Yoshikawa, she crossed to the door.

"Nice to meet you," came the mother's voice from behind her back.

The rainstorm hadn't let up at all. In the time it took to open her umbrella Takiko was wet from head to foot. The sound of the rain was all she could hear. Akira stirred in the blanket.

After she'd trudged back to the bus stop through the rain

and the mud puddles, on the spur of the moment she jumped into a taxi that happened to stop for a red light.

The taxi moved off in the opposite direction from home, toward the center of the city.

If she went straight home her father would still be there alone, lying around in the main room. He would probably be groaning as he listened to the pouring rain. He too was waiting for something. Her mother and Atsushi wouldn't be home till evening. She had with her one portion of formula and a change of diapers in a tote bag. There was no need to hurry home. She decided to drop in at her favorite coffeehouse, the one that had been a hangout of hers in her high school days, and where she had often gone while she was pregnant.

Akira in her lap kept screwing up his face to cry, then going back to sleep. He must be getting hungry by now, and his diaper was sure to be dirty.

The taxi plowed ahead through heavy sheets of water. They were quite snug inside the small cab, enclosed in a world of water they had all to themselves. The baby was in her arms: the warm infant body that she couldn't have imagined a year ago. This living thing, covered in heat rash, that cried and strained and yawned.

"Well . . . are you planning to keep him?" her mother had asked a few days after they returned from the maternity hospital, when her father and Atsushi weren't around.

"I know I shouldn't try to tell you what to do, it all depends on how you feel. Of course I'd love to have him here with us. It'd break my heart to give him away now. Believe me, I'm ready to do whatever it takes, but . . . well, there's no telling how much longer I'll have my health. And you, you're still

young, you could even get married. But it won't be easy with
the baby. No, you're in for a hard time. I hope you realize
that, if you're planning to keep him. I'm just not sure what's
the best thing for you, Takiko. You don't seem to realize what
you're letting yourself in for, you're taking it all so casually.
If you'd like us to, we could even adopt him. Only on paper,
for the family register. Apart from that it'd make no difference,
but if it would make life any easier for you, I think it's worth
trying. I'll talk to your father myself."

Takiko had stared at her mother's face in amazement.

Her mother didn't look well. Not that she'd ever had a very
bright complexion, but now it had a chalky pallor. In fact she
hadn't seemed well all summer. She was a sturdy woman who
had never been ill to speak of till now, but did that mean there
was no cause for alarm? Takiko recalled her mother's flushed
face when she'd come visiting the hospital every other day at
the height of summer. The peaches and the arrowroot jellies
she'd been sure to bring. All Takiko had to do was enjoy them,
but those visits might not have been too easy for her mother.
Takiko pictured her lonely figure from behind, tottering along
the road under the scorching sun in the few hours she could
snatch from her work. As she walked she brooded aloud, "The
baby, the baby."

However, there was nothing Takiko could say to set her
mother's mind at rest. She couldn't help being impatient with
her: Why must she disregard Takiko and distress herself so?

"I didn't have him for that. Adopt him! Are you kidding?
He's a perfectly ordinary baby I had in the usual way. You see
him every day—can't you get that into your head? Or is there
something wrong with him? Like you'd expect in an illegiti-

mate child? I just don't see what you're making such a fuss about."

"I'm only talking about the formalities. I wish you wouldn't get so worked up about everything."

"For pete's sake, leave me alone. Anyway, I'm moving out soon."

"There you go again. Nobody on earth is going to put you two before themselves, you know."

"Great! Fine! Just as long as they let us live. I don't want anybody around. You're always interfering. Everybody does."

The taxi stopped. Takiko set off through the rain again, carrying Akira. He had started whimpering.

This part of town was full of students from high school and college, in their late teens and early twenties. A large cramming school for university entrance exams was headquartered there, along with a group of design and beauticians' schools. There were also many coffee shops and snack bars. Takiko had often stopped off on the way home from school and stayed there till after dark. Although she had no business of her own there, she'd had several boyfriends who went to the cramming school. She would sometimes walk with one of them to its front steps and then drink a glass of fruit juice somewhere while she waited for him, or even join him in the classroom and pretend to be an eager student.

Going home had been painful even in those days. She would have liked to roam around forever. She never had anything particular to do; she just wanted to stay out. She'd had more boyfriends than most of her classmates, though the sort of romances that the other girls suffered over played no part in her life, and she was an ungainly girl with nothing very striking about her apart from her features and her height. She wasn't popular with teachers or the other girls. Nor did she feel any special emotion for the boys she dated. Yet even when her father called her a little tramp and thrashed her because she came in late, she didn't stop seeing her boyfriends. It was fun, after all.

From the busy main street she turned down a narrow alley and opened a familiar dingy wooden door on the right-hand side. At once the sound of a jazz piano enveloped her.

"Hey, look who's here. It's Odaka-san. And she's got the goods."

Takiko sat down at the counter and smiled at Watanabe, the owner, lifting Akira up to show his face. Akira burst into wails that nearly drowned out the music.

"He's not for sale! This is a perfectly good little boy."

"Well, well, so he's arrived, has he?" Kawano, the student who worked part-time behind the counter with Watanabe, seemed to find this strange. Takiko smiled at him as well and nodded.

"Sorry, but could I have some hot water? I want to fix his bottle. He's starving."

"Okay. . . . Incredible—they really do get born, don't they?"

Takiko took out the bottle containing powdered formula from her tote bag and handed it over to Kawano.

"You fill it with hot water to this halfway mark, see? Then you shake it well and fill it up with cold."

"Get it right," said Watanabe. "That's a heavy responsibility."

Two or three of the customers sitting at tables who knew Takiko by sight gathered around. The others had all looked over in surprise at the unlikely sound of a baby crying.

She moved to a sofa and changed Akira's diaper. As she hadn't brought a plastic bag, she threw the old one away among the vegetable scraps with an apology to Watanabe.

"Will this do?" Kawano brought her the baby's bottle.

She held it to her cheek and nodded. "That's fine. Thanks a lot."

She began to feed Akira immediately. The sound of the piano filled the room.

Kawano sat beside her, his mouth open a little, watching Akira's face as he gulped the milk. Takiko looked up to find half a dozen men surrounding her and Akira. She murmured, looking from one face to the next, "I'm sorry . . . I just felt like dropping in."

"No need to apologize," said a student she knew by sight.

"Right. You don't see any signs saying 'No babies allowed,' do you?"

"Look at that—properly born and properly drinking his milk," Kawano sighed.

"That's right." Takiko smiled again. "He's even got a proper name. He's called Akira."

"Yeah? Akira, is he?" someone said. Takiko went on talking to Kawano. He had been a few years behind her at the same high school, and he loved modern jazz. Both his face and his build reminded her of her younger brother, Atsushi. While she was pregnant he had played her records which, according to him, would be good prenatal education for the baby. And he had offered to let her have his part-time job at the coffee shop if she were ever short of money—she only had to ask. As Takiko had never considered herself a great fan of modern jazz, she didn't particularly appreciate Kawano's kindness.

"I haven't really gone out since he was born."

"When was he born?" Kawano asked.

"August. August twenty-eighth."

"Ah . . . Well, it's good to see you. The boss and I were wondering how you were getting along. Looks like everything's going well."

Takiko nodded. She remembered her father at home. What was he doing on his own? She had never told either Kawano or Watanabe much about herself. But whatever they might have imagined, it probably wasn't too far from the truth.

As three more customers had come in, Kawano reluctantly went off to serve them. The cluster of acquaintances around Takiko returned to their seats. One of the new customers sat down beside her.

"Hi, haven't seen you for a while. Is that your baby?"

Takiko looked at his face. It was a young man she'd gone out with a couple of years ago, who worked as a designer's assistant. He too was a regular at the coffeehouse. She gave him a smile in reply.

"Really? Unbelievable."

She kept smiling, her eyes on Akira's face.

Watanabe brought her a cup of coffee. The young man ordered one for himself. After checking that the bottle was empty, Takiko took it from Akira's mouth and set it on the table. Akira, who was almost asleep, opened his eyes and trembled but didn't cry when he suddenly lost the nipple. He began to stare dubiously at the ceiling lights. Takiko propped him up, supporting his back with her left hand while she sipped her hot coffee slowly. It was a long time since she'd had anything but instant coffee.

The young man lit a cigarette while studying her face.

"I'd heard rumors, but still it's a shock to see you like this. Have you lost weight?"

Takiko nodded.

"It must have been rough. I can't even imagine what it would be like. But on your own . . ."

Takiko was struggling to remember the young man's name. She'd been nineteen when they'd gone out on Saturday nights to all-night movies, or a pool, or a beer garden. Two or three times he'd gotten her into bed. This much she could remember. But she felt strangely unsure that any of it had ever happened. Though it had only been two years ago, at that time she could never have foreseen Akira's birth.

Takiko had lain blankly with open eyes under the young man's body. She had flung out her limbs and said nothing, lying there like lumber. The image came back to her as if it were a scene from early childhood; she could even believe she might have dreamt it. So too with her memory of Hiroshi Maeda's body. Without his body, however, Akira could not have been born.

"It's not all that rough," Takiko muttered in reply to the young man whose name she didn't remember. The piano music that had been playing in the coffeehouse suddenly switched to lively brass. Akira's body quivered alertly.

"Well, you were never like other people to begin with. You've done well, though. The baby seems to be coming along fine. . . . Have you got time for a drink? Let's celebrate."

"Not today," Takiko said without hesitation. "I'm out of milk for him already. I'll have to go home soon."

"He'll be all right, what's the rush?" The young man was looking down at Akira's face.

"I'm out of milk *and* diapers. I have to go," Takiko muttered.

"Doesn't look much like you, does he? Or maybe he does, I can't really tell with babies. Tell me, what's it like having your own kid?"

Kawano brought the young man's coffee.

"Oh, nothing much. He's only just been born."

Takiko smiled at Kawano. He gazed at Akira and said, "I'll wash the bottle. Won't the air in here be bad for a baby?"

"I'll be going soon. I wonder if it's still raining?"

"Yeah, pouring," said the young man.

"Oh . . ."

Kawano took the used bottle back to the counter. The young man fell silent. Takiko had nothing more to say either.

Kawano came back at once with the clean bottle, and she got up.

"Come again, any time," he said. The young man had raised his eyes and was watching her.

"Thanks, though it won't be too easy."

"Oh," Kawano added, "you remember that tall girl? The one who was kind of like a ghost?"

"A ghost?"

"She smoked a lot, and was fed up with men. . . . You remember, she gave you a hard time once . . ."

"Oh, her, yes. I vaguely remember," Takiko answered, jiggling Akira, who looked ready to cry at any moment. She did have the impression that, quite some time ago, there'd been a woman who'd put an arm around her shoulders and tried to nestle her cheek against Takiko's while remarking, "Mm, I like girls like you, isn't she cute?" Takiko had twisted away, and she seemed to remember the woman, who was extremely drunk, starting to cry. Takiko supposed she must have been glaring in irritation at the woman's behavior. She would certainly have wondered how she could expose her emotions so completely.

"What about her?" Takiko asked, leaning closer to Kawano, over the rising volume of the music.

He spoke close to her ear also: "Says she's having a baby. She was here the other day. It's quite a recent thing, but she's put on so much weight I hardly knew her. More like a dumpling than a ghost."

"Oh."

"But she's not getting married. Even though she's living with the guy. She says he's going to recognize the child legally,* and that's enough. People sure do change—we were all pretty surprised."

"Oh."

Takiko regarded Kawano inquiringly. What did all this have to do with her, she wanted to know. A slightly embarrassed look came over his face.

"Not that it matters one way or the other. It's just that the boss was saying we're having a baby boom around here lately."

"Was he? . . . Well, be seeing you."

Still unable to guess what Kawano had meant, Takiko was beginning to vaguely regret her detour to the coffee shop. As she settled Akira, who was getting restless in her arms, she happened to glance around at the young man. He was drinking his coffee without taking his eyes off her. Flustered, she smiled back and, after paying Kawano for the coffee, went outside.

*That is, by having his name recorded as the child's father in the mother's family register.

It was still pouring.

She took a taxi home. It wasn't yet four o'clock. Her mother and Atsushi hadn't come in and her father was alone, mending an old umbrella. It was a man's umbrella. Maybe he intended to go somewhere in the rain. She pretended not to notice the large umbrella as she headed straight for the storeroom, and her father merely raised his head without speaking as she passed.

Perhaps as a result of his tiring day, Akira fussed and cried for a long time that night. No one in the house could sleep. Takiko tried singing lullabies, she tried uncovering her breasts (which had even lost some of their original size now that her milk had completely stopped) and letting him suck her nipple, she tried standing on the futon and rocking him, and ended by dumping him down on the futon while she covered her ears and shut her eyes. Shutting her eyes only made his voice sound all the sharper, and its sharpness was aimed toward his mother. Her whole body hurt and tears oozed out. All the day's events vanished into Akira's crying—which was not, however, such an unusual end to the day.

Two days later she had a phone call; it was a man's voice. Her mother handed her the receiver suspiciously.

"Hello. I was wondering where you were. So you're there at home with your parents? That's a surprise. But I guess it's easier that way. No need to pay rent, and . . ."

It seemed to be the young man she'd met at the jazz place. It was an unexpected call. Her mother stood close by, still looking as if she suspected something. Takiko blurted out, "Hello? What on earth are you talking about? It's you, isn't it, um—"

"Abé! Hey, don't tell me you've forgotten?"

"Never mind that. How do you know this number? And what do you want?" She didn't sound at all pleased. As she spoke she glowered at her mother, who sighed and moved away from the phone.

"Don't be like that. You're getting grouchier than ever, I see. I've known your number for ages."

"Oh? . . ."

"Sure. Listen, how about coming out for a while? Bring the baby, I don't mind. I'll buy you a meal."

"Now? I can't do that." It was time to start fixing dinner. Takiko began to feel infuriated by the casual voice she heard coming from the phone.

"Surely you can go out? Your old lady will mind the baby, won't she? Knowing you, I bet you could do with a break from the kid. Come on, I'll treat you."

"You think I've got the time? Don't be ridiculous. And don't call me at home for no reason," Takiko answered back, her face reddening.

"You've certainly changed—I half thought so when I saw you the other day. You used to be kind of—how shall I put it?—a bit short on personality. It's hard to believe you'd turn down an invitation. But I like that, I like it a lot. After all, you're a mother now, aren't you? . . . So you're going to bring the kid up yourself, are you? Don't go getting married, now, that'd be a bore."

"I don't have to take this from you. If you don't have any reason for calling, I'm hanging up." Takiko's voice had grown louder.

"Don't be so touchy . . ."

"And another thing, I'm leaving here very soon, so stop jumping to conclusions. I just happened to still be here today.

So—goodbye." Takiko put the receiver down without waiting for an answer. She was choking with rage.

The following day, she took Akira and went off to look at the advertisements in the local realtors' windows. She couldn't rest until she'd done it.

The sky was blue, the first fine weather in quite some time. There was a chill in the wind.

From the house to the National Railways station was a twenty- or thirty-minute walk, down the hill, left at the intersection, then straight ahead. There were several realtors along the way. Because of the big public cemetery on the hilltop to the left, there were also a number of florists' shops. The municipal junior high school that Takiko had attended was another fifteen-minute walk beyond the station. When flowers had been needed at school for a PTA meeting or graduation ceremony, or to take to the funeral after a death in a classmate's family, one of the pupils was always sent to buy them at the florist's by the station, a job that had several times fallen to Takiko. She had always enjoyed these errands. Unlike shopping on a regular day off, strolling through the shopping district during school hours gave her a heady sense of unexpected freedom.

She would walk in her indoor school shoes, peering curiously into each of the stores along the very familiar street. The bakery, the pharmacy, the grocer's, the furniture store, the haberdasher's, the coffee shop she hadn't been inside yet, the small bar whose shutter was always down when she saw it. But even though she wanted to prolong her stroll, she never read the realtors' ads then. Their shop fronts papered with notices had been uniformly drab and of no possible interest to her.

Working her way toward the station, now she studied the

signs in the window of every realtor she came to, crossing from the right pavement to the left and covering both sides of the shopping arcade. By the time she reached the station she had had drummed into her an accurate idea of the minimum amount required for her move. To rent a small single room with a shared toilet and no bath would cost her around twenty thousand yen a month. By now her ready cash was down to less than fifty thousand yen.

There was a yellow bench by the station bus stop. She lowered herself onto it. It was more than an hour since she'd left the house. Both arms were growing numb with Akira's weight. He'd been heavy at birth and now weighed over thirteen pounds. He had a big head, big hands, and big feet. From her lap, he stared querulously at the soda machine that stood beside the bench.

There was no point in looking at any more realtors' ads. First she had to find a job, that much at least was clear. But when she found one, how long would it be before she could move? Once she started leaving Akira at Midori Nursery she'd be paying nearly forty thousand yen a month in fees. The money she'd said she would give her mother as rent also remained unpaid. But it's sure to work out somehow, she thought as if it was someone else's problem. It'll work out.

A bus pulled in, taking on several people and letting off nearly a dozen. Akira's eyes were drawn toward its pale bulk. It rumbled off leaving a smell of exhaust fumes. Directly in front of her she could see the railroad embankment. There was a siding for freight cars and also, she noticed, cosmoses blooming among the weeds. To the right she could see a long bridge that spanned many railroad tracks, and the factories on the other side of the station. The pale blue sky was almost bewilderingly wide. On the left, a bluff reinforced with concrete rose steeply. Looking up, she could see the dull green of the cemetery along its top.

Abé's voice over the phone was dinning in her head.

"I guess it's easier that way, no need to pay rent, your old lady will mind the baby, won't she? I guess it's easier that way, no need to pay rent . . ."

Takiko had no idea how many minutes she'd been sitting on the bench. Akira had begun to cry, so she got up and walked home. It was time for his bottle.

That night she had a dream.

She was in a great meadow where cosmoses bloomed here and there. She was among a group of schoolchildren in their early teens—perhaps it was a school trip—and she was one of them herself. They were in a meadow filled with bright, soft sunlight. Takiko was walking through it, entranced. Then she ran, laughing, like a child. She felt as though her body were melting into sweet honey.

The meadow ended abruptly and the sea appeared, shining with a strange color. Something was swimming in the water. How pretty it was. Takiko wanted to go down to the sea. It spread away below a sheer black cliff. She felt dizzy. She backed away from the edge and turned her head to look behind her. No one was there. She set off at a run across the meadow. There was no one anywhere in sight. Pale and uneasy, she kept running. Had the school party moved on? Hadn't anyone noticed she was missing? She'd only been a moment looking at the sea.

She tried shouting. "Hey! Hey!"

Not a sound. Takiko ran on in tears. She'd been left behind. She couldn't go anywhere from here on her own. She was afraid. If she stood still in the meadow, alone, she would collapse. She went on running, weeping aloud.

She woke to feel teardrops rolling over her cheeks. There was a faint sound in the dark storeroom: Akira grunting in his sleep. For a while, as she listened to his grunts, Takiko shed tears of relief while unable to forget her terror in the dream.

They were due to start at the nursery on October 15.

As the staff had instructed, Takiko began to keep a detailed daily record of Akira's behavior. When he had his bottle, how much he drank, when he had bowel movements, what the stools were like, the hours he slept, when he had his bath, the times of day he was contented or cross . . .

In addition, she was supposed to see that he stayed awake for as much of the day and slept for as much of the night as possible, so that he would adjust to the new routine at the nursery, but she hadn't been told how this was to be done. She continued to put him down in the storeroom by day and night. She didn't want to leave him anyplace where he would attract her father's attention. And not only her father; she didn't much want her mother going near Akira either. She was grateful that he would stay asleep in the storeroom during the day, especially when there were other people in the house—visitors, or friends of Atsushi's. They never remembered the unseen sleeping baby. She had no intention of hiding Akira. It was just that she hoped to avoid the awkwardness she nearly always felt come over everybody when they did remember.

Takiko didn't know how her mother was going about explaining her daughter's child to the neighbors, relatives, and others with whom she would have to stay in contact. She was aware, though, that her mother had begun to talk about Takiko's child a little at a time, making excuses as she went. "She is doing her best, really, to take good care of the baby. She's only twenty-one, and when you think most people are still out enjoying themselves at her age . . . The baby doesn't take after her one bit, you know. He's dark and has a very big head. Well, as long as he's healthy, that's the main thing, I suppose."

She had once heard her mother talking in this way at the front door. What she was saying was remote from Takiko, and no doubt from her mother as well. Meanwhile the remarks she'd begun nonchalantly dropping to Atsushi and their father, and even to Takiko, displayed such pride in Akira that anyone would have thought she'd made him herself. His nose was a nice shape, his hair was thick, his lips and his eyes were very masculine, he was an intelligent-looking child, he was too good for Takiko . . .

Her mother bought a baby carrier, and in her spare moments started on a coat for Takiko of the sort that would fit over Akira on her back, telling her that she couldn't do without one when winter came. She also bought a number of brightly colored plastic toys.

Takiko bought a batch of résumé forms at a stationer's and sent them off to various jobs that she saw in the paper. Akira's pre-enrollment checkup was successfully completed, and the long-awaited day drew steadily nearer.

The night she discovered a small abnormality in Akira's body was the same night that her father first turned his pent-up emotions on her in the shape of his fists—the night before they were due to start at Midori Nursery.

Both things, it seemed to Takiko, had been bound to happen. In fact, for the first time since Akira had entered the world she felt able to calmly let out a deep breath: Ah, she thought, so that's it. She couldn't help sensing at her fingertips what she'd wanted to know.

She took a bath alone a little after ten o'clock that night. Akira was fast asleep in the storeroom. Her father had come in quite drunk around eight and settled down to go on drinking at home.

Although there was no formal enrollment ceremony and no new job to go to, Takiko wanted to bathe and wash her hair so that she'd be clean and ready for the new time that would be hers in the morning. Her hair, last cut while she was pregnant, came down to her shoulders by now. Surprised at its mass and heaviness, she used plenty of shampoo, lathering up the tiny bathroom.

Once she was scrubbed and soaking in the tub, she thought of the public bathhouse she used to go to with her mother when she was little, and what it had felt like in the bath. She had clung to her mother's chest, afraid of the huge pool of hot water. Big breasts loomed on either side of her face—bigger than her face, soft, yet impassive. Squeezed between them, Takiko could see nothing but her mother's flesh. It was more than strange, it was frightening, and she would edge away from her mother's body. Then she'd remember the deep, hot water that surrounded her and would be afraid to leave her mother.

She must have been very small at the time. But why had her mother's breasts seemed so large? Her small bony frame had no suggestion of soft flesh about it. Perhaps it had been around the time she'd had Atsushi. As this occurred to her, Takiko looked down at her own breasts in the water. They were small and childish. Beneath them her belly was a darkish color, and wrinkled like a deflated balloon. She tried to picture her mother's belly, but couldn't remember her being pregnant. All she remembered was the size of her breasts.

She began to count. She had to stay in the hot water until she counted to fifty. So she'd been taught long ago by her mother, and the habit had stuck.

By the time she got out, Akira was crying in the storeroom. She couldn't bring herself to hurry to him, though. She dried herself in a leisurely way, toweled her hair, and put on her nightgown in the changing area by the washstand. Then she gazed at her reflection in the mirror. It was a long time since she had taken a good look at it. The mirror revealed a face both unchanged since childhood and so unfamiliar she didn't know whose it was.

Akira was still wailing. He'd had a feed only an hour ago; surely he wasn't hungry again already. Perhaps he would quiet down soon if she left him alone. She studied her face more closely while Akira cried on, unheeded, in the background. She tried smiling a little, and made a face: tight lips and fierce eyes glowering from under her brows. Perhaps because she was fresh from the bath, she looked the very picture of health. Her lips and cheeks were a bright color. There was a time when she'd been very worried about her face, when she was ten or eleven years old. She had particularly disliked her poor coloring, the somber cast of her skin. It was her mother's complexion. She had longed to be old enough to highlight it with lipstick and blusher.

That's an idea, she thought: Shall I wear makeup tomorrow morning? Since she very seldom used it, she still had the lipstick and powder she'd bought on leaving high school.

From the bathroom she went into the kitchen: she was thirsty. Akira was still crying. She went to the refrigerator for the barley tea she'd made that morning and poured herself a glass.

"Go take care of him, dear. The poor thing's been crying nonstop."

Her mother called to her from her seat by the sewing machine, where she was putting buttons on a finished garment. At her mother's voice, her father also turned to look at Takiko. As he stared, she realized how sloppy she looked: her nightgown was slipping open at the chest and her legs were exposed almost to the thighs. She hurriedly pulled the front opening together and retied the belt, then met her father's look.

His eyes had narrowed and his lips were twisted. When his eyes met hers, he let out a sound that was close to a groan: "Oi."

"What are you doing," her mother put in, "leaving your child to cry?"

"Oi," her father grunted again. How much had he had to drink? More than a little, at any rate. For a moment Takiko felt herself on the point of responding obediently to his call; then she flushed.

"Huh." She sniffed and turned her back. A glass crashed over. She ran in fear to the storeroom. Then all at once Akira's crying changed in kind.

They were no ordinary cries, she could tell. They had a fierceness she'd never heard before. The message of great pain was inescapable.

She rushed over to Akira and peered into his face. He was bluish around the lips from the violence of his yells. Yet there was no blood spurting from any part of him, no part of his body had fallen off. Terrified by the pain in his cries, all she could do was stare, unable even to pick him up.

She heard her mother's voice. She couldn't make out what she was saying, but as if urged on by its sound she timidly put out her hands to Akira's body and began undressing him. Arms. Chest. Stomach. Back. No, there was no blood flowing anywhere. No reddened swelling or purple blotch. She took off his diaper and examined his buttocks and crotch. Still no sign of blood.

Her mother seemed to have spoken again just behind her. Takiko started to shake. What possible pain could Akira be feeling? What intense sorrow could have come over this tiny baby? Was it not his body that was in such distress? Trembling, she began again to examine him minutely. Ear holes. Nostrils. Inside his mouth. Though she couldn't be absolutely certain, there didn't seem to be anything physically wrong. Why, then? What was happening? Takiko began blindly caressing the baby's naked body. Was this to be the answer she received, she who had given birth to this baby? The thought began to illuminate Takiko's face like light from Akira's body.

Suddenly her hands, which she'd been moving in a frenzy of anxiety, met with an odd sensation. A slipperiness like rubber or a tentacle of raw squid.

She stopped trembling. Her terror vanished. She began going carefully over Akira's body to find the source of that peculiar sensation.

"What is it? You found something?"

Her mother, beside her, was watching her hands move.

Buttocks. Chest. Stomach. Her hands inched closer to his groin.

At the base of his right leg, she finally came across that peculiar sensation again. The place appeared barely swollen, but under the skin in that one spot she could definitely feel something like a squid's tentacle.

"Here," Takiko murmured.

"What?"

"It's here."

She tried pressing the place a little harder with her finger, and thought she felt the slippery thing being sucked up inside his body. She went on pressing with no idea of what was happening.

Akira's crying suddenly stopped.

"What's there? What's the matter with it?" Her mother stretched out her hand to Akira's lower abdomen. Atsushi's solemn face craned in from behind her. Takiko's finger couldn't feel the slippery thing any longer. And Akira's pain seemed to be over. It had gone away too easily.

Takiko couldn't bring herself to speak at first. She continued stroking his stomach and chest. He opened his eyes, which seemed to have rapidly grown bigger in the last few days, and kicked his legs. There were tears still gathered at the corners of his eyes.

When she'd dressed Akira, who wriggled happily, and was holding him to her breast to reassure herself with the weight and warmth of his body, Takiko began to tell her mother about the peculiar thing she had touched. She hadn't quite calmed down yet, and her voice rose as if something hot were sticking in her throat.

As soon as she heard Takiko's description, her mother said, "That sounds like a hernia," and nodded to herself. "He does strain himself an awful lot. I wonder if he could have given himself a hernia?"

"A *hernia*?" Takiko burst out laughing in spite of herself, though she still looked as though she wanted to cry. Atsushi laughed too.

"Yes, I think it's that. Dear, oh dear, a hernia! They don't run in our family, I'm sure."

"Ha, just like you to have a kid with a hernia," Atsushi murmured as he peered at Akira in Takiko's arms.

Their father's voice was heard from the direction of the living room. It was angry. Nobody bothered to reply. Takiko was too busy asking her mother the meaning of "hernia," which she knew only as a word that children chanted in playground rhymes. Her mother, unsure of the precise meaning, was lost in speculation: it probably meant that there was a sort of bag in the abdomen wrapped around the intestines, and that part of them slipped out—though not out of the body—through a tear in it. Maybe it was a defect that some people were born with. She'd never heard of anybody dying of it, but could you be sure? You'd think it might be serious if the intestines got twisted or tangled, after all they did have a very important function . . .

"What the hell are you doing?" Having called their mother repeatedly, in the end their father got up and bellowed down the corridor. Startled, Akira began to cry. Their mother turned her head, clicking her tongue impatiently.

"Now look what you've done." Then to Takiko she said, "I'll hold Akira while you make him a hot honey drink or something."

Atsushi turned and strolled away as if to say, "The show's over," brushed past their father by the doorway of the living room saying, "Move over," and withdrew to his bedroom. Their father likewise returned to the living room.

Takiko handed Akira over to her mother. "Okay, I'll go make a honey drink. Would you take him for just a minute?"

As she went out into the corridor her mother followed, holding Akira. The change of scene quieted him and he began to look around, turning his head. From the corridor Takiko cut across a corner of the living room and into the kitchen. Her mother followed her there. Atsushi had already slid the doors of his room neatly and firmly shut. Their father had gone back to his drink.

"Oi . . . anything wrong?" he said.

Her mother replied, while dandling Akira, "No . . . well, nothing serious. Though for a moment I thought something terrible must have happened. It seems the little fellow has a hernia. A hernia, of all things—wouldn't it make you sick? Though I suppose it could be worse. We can't complain, can we, Takiko?" Her mother chattered on by herself. Takiko was holding the baby's bottle full of honey and hot water under the cold tap.

"They say that babies with hernias grow big, that's what I heard when I had the two of you. Actually, he's already a very big boy. I'm sure there's nothing to worry about. I expect this hernia thing's probably a sign that he's sturdy. You ought to have the doctor look at it, though, to be on the safe side."

Takiko answered without raising her head, "*I'll* decide what to do."

"Is that any way to talk to your mother!" Her father's booming voice gave Takiko such a start that the bottle hit the tap and broke. With a sigh she glanced at his face. Akira meanwhile started crying again.

"Do you have to shout about every single thing?" said her

mother. "What a fright your grumpy old grandad gave us, didn't he?"

"You stay out of this. Takiko, are you keeping this brat? So now he has a hernia, does he? Hey, you come in here."

". . . The bottle's broken."

"Come in here!"

"No. Why should I keep a drunk company?"

"Get in here, you hear me? A drunk's still better company than a bastard with a hernia."

"What? What do you mean by that?" Takiko glared at him.

At that moment, she and her father were possessed by the same rage. Her father yelled something, Takiko yelled back, he moved, she moved too, and their pain crossed.

The next thing she knew, he had her pinned face-down on the tatami. Akira's cries reverberated.

She shrieked at him, rearing up her head and lashing out with her arms and legs. At every few words her father's right hand pushed her head against the tatami, and when this didn't stop her screams, pain would descend on some part of her near-naked body.

"Shut up, damn you! Who do you think raised you, then, eh? You stupid, selfish smart-ass. Can't you be grateful at all? Or sorry for what you've done?"

She had her eyes open but could no longer see for tears. Akira's crying sounded right in her ear.

"What do I care? A whole lot of good you are! I'm sick of your father act. Who needs it, when you can have a baby just fine without it. So there! And we're not in your family register either. Yeah, sure he's illegitimate, and why not, what's wrong with that? I bet you're afraid of him. That's why you can't look him in the face. You lousy, no-good, useless bum. I'm the only one you can pick on, aren't I!"

"You're crazy!"

With her father's shout, Takiko's head was lifted and her forehead and nose were dashed against the tatami. Unable to continue for the pain, she wept aloud. Sobbing openly, she felt her body being gradually and gently healed by the sound of her crying as it was when she was a child. Not thinking either of her father or of Akira, she sobbed without restraint.

"Look, when are you going to stop crying?"

She finally roused herself when her mother tapped her shoulder. Her father was snoring nearby. She was worn out and heavy with sleep herself. She picked up Akira, who, left in a corner of the room, was crying still.

"I don't know what to do about you two, for the life of me. . . . It makes me want to bring up Akira-chan away from you and Dad, for *his* sake."

Takiko nodded meekly. On her way to the storeroom with him in her arms, she envied baby Akira intensely. If only someone would hold her like this too.

WINTER

Wed., Nov. 1 (rain)

6:00   Formula (180 cc).

8:30   Asleep all the way to the nursery.

       □

9:50   BM.

       Exercises, rubdown.

10:00   Fruit juice (60 cc).

Not long till bottle time. Squirming very happily.

10:45   Formula (180 cc).

Nodding off as he drinks. Opens his eyes big and bright just as he finishes. "Oh, that's right, I was having a drink of milk, wasn't I?" Opens and shuts his mouth, but seems satisfied. Smiles when I call him "Akira." Does he know his name already?

12:10   Asleep.

12:40   Awake.

12:55   Asleep.

3:25   Formula (180 cc).

No burp but he's not worrying. He's smiling at the owl wind chime. I've put Kazuya-kun down beside him, but they're not interested in each other yet.

—Midori Staff

6:00   Home. Playing quietly by himself.

7:00   Began to cry.

7:15   Formula (180 cc).

Crying louder.

8:30   To sleep.

Woke up right away and yelled.

9:00   Bath.

He loves the bath. Lolls back in the water.

9:30   Hot honey drink (100 cc).

In a good mood at last. Awake and playing by himself.

10:30   To sleep.

Mon., Nov. 20 (fair)

5:15 Formula (180 cc).
Back to sleep.
8:30 Large BM.
Leaving for nursery.

□

9:00 "I'm bored 'cause Akko-chan and Kazuya are both away with colds." Lying quietly in bed.
9:15 Dozing. Isn't it a lovely warm day?
9:40 Wakes up bright-eyed and starts to cry.
Exercises, rubdown.
We're too worked up with sobbing to manage the exercises, aren't we? Just a quick rubdown today.
10:10 Fruit juice (90 cc).
Didn't seem to mind me taking the nipple away when he'd finished. The moment I tried to put him to bed, though—waah! Held him for a while.
10:30 "You can put me to bed now, I won't cry." Grips one edge of the musical merry-go-round and gives it a good tug. Wow! Look what you've learned to do.
10:45 Asleep.
11:30 Awake and playing quietly, pulling on the merry-go-round.
12:05 Formula (180 cc).
Gulped it all down. Quiet for a while, then decided this wasn't enough after all and started whimpering.
12:35 Regular health check.
He has a slightly wheezy chest, but Nurse says it doesn't warrant a trip to the pediatrician.

12:45   Whimpering, so gave him fruit juice (70 cc). All gone in 5 minutes and still not satisfied. Boo-hoo.

12:55   Hot honey drink (140 cc).
        This seems to have settled him at last.

1:05   Wriggling in bed. "I've got a full stomach and I feel just fine."

2:35   Sleep.

2:50   Bottom's a bit poopy. Diaper was sopping wet—had to change his shirt too. Now he's waving his arms and legs happily, all smiles.

3:10   Was quietly looking at the ceiling decorations but now he's dropped off to sleep.

4:53   Formula (180 cc).

                                              —Midori Staff

6:00   Home. Still asleep.

6:45   Woke up and was lying quietly by himself. Gave him a toy, which he held firmly and waved around. But then he banged himself on the forehead and threw it away.

8:00   Started to fuss a little but soon fell asleep.

9:00   Formula (180 cc).

10:00   To sleep.

Mon., Dec. 4 (fair)

8:00   Formula (200 cc).

                    □

9:30   Sunbathing, rubdown, exercises.
        Feeling cross. Yelling nonstop.

10:00   Fruit juice (100 cc).
        Afterward he dropped off to sleep while I held him,
        but the moment I laid him down (ever so gently) he
        woke up with a squawk.
10:15   Sleep.
10:35   Contentedly waving his fists.
11:00   Sleep.
12:20   Wakes up quietly, waves his fists and stares at them.
        Seems not to notice he's hungry.
12:25   BM. Very good stool. I'm glad he's over that diarrhea.
12:30   Formula (220 cc).
        I made up 220 cc by mistake, but Akira took it in
        stride. He drank it all down with his usual expression
        and beamed when I wiped his mouth with gauze.
12:55   Smiling in the cradle.
 1:30   BM. Just a little, but on the soft side. He's a bit fretful,
        but perks up at once when I change his diaper or move
        him.
 2:40   Sleep.
 3:20   Akko-chan was making such a row in the next bed
        that she woke Akira. I sang to him and shook a rattle
        till he cheered up.
 3:40   Sleep.
 4:50   Woke him for a feed.

                                            —Midori Staff

 6:45   Started crying.
 7:00   Honey drink (120 cc).
 7:30   Went to sleep.
 9:00   Bath.

9:30   Formula (200 cc).
10:00   To sleep.

Wed., Dec. 20 *(fair)*
4:40   Formula (200 cc).
         Back to sleep.
8:00   Out of bed. BM: large amount, good stool.

         □

9:00   Arrives at the nursery.
         Sunbathing, exercises, rubdown.
9:50   Fruit juice (80 cc).
10:10   Formula (180 cc).
10:20   Smiles delightedly every time he sees an adult's face.
10:50   Solid food: cream stew.
         I didn't think he'd want much after his bottle, but was
         I wrong! He gobbled it up, opening wide and quivering
         all over. Had a second helping, and in the end he put
         away a whole cupful.
11:30   To bed.
         Asleep.
1:55   Whimpering. Too soon for a bottle, so let's have a
         little game.
2:45   Formula (200 cc).
2:55   When he finishes, waah. Don't tell me that's not
         enough! Playing with toys.
3:45   To bed.
         When I went over to him with the olive oil for the
         rash on his head, he gave me a look that said, "Oh
         boy, she's got something for me." I dabbed the dry

spot at the corner of his mouth while I was about it, and he opened wide. "Aah."

4:00   Sleep.

—Midori Staff

6:30   He was restless and seemed to want something to eat, so I tried putting a crust of bread in his hand. He sucked on it quite expertly till he'd eaten it all.

8:00   Formula (200 cc).

He should be full, but he's watching me—he smiles when I go near and cries when I move away. Even though his grandmother's holding him, he keeps gazing around searching for me.

9:00   Bath.

9:30   Fell asleep at once.

. . . The hands of the restaurant's clock were already approaching five. According to their agreement she was supposed to be allowed off fifteen minutes early so that she could collect Akira from Midori Nursery by five, but when it came down to it, it wasn't easy to get away on time. The other three women all stayed on past four-forty-five and well into the evening. Two were in their early forties, married with children, and, like Takiko, living in the neighborhood; the third, who was exactly her own age but had worked there for five years, lived with the owner's family.

Lunch hour was their busiest time, as the restaurant was near a station on the main loop line, but they also did a fair amount of business from early evening through dinnertime. The owner had been looking for a part-timer who could work at least until six o'clock. He had nevertheless agreed to the awkward hour of a quarter to five, perhaps calculating that someone as strongly built as Takiko could comfortably handle the cleaning and vegetable buying in the morning and go out with deliveries as well. He didn't go so far as to prompt her to leave on time, however. The other women were also indifferent to Takiko's hours. If she wasn't keeping an eye on the time herself, four-forty-five would pass unremarked.

"Well, I'm off."

Takiko dashed in from a delivery run, shed her blue smock, tossed it onto its peg and was almost out the door again, not looking at anyone's face as she murmured the words.

"Just a minute."

She glanced around to see Michiko Hashimoto, the waitress who lived in, glaring at her behind the cash register.

"I'm sorry, I'm in a hurry," she answered shortly, avoiding her eyes, and kept on going.

"Odaka-san! Wait, will you!" Michiko's voice rose. Takiko hesitated a second, then gave up and came back inside. She found it hard to get along with Michiko, who was trusted by the owner and expected to supervise the other staff. Michiko appeared to find her exceptionally dense and cheeky besides.

"What is it? Sorry, but I'm already running late." Takiko couldn't help sounding impatient. She was late more often than not, and Midori Nursery was strict about being on time. She had once overheard another of the mothers—who, unlike Takiko, held a full-time job—appealing to the nursery staff.

"Couldn't you possibly allow us an extra ten minutes? Just ten? If I leave the office at five I can make it by ten past. I can't ask them to change my hours especially. It's only ten minutes. Please? All you'd have to do is let her sit here."

The answer had been firm: they could not extend the nursery hours, by ten minutes or by one minute.

"If we had the staff, of course, we could keep the children until six. But you know how things are—we've got four babies to one helper. Once she's a year old we can take her till six o'clock, but until then I'm afraid you'll have to work something out for yourself. Everyone has the same idea, you see—just another fifteen minutes or another half hour. But we have our limits too. If you like, we could help you find a baby-sitter in the neighborhood—a student wanting part-time work, say. We've already made arrangements for one of the babies: we take her to her grandmother's just down the street. If there's anything of that kind that we can do . . ."

Takiko had been thinking of making exactly the same request. There was no need to hear the answer twice.

The mother she'd overheard must have worked something out, because she now managed to show up at five. Kazuya Yoshikawa, who'd started on the same day as Akira, was collected at five by his father. And quite a number of fathers brought their children in the mornings. Takiko found the sight of them refreshing. It seemed an odd thing to feel. Far from being envious, she actually felt her spirits lift at the thought of being involved in the same place and tied by the same hours as these fathers. She would even have liked to tell someone about it with pride.

Amid the daily rush, Takiko had begun to grow attached to the brief spells of time she spent at the nursery.

"In a hurry? Only to get to the nursery, right? Is getting there on time more important than your pay? Imagine that," Michiko said without expression.

"Oh! That's right. It completely slipped my mind." At the

word "pay" Takiko smiled. Though she'd had in mind that it was payday all that morning and most of the afternoon, at the last minute she'd been distracted by the clock. "Can I have it quickly, then? I really don't have time."

From the drawer of the cash register Michiko took out Takiko's pay envelope and ran her eye down the itemized statement on the front. "Hmm. I must say you've been away a lot, and late too, Odaka-san. And you leave early."

"Look, can I have it quickly, please?"

"It's no wonder you don't make much money. Is this good enough for you?"

"No, but it can't be helped, can it? Babies get sick. Look, please . . ."

"A bit like a child's allowance, isn't it? Here's your pay, then."

Michiko thrust the envelope at her, still without expression. Takiko grabbed it and stuffed it into her cloth shoulder bag as she broke into a frantic run. It was exactly five by the restaurant's clock.

It would take her ten or fifteen minutes by bus—if the bus came at once.

Spotting an empty taxi as she emerged onto the street, Takiko raised her hand without a second thought. If she took a taxi she could make it to the nursery in five minutes.

Once they were under way she heaved a sigh, took the pay packet from her bag, and checked its contents. There was scarcely enough there to cover the cost of her meals, let alone rent an apartment of her own. It would all be gone by the time she'd paid for Akira's day care and his formula, plus the taxis she was forced to take, like this one.

She had to find a decent job. This was becoming increasingly obvious, but at the same time she was increasingly unsure of how to go about it. Before being taken on at the restaurant she had sent out any number of résumés with copies of her family register. She'd had several interviews. But not one company would employ her.

"Well," her mother had said, trying to cheer her up, "let's face it, who'd want to hire somebody like you? That's why I say you're taking things too casually. Why not go in for dressmaking? I'd teach you. In any case, there's no need to rush into anything."

She could see what her mother meant, but all the same, her failure had come as a surprise to Takiko. She was as motivated as anyone could be: she needed money, she wanted work. And she'd assumed that this was by far the most important factor in finding a job. While she hadn't really supposed that her new family register would pass unnoticed, she had somehow taken an optimistic approach. Shouldn't she be more employable now, when she wanted so badly to work, than when she took the hiring tests at the end of high school? Why did she have so little trouble back then, when it had meant so little to her? She hadn't even been very excited when she passed. Though she hadn't wanted to go to college, she hadn't especially wanted a job either.

Takiko couldn't argue when her mother referred to her as "somebody like you."

Akira was a very ordinary baby by any standard. He was above average in size, was teasingly known at Midori Nursery as "the big eater with the big grin," and apart from the peculiar thing called a hernia he was thriving in every way. That was all there was to it. Nor should there have been anything remarkable about the fact that she was rearing him. Each time

Akira laughed, or listened inquiringly to her singing, or gaped like a baby bird for a mouthful of food, Takiko simply basked in pleasure and thought for a foolish moment that she'd been given the most lovable thing in the world.

This was all that Takiko plus Akira amounted to, yet they clearly weren't regarded as anything so simple. She sensed that people seemed afraid of them. But what on earth was there about her and Akira that could make people wary?

She remembered the word "illegitimate" more often.

She'd run out of time. Unable to fritter away any more days without working, she had begun to search for a temporary job in the neighborhood.

Finally she'd been hired by the noodle place in front of the station and started making the daily trip between Midori Nursery and the restaurant, always worrying about the time. The days went by without a moment for reflection. Akira, meanwhile, caught a cold, had a bout of diarrhea, and at one point developed a worse problem with his hernia, the intestine protruding all the way down to his scrotum so that Takiko was no longer able to make it go back with a press of her hand. On each occasion she'd had to take time off for a visit to the pediatrician. The clinic had advised surgery and referred her to a university hospital. She'd been able to book him for next spring, but now she also had the hospital costs to think about.

"Sorry I'm late again."

She clanged up the iron stairs and burst into the infant room on the second floor. A crowd of faces all turned to her at once in the confined space under the room's electric light. Normally the nursery was bare and quiet at the day's end, with one helper left minding Akira and a mother or two on the way out with their babies. Takiko stood stunned for a moment in the entrance.

"Please come in, Odaka-san."

It was the other parents of Akira's group, the Dandelions, gathered in a circle on the floor. The two helpers' faces were also visible among them.

"You forgot the group meeting today, didn't you?" someone said laughingly.

"Looks like you ran flat out to get here."

"Odaka-san is always like that," the younger helper teased her in an amused tone.

"Anyway, sit down. The meeting's only just begun."

"I'm very sorry. I've been awfully absentminded today." Takiko lowered her head and sat down in the nearest spot.

"Oh, that's nothing new, is it?" observed Kazuya Yoshikawa's mother, who was sitting next to the staff. Having enrolled on the same day, they were more familiar with each other than with the other parents.

"Well, no, I suppose not," Takiko murmured red-faced, sending up a laugh from everyone present. Takiko brightened too.

"Please, would you try and keep the noise down or you'll wake the babies." From across the room, the helper who normally looked after the one-year-olds poked her head around the corner to complain. Behind a set of shelves there was an alcove like a large closet that contained a bunk bed for the Dandelion babies, who couldn't move around yet. As it was beside a north-facing window, the bed didn't look as though it'd provide much warmth. The babies were placed there in a row each morning, the first arrivals commanding the best spots in the top bunk. Takiko's baby Akira generally went into the bottom bunk.

"Sorry. We'll be good," answered one of the Dandelions' helpers. The parents, especially the younger mothers, laughed again. The two fathers present were also grinning in the direction of the corner where their children should be asleep.

It was one of the monthly gatherings known as a group meeting.

As had been made clear when they enrolled, there were quite a few meetings to attend. Nearly all were held at night, directly after the nursery closed, while the babies were minded by one of the staff or one of the parents on a roster. So even if they wanted to skip a meeting or simply forgot, it was difficult not to attend. In fact, Takiko looked forward to these events, even with her hectic routine. Tired as she was, they were never a burden. She particularly didn't want to miss the group meetings, where she could hear how Akira was doing at the nursery and watch the other parents chatting together.

Two of the fathers attended the Dandelions' meetings without fail. One, she'd been told, was still in graduate school. Apparently he was almost solely responsible for looking after the baby, whose mother was a nurse. The other was an office worker who looked closer to forty than thirty and had two other children. He carried a large briefcase. Takiko hadn't heard what kind of work he did, but she guessed it was something to do with finance, as he was always trying to help Midori Nursery out of its difficulties, compiling, copying, and distributing financial reports and tables of alternative fund-raising plans for replacing the prefab building. The children's mother was in the hospital with some complicated illness. Takiko had heard him talking to one of the staff.

". . . They still don't know what's causing it or anything definite at all. They think it might be bacterial, hemolytic strep or something like that, but they're not sure. At this rate, we have no idea when she'll be out of the hospital." With that, the father had given a loud laugh. He was a short, stout man with glasses and his hair parted neatly on the side.

The young father in graduate school wore glasses too; he was a dark youth with longish hair.

To Takiko, there was something fresh about the sight of these two fathers. Two men whom she'd be unlikely ever to meet elsewhere were here on the second floor of the old building known as the Midori Nursery, gazing as intently as she did at the faces of the helpers who recounted the gradual growth of each of their babies, looking down at the handouts mimeographed on cheap paper, appealing to the staff with the same small worries as her own—worries about weaning and illnesses. This was an image of the opposite sex that Takiko hadn't known, or had a chance to know, till now.

How could she have forgotten this meeting? And that it was payday. I'm really not myself, thought Takiko, feeling her weariness and disappointment in herself return. As she listened to the helper who was beginning to describe the babies' lives over the past month, she wondered why her mind was always such a blank. The thought brought a hot, choking lump to the back of her throat which, if it weren't for the people around her, might well have flooded her eyes with tears. Ever since Akira had been born—and though she still wasn't getting anything done—she would give way to a numbing lethargy at the end of the day even before he was asleep. Sometimes she would catch herself tumbling down the tunnel of sleep while she was in the bath with him, or folding the diapers that she'd hung out to dry in the morning. Why couldn't she get anything done? She couldn't help finding fault with her wimpy body. Why can't you work up more energy? There's something wrong here.

Yet no matter how she pushed herself, she couldn't manage anything apart from the round trip, toting Akira, between home and the nursery and on to the restaurant. A day, a week, a month had gone by like sand sifting past her body, odorless and tasteless.

The main topic at that day's meeting was the solid food on which four of the babies—Akira among them—were just being started. Akira seemed to eat plenty of whatever was going, but one of the others disliked mush and preferred big white noodles. One liked to suck on hard things. And one showed no interest at all. At this stage of weaning the idea was simply to get them used to the feel of a spoon, the helpers explained, and it was quite all right to continue bottle-feeding at home. They went on to advise on how the babies should practice lying on their stomachs, and have as much fresh air as possible even when the really cold weather set in, and so on. In closing, the staff mentioned that they wanted each of the parents to put up ten posters near their homes for the bazaar that was coming up a week from Sunday. This was to be done that night if possible, or by Friday—in two days' time—at the latest.

Taking ten of the mimeographed posters each, the parents hurried over to their babies. Takiko elbowed through the crush of bodies and looked for Akira.

He was in the helper's arms, being given a bottle. Takiko took him over and sat down on the floor to feed him the remaining half of the milk. The graduate student was efficiently changing his baby's diaper. The other father was the first out the door, clutching his baby to his chest with one arm and his briefcase in his free hand. The other mothers collected their children and made their way out one by one, exchanging goodbyes, the graduate student left with his baby in his arms, and once again only Takiko and Akira remained.

It was after eight when she reached home. She was almost sick with hunger. The mothers who lived at a distance bought sandwiches or rice balls to eat during the meeting. She always meant to do likewise, but when the time came she never had a moment to stop at a bakery.

At home, everyone had finished their meal. There was no sign of her father; perhaps he was out drinking at a local bar. She'd hardly run into him at all, in fact, since she'd started work at the restaurant. When she went out in the morning he was still asleep in the middle of the living room. And he seldom stayed home in the evenings now. By the time he came in, Takiko was so sound asleep that he wouldn't have woken her even if he'd kicked her. It must have been two or three weeks since they'd last seen each other face to face. That had led to a quarrel over some trivial thing which ended with her father striking her and Takiko breaking into tears while still trying to hurt him in return.

Atsushi was keeping to his room, and their mother was at her sewing machine as usual.

Having carried Akira in her arms all the way from the nursery, Takiko put him down on the tatami and went to look for leftovers in the kitchen. Not bothering to warm them up, she ate her supper in the living room. Akira was crying loudly all this time.

"It's not right, you ought to think of Akira-chan a bit more." Her mother stopped the sewing machine and burst out as if unable to contain herself. "Poor thing, he cries all the time he's at home. I can't bear to see him being taken out and left somewhere till this hour of the night—he's not even four months old. Can't you stay with him for a year at least? What's the use of rushing off to some silly job? I don't see why you have to pay good money to leave your own baby with complete strangers. It's time you stopped this nonsense. Look at him, he's not putting on weight any more, and his hernia's getting worse and worse. Didn't the doctor tell you he shouldn't be allowed to cry?"

"He wants to be held, that's what he wants," Takiko answered without raising her head, and carried her dishes out to the sink. She suddenly remembered the posters for the sale. She could leave them till tomorrow, but it seemed a better idea to go around at night when she wouldn't be seen. If she did it tonight she could slap the ten posters up wherever she liked and get it over with.

She picked up Akira, who was screaming.

He stopped crying at once in her arms, but she changed her mind and put him down on the tatami again. She couldn't see how she could manage the posters if she was carrying him. Although his head still wobbled precariously, maybe it would just be possible to take him on her back; some of the Dandelion babies of the same age had been riding on their mothers' backs for quite a while now. And not just this one time: how much easier it would make the trip to the nursery if she switched to using the carrier.

She fetched the sling that her mother had bought her some time ago out of the storeroom. But she didn't know how to position Akira, who was crying again, and strap him onto her back.

After picking him up and hushing him, she called to her mother. "Mom, could you come here a minute, please, and show me how to use this?"

"Eh? What's up?" Her mother glanced around.

"How do I get him into the carrier?"

"The carrier? Whatever for?"

"It's not too soon, is it?"

"I guess not, but why now?"

"I have to go out for a while, and I can't leave Akira." Takiko pointed to her quota of Midori Nursery posters and explained, reluctantly, that she was to put them up in the neighborhood. "The staff's bonuses are paid out of the proceeds. All the private nurseries do the same. So we're supposed to put up ten posters each. I can't be the only one who doesn't, can I?"

However, as she'd expected, her mother stood up with a changed expression. "What's this?"

"I told you . . ."

Before Takiko could answer, her mother had unrolled the posters on the table and was staring at them. " 'Big Winter Bazaar'? 'Organized by Midori Nursery. Second-hand clothes, wholesale goods . . .' You weren't seriously planning to put these things up around here, were you? How stupid and naïve can you get? Do you want the whole world to know your baby's in a place like this?"

"What of it?"

"Are you out of your mind? To go and disgrace yourself like that! Besides, if Dad saw them you'd be crippled for life. Anyway, I won't have it, and that's final."

Without listening to anything Takiko might say, her mother briskly ripped up the ten posters.

Mon., Dec. 25 (fair)
 8:00   Formula (200 cc).

         □

         Thanks for your help with the bazaar yesterday. A
         report will be distributed later.
 9:15   Sunbathing, exercises.
 9:50   Fruit juice (70 cc). This seems to be enough today.
10:10   I've put him to bed, but he's secretly holding hands
         and having fun with Akko-chan next door. As they
         don't appear to be sleepy, I rattled the bamboo wind
         chimes in the middle of the room, and made them
         both smile.
11:05   Puree (¼ cup), meat broth (small amount), boiled
         spinach with soy.
         As soon as one mouthful is gone he cries for more. I
         pop in another: mumble mumble, all smiles, then
         another squawk. I'm afraid I may have given him too
         much in the end.
11:35   He was out like a light the moment I let him down
         from the rocking cradle. Both he and Akko-chan are
         fast asleep with their arms and legs stretched out.
         To bed.
12:45   Boo-hoo, I'm hungry.
12:55   Formula (200 cc).
         He sucks so hard he keeps flattening the nipple. Howls
         every time I go to fix it. "You've taken it away!" Drank
         it all in only ten minutes.
 1:10   Cradle.

1:50   BM. Good stool.

When I hung a rattle from the bamboo wind chimes and set them swinging, he was very impressed. After he got bored with that he started smiling at me, and when I spoke to him he pushed against my chest and sprang his legs up and down.

3:00   Starting to whimper. "Oh, I'm so bored."

We've been to observe our friends the Violets crawling. They've got a nice sunny spot.

3:40   Hot honey drink (130 cc).

4:00   Nodded off as he finished. Didn't wake even when I put him to bed.

4:55   Formula (200 cc).

—Midori Staff

6:00   Home.

6:30   Juice (120 cc).

Made short work of that and started to cry. Smiled when I picked him up.

8:30   Bath.

9:00   Formula (200 cc).

Bed.

Fri., Dec. 29 (fair)

8:00   Formula (200 cc).

☐

9:40   BM.

Exercises, rubdown, lying on stomach.

When I lay him on his stomach he rolls right over. He's gotten very good at turning from front to back, hasn't he? But going the other way's hard work. If I hold his feet and cross his ankles for him he can take over from there.

10:00 Fruit juice (60 cc).

10:55 Baby food (¼ cup), miso soup (⅓ cup), mashed yam (small amount).

He started out chewing happily but soon burst into tears. When I offered the spoon he just slurped on it. Fifteen-minute nap in the cradle. When he woke up I tried him with the food again, and this time he was ravenous. He struggled to take the cup and spoon out of my hands and thrust his face forward, demanding, "Quick, quick!" After a while he got frustrated with the business of swallowing. You'd rather have milk, would you?

12:00 Formula (200 cc).

Glug-glug. He's drinking away by himself, concentrating so hard that nothing can distract him.

12:25 Bed.

2:50 Akira's little whimper was almost drowned out by all the noise in here. He soon gave up and started playing with a towel, and before long was quite happy.

3:20 He looks contented rocking in the cradle. Sucks his fingers, gazes around and smiles.

4:00 Everyone's assembled in the middle of the room. Our last day together this year. See you next year.

(Please keep up the notes during the break.)

—Midori Staff

Mon., Jan 1 (cloudy)

7:15	Formula (200 cc).
	Bed.
10:10	Playing on his own.
11:00	Pumpkin puree (small amount).
	Formula (200 cc).
11:50	Started crying.
12:10	Bed.
1:00	Woke up and started crying.
1:30	Juice (120 cc).
3:00	Formula (200 cc).
4:30	Very bad temper.
5:30	Bed.
6:00	Started to howl.
6:20	Gave him a crust to suck.
	BM.
7:30	Formula (200 cc).
9:00	Started to cry.
9:30	Bath.
9:45	Juice (120 cc).
	Bed.

Tues., Jan. 2 (snow)

6:50	Formula (200 cc).
10:50	Formula (200 cc).
12:45	Hot honey drink.
	Bed.
2:30	Started to cry.
3:00	Formula (200 cc).
5:00	Bed.

6:00   Pumpkin puree (three mouthfuls), apple juice (100 cc).

Started to cry again.

7:10   Formula (200 cc).

9:30   Bath.

10:00   Juice (120 cc).

Bed.

Midori Nursery's New Year holiday lasted through the fourth.

Toward the end of December, Takiko had been told by the restaurant owner that he wanted her to come in on the second if at all possible, or else the third. She replied that because of the day-care arrangements for her baby she could only work from the fifth. Also, she added, she couldn't come in on the thirtieth or the thirty-first.

The owner had not looked pleased. New Year's Eve, with its deliveries of the traditional noodle dish, was the busiest night of the year. He would have to find another part-timer in a hurry. "I've been keeping an eye on the situation," he said, "and I'm afraid your schedule just doesn't seem to agree with ours." Takiko had returned his hard look, growing pale, and said finally, "In that case, I suppose I'd better quit." And so she had lost her job at the restaurant.

Over the holiday she didn't tell her mother, let alone her father, that she had quit. She saw no reason why she couldn't wait to tell her mother until she'd lined up another job right after the New Year.

At the nursery there were two people, both mothers of toddlers, who sold cosmetics door-to-door. One had a permanent job with the cosmetics firm and the other had only recently started with her help. Takiko had overheard them discussing the job with someone. Their good grooming and careful makeup made them stand out among the other mothers. Takiko herself was one of the many who didn't have time. Although she thought nothing of it when she passed fashionably dressed college students of her own age on the street, she was uncomfortably aware of her changed appearance when, after tripping or being clumsy on the bus or at work, she was greeted with obvious impatience instead of the smiles she would once have received from young men.

The two women who sold cosmetics projected a bright aura of confidence which had almost escaped Takiko's notice. Sometimes after a meeting broke up they would begin to promote their products to the staff and other mothers, and once or twice they gave expert facial massages "at no extra charge." As they made up one of the group their model would watch excitedly, amid peals of laughter, like a child with a new toy. For the moment each woman's face would become a young girl's again.

That looks like fun . . .

Takiko watched these scenes uncertainly from a distance.

Though she'd never heard of the brand, it was probably a reasonably large company. Perhaps, if she asked, she could have a job like that. She was fairly sure she could handle it. She'd make herself up properly, take care with her clothes, and use refined language. Just think how surprised everyone would be.

She didn't want to admit any doubts about this idea.

On the second it snowed. The snow fell quietly until evening. Akira cried all day long, and every time he yelled his intestine slipped through the rupture and bulged down into his scrotum.

Atsushi had stayed out from morning to night since the thirty-first. Their mother had had a batch of work that took her till New Year's morning to finish and must have worn her out, for she was still in bed in Atsushi's room, while in the living room their father was drinking saké with two childhood friends he'd run into recently and brought home the night before. They talked of one subject, their hometown in the north, of which Takiko too had a faint memory.

She would have liked to keep out of their way, but with her mother in bed she couldn't stay shut up in the storeroom with Akira. She prepared some snacks from the holiday food supplies for her father and his guests, and went around refilling their glasses with cold saké whenever she was asked. When they were dead drunk she covered them with blankets and cleared a few dishes off the table.

Though her father's leg should have been bothering him because of the snow, he was still in a good mood that evening. The visitors began to drink what they called "the hair of the dog," joking with Takiko and complimenting her looks extravagantly, showing every sign of having settled in for another night.

As soon as she'd finished one of her tasks, if she had ten minutes or half an hour to spare, Takiko would race to her room, not even checking how her mother was, to make sure that Akira was all right on his own. He cried each time he woke, then fell asleep in an unnatural position once he'd tired himself out. Though he couldn't yet go wherever he wanted, his arms and legs were growing stronger and she would find him in different places—once with his face hard up against the little grating, and once with it buried in the futons. He always woke at her touch and began to cry, putting out his arms. With a sigh, she would pick him up and hold him to her breast. Though he was well wrapped up in a wool sweater and pants, his hands and face were cold. The electric warmer she'd placed between the futons was a good distance from him.

"Stay under the futon or you'll catch cold. It's snowing today, you know," Takiko murmured while pressing her warm cheek to Akira's chilly one. On an impulse, she opened the window an inch or two. The snow was still falling. Two or three flakes strayed into the storeroom, like insects on failing wings. Snow was piled almost an inch deep on the windowsill and sash bars and on the neighbor's holly bush. From time to time the holly leaves shuddered under their load and sloughed it off to reveal a snow-washed surface that was a strangely vivid green. The snow at the foot of the bush was pocked with little holes.

Takiko put out her hand and, scooping up some of the drift from the windowsill on her forefinger, she first licked it herself then put it in Akira's waiting mouth. His happily expectant face contorted for a second as the coldness met his tongue, and he shivered. Yet he didn't try to spit out what went into his mouth.

Takiko smiled. "See, this is snow. That's what it's called, *snow.* . . ."

Akira sucked his mother's finger, then yelled in protest when he found the cold thing no longer there. Lately he had taken to arching his body back and pushing away with his legs as he cried.

"So you like snow, do you? Want some more?"

She scooped up some more for him from the sill. Without pulling a face this time, he began to lick the white, cold substance intently, making sounds with his tongue. She remembered the scene of the snowfield again. The men who raced over it in dog sleds, cutting across the dazzling plain in a single sharp line. A distant scene in a dream. But if Akira were to ask her, Takiko intended to answer: It was one of them—I don't know his name or where he is now—who gave me a baby, and that's you.

She would go on telling him the same thing even when he was old enough to laugh at her.

Oh yes, he was a wonderful man. He was born and grew up there in the snow, and that meant he didn't bother with unimportant things. He'd just run his sled at incredible speed, like an animal himself, over those broad spaces of pure white. For a long time all I did was watch longingly from the distance . . .

Akira had gone cross-eyed with concentration as he sucked the snow.

That night, with more to be done in the kitchen, Takiko made up her mind to keep Akira with her in the carrier since he cried constantly if he was left alone. It was the first time she'd carried him around the house on her back. But her father seemed too sodden with drink to notice, and so did the other two. The television was left on in the background. One of the men kept repeating loudly and thickly, "It's no use, can't do a damn thing about it," and each time her father and the other man grunted their agreement.

She threw together a meal for herself and her mother, served her father and his friends only those dishes they'd want while drinking, then sat Akira down at her mother's bedside and ate her dinner there. Her mother didn't feel like eating and spent the whole time playing with Akira. She was an unhealthy color and had lost a little weight, which was perhaps why she looked so much older.

"The doctor should be back the day after tomorrow. Go and get yourself looked at properly," Takiko said as she put a helping of pork on her mother's plate.

"I expect another day in bed will set me right," her mother said. It wasn't like her to seem so unsure of her health.

Takiko fed Akira stewed pumpkin and fruit juice, then heated a little water and gave him a quick bath without taking one herself. As nobody else was likely to want one, she emptied the tub. Akira was crying with hunger and sleepiness. His day always ended in wails.

The bottle she gave him didn't quiet him. Taking him on her back, she went to wash the dishes. Her father and his friends appeared to have more or less passed out. Akira's crying occasionally made them raise their heads and gaze fuzzily around. Only the noise of the festive New Year's game shows blared in the living room. Atsushi would probably be home as late as he had on the night of the first.

Takiko tossed a half-washed dish back into the sink, abruptly sat down in the living room between the two guests and poured herself a glass of cold saké, which she began to drink while watching TV. The large man sprawling with his face on the table beside her roused himself and gave her a bleary smile when their eyes met.

"Hi there, Taki-chan. Having one too, are you? Don't hold back, now, that's what I say. . . . You're a pretty girl, Taki-chan. Just the age when a girl's at her best. But your husband's away at the New Year and you're stuck with us, eh? Don't mind what your old dad says. If that is your dad. Drink up. Guess it's not much fun for you, either. Not much fun for a cute girl like you, Taki-chan, eh?"

With his arm around Takiko where he'd been stroking her arm and patting her thigh, he slumped against her and began to breathe evenly. Akira, on her back, also seemed to have fallen asleep at some point.

She continued to drink saké alone, gazing pensively at the TV. After a foreign film came one of the popular specials of the season, a show in which stars displayed unexpected talents.

Eventually Atsushi came home. At the sound of the front door opening Takiko tried to struggle to her feet. The effects of the drink, which she'd hardly noticed till now, spread hotly through her body. Under the weight of Akira she sank back onto the tatami.

"What are you like that for?" Atsushi muttered as he came in to find her flopped on her behind and unable to get up.

"Help me, Atchan. I'm too drunk to move."

"Oh, yuck, have you been drinking with these guys?"

"Are you kidding? Help me up, quick."

Atsushi hauled her up roughly by the arm.

"Ow! You'll pull my arm off!" she hissed. Without replying, he held her by his side and got her to move her feet. His body had a strength that made Takiko want to lean dependently on him, which confused her and made her giggle.

Sitting down on the futons in the storeroom, she took Akira out of the carrier. Her pulse was racing and she was short of breath.

Atsushi said something.

"Huh? What?"

"I'm going to throw those guys out."

She wanted to look at his face, but her eyes were too heavy to see straight.

"No, don't be silly."

"I can kick them out easily." His voice sounded a long way away, too.

"Leave them alone. They're not doing anyone any harm, are they? It's New Year's. Only comes once a year, New Year's."

"New Year's—I've had it up to here."

Atsushi went away. As she crawled fully dressed into bed and tried to make out what he was doing, the television went quiet, the living room light went out, and silence fell throughout the house.

Takiko closed her eyes and relaxed. The bed was slow to warm up. The snow outside had given the room an icy chill, the first real cold of the winter. In the living room the kerosene heater would still be burning with a bluish flame. There might well be an earthquake in the night, or one of the men might knock it over with his foot and start a fire. But so what if there was a fire? Since Atsushi would no doubt rescue their mother, at worst those three men would burn to death, and she and Akira as well if she didn't wake up; and the house would burn down. That was the worst that could happen, and it wouldn't be any great loss. If she turned the heater off the three men might freeze to death in this drafty house. Seeing as how they were such old friends, born in the same town, that might not be such a bad way to go. But if everyone were calmly to wake up tomorrow morning without having burned or frozen to death, that wouldn't be a bad thing either.

Takiko tried—while her whole body seemed to lurch drunkenly from side to side—to remember her father's hometown.

Her parents had taken her there once or twice when she was small. How old would she have been? She had an idea that it was not long after her parents, who had separated, decided to live in the same house again.

The town was a dark, foul-smelling place. What could that smell have been?

It was a port. The railroad station was right on the waterfront. The sea was black. A black expanse of water—perhaps she'd seen it at night? She'd been terribly cold. There'd been a big ship directly alongside some freight cars. "That's the boat that goes over the sea to the north," her father had told her. "It's much, much colder over there," he'd added.

Wherever they walked it was wet underfoot. She seemed to remember it being wet in the station, on the streets, outside the stores, even inside the houses. She thought there might have been powdery snow whirling in the air too. Perhaps it had been very early in the big spring thaw. She'd been numb with the dank cold that seemed to seep right through her body.

She remembered very little else. Only that she had felt forlorn and miserable. She was afraid of the sea that stretched away to the north. She was convinced that if she relaxed her guard for a moment she would tumble in. But there was a boat that crossed that sea. What would make anyone go to a place colder and darker than this? To the very young Takiko, the ferry that left from the wharf seemed fraught with some utterly terrifying purpose.

Though she'd never expressly asked, she had the impression that it was this trip that led to her parents' reconciling. Atsushi had been born after it. She'd been used to hearing her mother use words like "drunkard," "no-good lazy bum," "woman-chaser," and "coward," but as her father wasn't living in the same house, she hadn't been sure just what his existence had to do with her. There was no way she could take as much interest in him as her mother did.

She couldn't say for sure whether her mother had told her they'd be living with her father again before or after that visit to the town where he grew up. Her mother had looked depressed. She'd also said something like: "I can't manage, not with a child. I'll just have to put up with him."

In any case, Takiko had been unable to make the first move toward him herself. Her father had been kind, she seemed to remember. Perhaps the return to his old home after many years had put him in a mellow mood. What did her mountain-bred mother think as she looked at that bleak, wintry sea? She'd grown up without ever seeing the sea. So she had told Takiko long ago with an incredulous shake of her head. "It's true! Isn't that a shame? I wasn't the only one who wanted to see the sea, all the children were longing to. We could hardly wait."

Her father had said, eyeing the black water, "It's much, much colder over there."

Takiko fell into a deep sleep while dreaming she was aboard the boat.

The two guests finally departed the next afternoon, her father accompanying them. Her mother decided to get some more sleep now that the house was quiet. Atsushi slept past noon too, their futons side by side, then went out to enjoy himself again. Takiko put Akira on her back, opened the glass doors of the veranda, and set to work energetically cleaning. The sky was clear and dazzling. The covering of snow from the day before melted by evening, gleaming all the while.

Her father didn't come home that night.

On the fourth, her mother dragged herself out of bed to

start work. "You must see the doctor, you're not as young as you used to be," Takiko said on the way out of the house with Akira on her back.

She had nowhere in mind to go. The day was as beautiful as the one before. There wasn't a trace of snow in the streets. She headed in the opposite direction from the main road on the hill, walking along a quiet side street parallel to a busy thoroughfare below. To her left a series of narrow lanes ran down the intervening steep slope. Each time one of these appeared there was a vista of blue sky and the city gleaming whitely in the sun. The flat white light extended up to where a haze lay on the horizon. A single line of brighter light stood out: that would be the water of the Sumida River. The maternity hospital where Akira was born had been near the river.

On the morning of the third she'd had a New Year's card from the woman who'd been in the next bed. It had said something like: "Our baby is growing fast—fifteen pounds already. I'm sure yours must be very cute too. Do drop in and see us whenever you like. All the best in the coming year." Takiko hadn't yet written a reply, nor did she intend to. Instead of being fondly reminded of the sender she'd recoiled as though she'd taken delivery of something that wasn't meant for her. Somewhere along the way, the bed in the maternity hospital had become a place she'd rather not remember.

Takiko had received only eight New Year's cards, counting that one. Two were from local politicians she'd never met. Then there were Kawano and Abé, a colleague from her office job, and two boyfriends from her high school days. That was all. Atsushi was the one who received the most cards, nearly all from his school friends.

There wasn't a sound to be heard on the deserted street. It

was lined with large old homes; a small pediatric clinic displayed a notice, OPEN ON THE 5TH, and at the police box the patrolman was passing the time repairing his bicycle.

Farther along, the large houses on both sides gave way again to small ones without walls or gardens, there were an increasing number of cheap apartment buildings and a few new expensive ones, and then the street met the bus route that descended the hill.

Following it down, Takiko went into the subway station at the intersection below.

Inside the station, she at last sighted several people in kimonos for their New Year shrine visits. Families dressed up to go out also caught her eye. By the fourth day of the holiday people were probably ready for a family outing. Fathers with children in their arms, mothers cautioning them about one small thing or another. Harried fathers piggybacking their children, mothers bringing up the rear with armfuls of belongings and equally bad-tempered expressions.

Akira, on Takiko's back, was fast asleep.

Takiko took the subway and found an empty seat. On her right was an old man who reminded her of her father, and on her left a sleepy teenage girl.

It wasn't as if there was anywhere she wanted to go. She simply wanted to be on the move with Akira, by subway or bus, through the vastness of the city. It seemed to her that only by staying on the move could she bring sights to her eyes and sounds to her ears, and remember the softness of her own body.

After riding the subway for about twenty minutes, however, she got up when she heard a familiar stop announced. She found the station more crowded than she'd expected. It connected with the city railroads and a private line as well. Takiko hurried away and, as if she'd had it in mind all along, headed without hesitation for the coffee shop where Kawano ought to be.

Watanabe, the owner, was alone behind the counter. There were a surprising number of customers. Kawano should show up in about an hour, she was told, so she first had them make up a bottle for Akira, who had just woken, and also changed his diaper. This time, unlike their earlier visit at the beginning of autumn, Akira was surveying the dimly lit interior with a smile on his face. Watanabe lent him a spoon to play with.

"You've lost weight, I see. Have you started working?" Watanabe asked her quietly, tickling Akira's chubby cheeks.

There wasn't a single face she recognized in the place. She gave Akira the bottle while gazing idly at the large photographs of jazz musicians on the walls.

Kawano arrived just as she'd finished feeding Akira and was lighting a cigarette, one of Watanabe's. As soon as he saw a baby on the premises he realized that Takiko was there.

"Hello." She greeted him with a smile when their eyes met. "Thanks for the New Year's card. You were the only one who addressed it to Akira as well as me." Kawano's startled face was slow to smile. "It was too much work to write a reply, so I ended up coming here. Today's my last chance to wander around." Kawano nodded at her lively tone and broke into a smile at last.

"Your face has changed, Odaka-san. Must be half the size it was last time you were here. October, wasn't it?"

"Really? Have I gotten as thin as that?" Takiko put her hand to her cheek.

"I was just thinking of you. And here you are. Gave me a

shock," Kawano murmured, smiling at Akira who was looking up at him. "Akira's getting to be a big boy, isn't he? Looks like he's gobbling up his mother."

"Don't be silly," Takiko laughed.

After joining Watanabe behind the counter and exchanging his leather jacket for an apron, Kawano returned to tell her that Abé had been in twice in December and had asked if she ever happened to drop by. She nodded without comment, and Kawano said nothing more on the subject. He was still on vacation himself, he explained, but had decided to come in anyway because he was more comfortable here than in his apartment.

"And here you are. So I guess I'm in luck. I'm not sure if it's a good or bad sign for the rest of the year, though."

Takiko followed him to the counter, carrying Akira, and took a seat there. He replaced Watanabe at the sink and went to work washing coffee cups.

After watching his turned back for a while she offered, "How about if I put Akira on my back and give you a hand?"

"On your back?"

Kawano stared at her and burst out laughing.

"It's kind of boring just sitting here."

"It's okay, that'd be too much of a good thing. Listen to the music. There's a great track on now."

A piano piece was playing quietly in the background.

"But . . . I'm kind of at loose ends."

"Want another cup of coffee? You'll have to go home soon, won't you, because of Akira?"

Takiko shook her head childishly. "I'll have a whiskey and water. New Year's is nearly over and I haven't done a thing to celebrate."

"Hm . . . Will he be all right?" Kawano glanced at Akira who was eagerly reaching for a dish of lemon slices on the counter.

"He's fine. And if anything happens I'm sure you'll cope." Laughing, Takiko handed Akira a slice of lemon. He delightedly pressed it to his mouth. Instantly he screwed up his face and shivered. He didn't cry, though, or let it go.

"You're impossible. Well, make it just one, then."

"Mm." Takiko nodded.

For a while Akira continued to play contentedly on her lap, but in less than an hour, perhaps needing to sleep, he began to fret. She took him on her back and started on her second weak whiskey.

It was still very early in the evening. Akira dropped straight off to sleep in the carrier. Sooner or later she'd have to get up and go home. But not just yet. She ordered another drink from Kawano. He didn't make it at once, but checked Akira's sleeping face before handing Takiko her third glass.

Akira stayed asleep for an unexpectedly long time. When he woke up hungry and started to cry, the hands of the clock had passed six and she was the only customer left. She was also pretty drunk by now, after at least five whiskey and waters.

"The boss says we're closing early today because it's New Year's. Why don't we leave together, Odaka-san? I'll see you to the station."

At Kawano's insistence, Takiko stood up. The floor swayed beneath her feet. Before she knew what she was doing, she clung to him.

"Gee, can't you even walk by yourself?" Kawano said as he supported her. Though she hadn't noticed him change out of the apron, he now had on his leather jacket instead.

By the time she'd paid Watanabe for her drinks and been helped into her coat by Kawano, Takiko was going under rapidly. Something white and bright whirled before her eyes and it was hard to breathe.

She made it to the street outside leaning heavily on Kawano. She couldn't hear his voice, or Akira's crying.

"I feel sick. I don't want to move. . . . I don't want to go home like this," she said in a tearful voice as she clung to Kawano.

He stopped a taxi, pushed her inside, and got in. It was such a relief to be carried along by something—no matter what—that she closed her eyes and fell asleep against him.

But in no time he was shaking her awake.

"Okay, go ahead. You can walk it, it's not far. Careful now—you've got Akira."

She could hear Kawano's voice. Nodding, she moved in a stupor. Then when he told her it was all right now to lie down, she smiled with pleasure, stretched out full length, and went back to sleep.

Waking suddenly, Takiko remembered Akira for the first time. He had gone from her back. She raised herself and looked around. Kawano was giving him a bottle.

"Oh! Why are you . . ."

She went over to him in astonishment. Kawano gave her a sour look.

"I couldn't let him cry like that, could I? And it was no use trying to wake you. So I found this in your bag. It's a good thing you'd brought milk powder. Get some more sleep. It's only been, let's see, half an hour."

"Half an hour? Oh. Where are we? Is this your room?"

"That's right," Kawano answered, more sourly still.

Gazing around with new interest, Takiko returned to the stale-smelling and evidently permanently spread futon and lay down again. It was the sort of room that contained nothing but a stereo and records. There was a small sink in the corner and green patterned curtains at the window. The bright blue of a small plastic bucket under the sink attracted her eye. It was a clean room, she thought. A gas heater's red glow filled its six-mat area.

Akira finished his bottle and began babbling happily.

"It's lucky for you I was here," Kawano told him with a smile, "or there's no telling what might have happened to you." Akira touched his face with both hands and went on making the same sounds.

"Aah-ooh, aah-ooh."

His fingers found their way into Kawano's mouth, up his nose, and nearly into his eyes. Kawano shook his head and dodged now and then, laughing.

Takiko watched them together dreamily. She was full of nostalgia, as if she'd seen such a scene before. She forgot to move or speak.

When Akira was laid down on the tatami, he discovered the empty bottle and began to play with it, alternately swinging it around with all his might and sucking on it.

"How do you feel?" Set free, Kawano came over to her. "Better now?"

Takiko only stared at his face. Who was this speaking to her? she wondered in the midst of her contentment. Who could it be? It wasn't like anyone she knew—not Kawano, nor her brother. But it was the person closest to her now. Just as Akira's body always communicated its moment-to-moment life, so this young man's body was imparting its soft weight to her.

"You're looking better. Good thing you didn't have to throw up."

Takiko stretched out her arms to him in the way Akira often did when he wanted an adult to hold him. With large eyes, she watched his face.

"Aah-ooh. Aah-oom." Akira made noises behind Kawano's back. Kawano turned his head, and she shifted her gaze there too. Akira smiled back while sucking the bottle under the two adults' watching eyes. His cheeks were pink.

"He's cute," Kawano murmured, and turned back to Takiko.

With a smile of pleasure she murmured in return, "Isn't he?"

Over her smiling face, Kawano's came falling softly. She put her arms around his body.

By the time Akira tired of playing alone and grew sleepy and started to cry, they were unable to move away from one another's bodies.

Akira cried himself to sleep, then after a while began to wail again.

Takiko sat up and, after laying her hand on Kawano's warm cheek, shuffled her naked body across the tatami to pick up Akira. Kawano watched her movements without speaking. Akira spotted his mother's exposed breasts and began to suckle with tears still running down his face. While with her left hand she brushed back her hair, now damp with sweat, Takiko vaguely watched his face as he sucked intently on her nipple from which nothing had come in a long time.

It was after ten o'clock when she put on her clothes, took Akira on her back, and left the apartment without disturbing Kawano.

When she reached home, before she'd had time to think about anything, she fell into a deep, healthy sleep.

Next day, the trips to Midori Nursery began again. Takiko went the following day to the local branch of the cosmetics company, with the saleswoman whom she'd asked for an introduction, and arranged to spend two weeks in training.

Wed., Jan. 26 (fair)
8:00   Formula (200 cc).

      □

9:25   Rubdown and exercises in the sun. Laid him on his stomach and lifted his legs as if for a handstand. He put his hands down nicely to support himself, with his head on the futon, and gave me a broad grin.
9:40   Fruit juice (60 cc) + honey drink (60 cc).
      As soon as I put the nipple in his mouth, both hands came up to hold the bottle. Wow, look what you can do! Later, when he was maybe getting tired, he let go with his right hand and used his left until he'd gulped it all down.
10:05   To bed. Making a snuffling noise.
10:20   Asleep.
12:10   Woke him up. BM.
12:15   Formula (200 cc).
12:30   Cradle. Gave him a rattle, but he seemed much more interested in the bamboo wind chimes. When I dan-

gled them within reach he swung them around and inspected them from top to bottom. Lost his grip and batted them with his feet instead. Kazuya and Akkochan were watching with big smiles.

1:00   BM (good stool).
        Gazing at the mobile in the middle of the room and chattering contentedly. "Ba-ba-ba, ahn-ooh."

1:35   Puree, spinach with soy, meatballs, leek soup. He's got a good appetite.

2:10   Honey drink.
        Practice at turning over. If I cross his feet firmly he can just manage to roll over, and beams happily.

3:40   "Ooh, I'm hungry."

4:00   Formula (200 cc).

                                        —Midori Staff

6:00   Fish-paste cake (three pieces), soup (two spoonfuls).

7:00   On his stomach on the kitchen floor going "ba-ba-ba." When I say "ma-ma-ma" Akira laughs his head off and goes "ba-ba-ba."

9:15   Bath time.

9:45   Formula (200 cc).
        Put him to bed but he won't stop crying.

10:30   Honey drink.

10:45   To sleep.

Wed., Feb. 28 (rain)

5:30   Formula (200 cc). BM.
        Playing.

7:15   Gone to sleep.

8:30   Started crying. BM.

□

9:30   Exercises, rubdown.
       When we practice standing up he rolls his eyes and
       looks pleased with himself.

10:00   Formula (100 cc).
        You weren't hungry yet, were you? Didn't cry when
        the bottle slipped out of his grasp. Flapped his hands
        and started to play.

10:15   Cradle.

11:10   Puree, omelette.
        Shuts his mouth tight and refuses to open up. Sleepy
        as well. Keeps rubbing his eyes.

11:20   BM.

11:30   Sleep.

11:50   Sprawling on the bed, fooling with some toys. Kazu-
        kun next door has swiped one. Still smiling, Akira
        paws Kazu-kun's face and grabs his shoulder. "Hey!
        Hey!"

12:40   To bed.
        Holds up his arms and talks in yelps. Ah! Wah!

12:50   Dropped off sooner than I expected.
        Asleep.

3:00   Formula (200 cc).

3:20   Cradle.

3:50   Whimpering. What a pathetic sound. Chortled when
       I picked him up. I carried him over to see the Violets.
       It's snack time—buns and bananas all over the table.

"Ooh, I want some too." He conned a rice cracker and came back home.

4:00 Cradle. Half the cracker and a bite of hot dog. Seems highly satisfied. "See, it pays to make a fuss."

4:25 Fruit juice (70 cc).

—Midori Staff

7:00 Formula (200 cc).

7:30 BM (carrot in it).

7:45 Spinach, hamburger patty, carrot.

8:30 At a friend's home.
　　　To bed.

Fri., March 23 (fair)

7:00 Formula (200 cc).

8:00 Out of bed.

　　　□

9:20 Rubdown, exercises, sunbathing.

9:50 Must have made him sleepy. He's nodding off while sucking the hem of his shirt. Ah yes, spring is here.

10:10 Fruit juice (60 cc).
　　　"I want more!" Did his best to take Taro-kun's bottle away. But a grown-up caught you, didn't she?

10:15 Bed.

11:15 Rice porridge, scrambled eggs, miso soup with seaweed, mandarin.
　　　"Wah, that's not enough!"

12:10   BM (good stool).

12:45   BM. Must have been left over from just now.
        Snuffle-snuffle, chatter-chatter. He's tumbling over
        and over and talking away in a very cute voice.

1:00   To bed.
        Goes right on talking, shaking his head and smiling.

1:10   Asleep.
        Oh, you haven't had a pee. To the potty. Nothing
        doing.

2:45   Cow's milk (180 cc).
        He's playing as he drinks. Unusual for him. Laughing
        and squirming.

3:50   Snack: steamed cake, cheese, tomato, sesame cracker.

4:30   When I put the clothes basket on the floor he reached
        out with a twinkle in his eye. "Uh-oh, can't quite
        make it." Thrashed about like mad trying to get at it.
        Now that he can turn over he's very active, isn't he?
        This is where the fun starts. But we'll be saying good-
        bye soon. We'll miss him.

                                        —Midori Staff

6:30   Home.
        Rolling about by himself on the kitchen floor.

7:00   Dinner: tofu, greens, banana, rice, clear soup.

8:00   In a good mood. "Ah-ah, wah-wah." Putting his big
        toe in his mouth and sucking it.

9:00   Bath. Cried the whole time.

9:30   Cow's milk (200 cc).
        Asleep.

Sat., March 31 (rain)

6:50   Formula (200 cc).
        Large BM.

        □

9:30   Rubdown, exercises.
        Hugging a toy happily, but soon lost it to Kazuya-kun.

9:45   Fruit juice (70 cc).

10:05   To bed.
        He looked sleepy, but next thing I knew he rolled out into the center of the room. He's sucking a corner of the towel that's wrapped itself around him.

10:20   Asleep.

11:05   Rice porridge, soup, soft noodles, salad, sausage.

11:45   Emptied the toy bucket and waved each one around in turn. I put him on his stomach and took his hands for crawling practice, but he laughed so much he couldn't use his tummy muscles to get anywhere. Then practiced standing up, holding the bar in the Violets' room, which he did with a smile—no trouble at all.

1:00   Cow's milk (180 cc).

1:30   Cradle.
        Talking with the adults. "Ee-hee-hee, hee-hee-hee."

2:45   Snack.
        A thin slice of apple. None of the others managed theirs. They all spat it out, but Akira-kun chewed his up and swallowed the whole lot.

All day long for some reason he's stayed close to Kazuya-kun, hitting his face, trying to climb on his back, making him cry. I wonder if he's sorry to be saying goodbye? It certainly looked that way. "Hey, Kazuya, I'm off to a different nursery tomorrow. You won't forget me, will you? See you again some-time."

—Midori Staff

YOUNG LEAVES

Gray concrete block walls stretched ahead. There was no one in sight on the broad asphalt road, and few cars passed that way. The road ran through a residential area in the central city, near a station on the main loop line.

The first time Takiko had walked along it with one of the senior saleswomen she had marveled at the number of trees. Tall deciduous trees displaying the intricate lines of their leafless branches against a background of sky. Low shrubs intertwining their crooked branches. And many kinds of evergreens, their leaves shining softly in the winter sun. All belonged to the gardens of the large houses that lined the street.

"Expensive old houses like these are no good, even for a real veteran," she'd been warned by the saleswoman, who was over forty, the mother of three children, and rumored to be making more than three hundred thousand yen a month. She didn't look her age at all, perhaps because of her skill with her own makeup.

"No matter how pleasant you try to sound over the intercom, you just get a 'Not today, thanks,' then click, and that's that. You can't see a thing over the gate—you're really out in the cold. So it's best to go straight past these places, since they're bound to be a waste of time. You'll probably have better luck in a less expensive apartment block like that one."

The woman was pointing to a six- or seven-story apartment building whose balconies were colorfully decked out with laundry, quilts and mattresses.

She was a kind teacher. She seemed ideally suited to the job, and Takiko could only look on in amazement as she went to work with obvious enthusiasm. If they came across a young mother sitting in the sun with a baby on her lap, she would take a look at the condition of her skin and offer advice on its care, sociably, yet without wasting words, then have herself invited in ("so much nicer than talking in the street"), open her large case packed full of products, and begin to describe their merits. When Takiko tried exactly the same approach it would result in a dirty look. She couldn't tell what she was doing differently from the older woman, who always sold at least a bottle of lotion. It didn't help to be told, "See, this is all you have to do"—she had no idea where the trick lay, and only grew more unsure of herself.

During her two weeks' training, Takiko had first been taught to make up her own face. Applying full makeup was a surprisingly complicated business. Before she had a very clear idea of how to go about it, she'd been drilled in such subjects as greeting and handling customers, facial massages, and even the structure and functions of the skin and hair.

She had still known next to nothing about cosmetics when she was handed various logbooks and ledgers for actual and potential customers' names and sent out for the first time, accompanying the experienced saleswoman. And four days later she'd had to start selling door-to-door on her own.

At first she had felt thankful and relieved in the freedom of her new hours (she wasn't even required to appear regularly at the branch office) and the knowledge that while there was no fixed wage there was no limit to what she might earn, either. She wouldn't have to bow her head to anyone on this job— unlike the restaurant—in order to go and pick up Akira from the nursery. Nearly all the saleswomen had children. A number of them worked only while their children were at school.

Once she'd lost her escort, however, Takiko had come to an abrupt halt. There was nobody now to tell her where to go or what to do.

"There must be something else you can do with your face, surely?" her companion of three days had cautioned helpfully. "The way it looks now, you'll put the customers off. You'll just have to keep practicing. . . ."

"I'm sorry." All Takiko could do was shrink and apologize in a small voice.

She was finding it off-putting enough herself. Each morning, she woke with Akira's crying, gave him a bottle, hung out the diapers, made breakfast, then rushed to the storeroom to open the sample case she'd been loaned and set to work, peering into the mirror inside its lid. First lotion, then skin milk and moisturizer; then she applied a little olive-toned base cream, smoothed foundation over it, patted on powder, put blush on her cheeks, brushed blue eye shadow on her lids, used eyeliner, darkened her lashes, and applied lipstick. Akira, who evidently saw his mother's cosmetic case as the ultimate in toy chests, tried to gain possession of it the moment she was off guard. The makeup progressed amid scoldings and—as he couldn't yet understand his mother's words—tears when he had his hand slapped. Since she wasn't used to makeup at the best of times, there was no way it could turn out a success.

Once she had more or less finished, Takiko would sit Akira beside her in the living room and start on a hasty breakfast. Her mother would take a long look at her face from the kitchen, or from where she sat at her machine on the enclosed veranda, and give an exaggerated sigh.

"Oh dear, do I have to get an eyeful of that face first thing every morning? You're so much prettier without all that. Can't you find yourself a decent job?"

Her father would already have gone out. After the New Year holiday her mother had seen a doctor and been told she had cardiac arrhythmia; she had to cut down her work load and her worries. A week later, Takiko's father had begun to do odd jobs at an amusement park.

Before she could even think of renting an apartment for

herself and Akira, Takiko first had to help make up her mother's lost earnings to meet immediate expenses at home and for Atsushi's schooling. Her father's new income was small—yet Takiko's was even smaller.

Her earnings failed to pick up in January, February, and on into March. It was all she could do to pay the fees at the nursery; she still hadn't managed to pay off the cosmetics she'd had to buy from the company, both for herself and for her sales. How could anybody make three hundred thousand or five hundred thousand yen a month at this job? Takiko was utterly mystified. But she didn't have time to puzzle over the mystery.

She tried asking for advice from the elderly woman who was head of her branch, and who was said to have been over twenty years in the business. Her only reply was "Look up everyone you know—friends, neighbors, relations, old classmates. Any kind of connection will do. You were taught that in the training sessions, weren't you?"

Takiko didn't have anyone she could call a friend. As for neighbors and relatives, when she thought of her mother's illness and her father's anger she knew she couldn't possibly try them. The thought of approaching her old classmates was almost frightening. Most were still at college.

Her sales still showed no sign of improving. She visited the woman who had sent her a New Year's card, who'd been in the next bed at the maternity hospital, and sold her a bottle of skin milk and a lipstick. Through introductions from Kawano she was able to sell two bottles of lotion and one pack each of nutrient cream, powder, lipstick, and blush. These were Takiko's total results for three months. She still hadn't made a single sale by knocking on strangers' doors.

She hauled out her graduation albums from elementary and junior high school, chose several names for a start and tried phoning them up. One had married and moved to a distant part of the country. Another's whole family had moved. The rest were still at their old addresses. There was one at college, one studying to be an interpreter, and several who had office jobs. When Takiko gave her name, each sounded hesitant as she said how nice it was to hear from her after all this time. Takiko explained about her job and asked if they'd mind meeting her and having a look at her products. Not one said she'd like to see her or them.

She also consulted the saleswoman who had originally introduced her to the job, the one who had a child at Midori Nursery. "It's all right," she was assured, "everybody goes through the same thing for the first three months or so. You'll gradually begin to do better. Just don't be in too much of a hurry." And the woman passed on one of her own regular customers—a housewife in her forties who lived over an hour away from Takiko—to cheer her up.

The early March weather had been alternating, cold one day and warm the next, at a dizzying rate. It was around this time that Takiko returned to the residential street she'd walked along once before, soon after she'd finished her training. The greenery was just as plentiful as she recalled. The changes that had taken place between January and March could be discovered in flower beds glimpsed through gates and gaps in garden walls. The jonquils and crocuses were in bloom, the sweet daphne were just coming out, and the plum blossoms, both red and white, were at their best.

It was a mild, clear day that followed one of cold and sleet. The blue of the sky appeared softly swollen with light. Takiko

walked along the quiet street with an unsteady feeling, as
though she were appreciating spring for the first time in her
life. The weight of her sample case, however, remained unchanged. After an hour of plodding about with it her arm was
always numb. In the winter, when the hand that held it was
stiff with cold, she had felt its weight only as pain. She had
often stopped at a department store and sat down in the lobby
to rest her hands and warm up. At times she'd almost dropped
off to sleep while idly smoking a cigarette, her body hugging
the sample case on her knee. She could hardly wait for the
evening, when she would go to pick up Akira. Even in the
mornings, only an hour or two after she'd left him at the
nursery, she missed the warmth of him on her back.

The coming of March and the end of winter had made little
difference so far. It had only increased the number of places
where she passed the time as, no longer needing to escape the
cold, she sat herself down on benches in railroad stations and
children's parks. It would all work out somehow. There was
no point in forcing herself to keep moving now. Takiko had
stopped thinking about anything while she sat and smoked on
benches. She became absorbed in watching children at play
in parks and all kinds of people coming and going on railroad
platforms.

At the end of February there had been a second training
session at the company's headquarters. There were different
skin-care products and techniques for winter and for spring.
She was made to study the effects of the seasons on the skin
as if she were still in high school. She'd also found that the
sales phrases she'd gone to such trouble to memorize were to
be replaced with new ones for the "spring campaign." She
took the course enthusiastically. She had to do something to

improve her sales performance. While the course lasted she was able to believe that she too could easily carry it off. It wasn't at all difficult. But when she set out on her rounds again, everything was exactly as before. When the time came, standing at a stranger's door, she stumbled over the words and couldn't even manage a smile.

Takiko had spent that morning in the usual way, walking around a public housing complex near a small station about thirty minutes out of central Tokyo, without any particular idea of where to find a customer. Before she had gone very far she had suddenly become aware of the spring sunlight on her body. All this time, while she'd been busily rehearsing the slogans for the spring campaign, she'd been unaware that spring itself was drawing steadily closer to her.

She stood still and looked up at the sky from a fourth-floor walkway. Its azure spread overhead, as bright as if it were tinged with yellow. The comfortable sound of futons being beaten here and there drifted into it. The voices of small children could also be heard as they played, watched over by their mothers, in sunny spots below.

Maybe she could see the shadowy masses of mountains?

She stayed there straining her eyes into the far distance. She felt sure she should be able to see the mountains' pale blue shadows from where she was. Somehow she was convinced that she'd simply forgotten to look out for them as she walked and walked. These days she quickly forgot important things.

However hard she looked, though, she couldn't make out the pale shadows of a mountain range in this tranquil, blue, suburban sky. The multicolored roofs of houses stretched away with only an occasional dark knoll of greenery to be seen.

Behind her, as she continued to search the skyline, a small

child in a navy blue smock—probably on his way home from
kindergarten—ran past and started banging on the metal door
at the far end of the walkway. Takiko turned her head to the
child and gave him a smile. He merely stared back impassively.
She let her eyes return to the sky.

"Mommy," she heard the child say, "there's one of those
pests coming this way. See, there she is!"

The mother's voice echoed faintly, and the metal door
slammed.

Takiko picked up the big black sample case that she'd set
down at her feet.

There were no silhouettes of mountains to be seen here.
How had she gotten such an idea into her head? She couldn't
see any mountains, much less the horse-shaped traces of snow
on a ridge that were said to float clearly into view when spring
came.

Takiko hurried down the stairs. What on earth was she doing
here? She felt suddenly fragile and alone. She couldn't help
wondering, too, what had come over her: Why remember her
mother's story of the horse of snow at a time like this? But now
that she had, it wasn't easy to shake off the vision of a horse
of unmelted snow crisply sparkling in the distant sky. The
sparkle was mercilessly driving her body to do something. It
was the light of spring. Transparent light that glittered on a
faraway ridge, beyond mountains receding peak upon peak.

She headed toward the station. For a start, she thought, she
had to go somewhere else. She bought a ticket for some con-
venient amount and walked onto the platform. The uptown
train came in first and she boarded it hastily. The car wasn't
crowded. A mother was dozing, tilting sideways, in the seat
opposite. The baby on her back was also asleep, its head lolling

forward. Takiko closed her own eyes for the duration of the ride. The shining figure of the horse on the blue ridge streaked in pursuit.

At the end of the line she changed to the central loop. She was being drawn toward the street with all the trees that she'd walked along in January. It hadn't occurred to her to head for the actual mountains where the first signs of spring were appearing. That wasn't where her baby was. The baby who could already turn himself over and appeal to his mother for a cuddle would be soaking up the spring light in the very center of the city.

She was able to find the street without any trouble. The quiet, bright light and the smell of spring were there in greater abundance than she had expected. The street was lined with those strangers' gardens that she couldn't enter; there was no sign of anyone about. She strolled down the broad asphalt road, squinting her eyes.

Along the way there was a white sign that read MISAWA GARDENS. The gray wall of concrete blocks to which it was fixed was so unremarkable that she might easily have taken the place for an ordinary house, if it hadn't been for the sign. The wide double gates stood open, and just inside them, to one side, there was a large greenhouse of semi-transparent plastic panels. The ground between it and the gates was covered with ornamental plants in pots. Even Takiko could identify the rubber plants, but she didn't know the names of any of the others. The multitude of tropical-looking ornamental plants, which she never saw in gardens, held her riveted there for a long time. It was such an unexpected sight. The springtime she'd so carefully sought out and drawn to herself slipped back into a vague blur. These clusters of green leaves had no season.

Or, rather, the light of each season seemed to have collected there. Summer light, winter light, and yes, that *was* spring light, dancing on the surfaces of the tropical plants' big, fleshy leaves.

At the back of the lot she could see a one-story house, probably the owner's. Perhaps this was the lunch hour, for there was no sign of anyone at work as she peered through the gate.

From then on, Takiko often forgot about peddling cosmetics and would go instead to have a look at this greenhouse on a residential street.

The spring light grew stronger every day, and the magnolias were in flower when she had a fight with her father that resulted in her having to go to the welfare office for the first time—to transfer Akira to a free public day-care center.

As usual, they had clashed over some quite trivial thing. Yet Takiko was injured seriously enough to have to rush to a hospital emergency center in the middle of the night. She was not in very much pain. She'd been flung backward by the force of a blow on the mouth and had hit the top of her head on the iron leg of her mother's sewing machine. While it hadn't hurt especially, the cut in her scalp had bled so badly it horrified Takiko herself. The blood streaming down her face and over her ear had been a very frightening sight. Her mother had cried and shouted, "You stupid no-good—," grabbed her father by the throat, and tried to throttle him until Atsushi caught her arms from behind. Then, bursting into loud sobs again, her mother picked up Akira, who was screaming nearby, when suddenly she turned pale and started to moan. It was her heart.

Takiko was sitting stunned, blood still dripping down her

face. Her father picked up Akira, who was crying convulsively on the floor where he'd tumbled off her mother's lap. For her father to hold Akira was unthinkable. Takiko felt a moment's terror and almost screamed. A baby's life could so easily be lost.

"Takiko," Atsushi said, "you'll have to get to the hospital, right away. I'll go with you." He had his hand on her shoulder. Akira was still crying in his grandfather's arms. "Akira's all right. And anyway, we won't be gone long. Come on. Don't worry about Mom, she'll be fine in no time if she's left alone. But unless you get that seen to you'll end up either stupid or dead."

Takiko left the house, clutching Atsushi's arm. The cab-driver who picked them up sounded guardedly curious about what had happened.

"Face the facts!" Her father's roar lingered in Takiko's ears. Akira had been in her arms, crying and refusing to settle down. Her father was drunk. "There's others to think of besides yourself. Why drag your whole family into this? Haven't you ever heard of baby homes? Stop playing games and put him in a home."

She didn't need to be reminded that her father had been tired and edgy since starting his new job at the amusement park, nor that he'd had to start this job because of her mother's health, which might never have taken a turn for the worse if she'd had a normal summer. Of this Takiko was almost certain. For her mother those days of summer must have passed without letting in a single ray of light. Takiko began to perceive one reply to what she'd done. A very foolish, reckless thing. Yet she didn't regret it, nor did she think she ought to go down on her knees and apologize to her mother. This wasn't something that an apology would solve. It wasn't something that allowed regrets and second tries. All she could do was go on giving Akira his bottle and watching her parents, her brother, and herself, without regrets. There was nothing else she could do: this was the conclusion she inevitably reached. She had given birth to a baby that no one had wanted her to have, a birth to which she alone had consented. Regrets were not permitted.

Since the New Year, however, the whole family had rapidly run into difficulties. There simply wasn't enough money. Her mother had been barely supporting the household by working three times harder than most people. When the doctor had shocked her with the news that she risked a fatal heart attack if she didn't slow down, she had cut back to a normal work load since, whatever happened, she had to be there to protect her daughter and her grandchild; things might have been different if she didn't have Akira to consider. In doing so she had counted on Takiko's income from the door-to-door sales, but Takiko's income had simultaneously dropped to near zero. Her mother hadn't blamed her. Instead, she had turned on Takiko's father. He was the one who should be working, she had wept. Never mind his bad leg, he could find work soon enough if he looked for it, and if he didn't plan to look, after all that had happened, she would really leave him this time. She simply wasn't going to put up with any more.

Takiko's father had found work. Cleaning, watering the lawns and shrubs, and sometimes taking the tickets at a large amusement park in the city center.

But they hadn't been able to count on his earnings for long. He had increased his drinking out of frustration with his new job, and began buying rounds for complete strangers. It was true that baby Akira was a burden on her family. Takiko couldn't argue with that. Even she had to admit that perhaps putting him temporarily in a baby home might be the most natural thing to do.

Why not put Akira in a home until she, his mother, could get back on her feet? A sunny place with a huge garden: Takiko didn't know whether her father had actually seen the one he spoke of, but from the proud way he talked you'd have thought he built it himself. He made it sound too good for even the richest child. Akira would be fed delicious foods, and wouldn't have to see blood streaming from his mother's head, or his mother in bed with a man—and what's more, he might be able to have his hernia operation for free. Takiko had already put Akira's name down at the same university hospital where she had her head wound treated. The surgery was scheduled for April. The way things were going, however, it didn't look as though she'd be able to take him in then. And there was little hope of the situation improving, even if she were to postpone the date from April to August, from August to December. The costs of the surgery and the hospital room wouldn't have been unduly hard for her to meet in the days before Akira's arrival.

Yet Takiko was unable to let Akira go even temporarily. She couldn't have said why herself. She'd spent a mere seven months with his tiny body. However close she might have grown while taking care of him, it hadn't even been a year.

It wasn't because she was his mother; she couldn't see it that way. The fact that she'd brought him into the world with her own body didn't make her especially meaningful to the baby. Akira would no doubt cuddle up to the staff who looked after him at a baby home in the same way he cuddled up to her now, with the same gestures and expressions. She couldn't say this would be wrong. Yet she couldn't contemplate parting with him. At the risk of further disrupting her family's life, and Akira's in particular, she wanted to stay in contact with his soft flesh. She could no longer discover time of her own anywhere else.

With a bandaged head, she went to the welfare department of the local ward office. There she applied for a place in a public day-care center and had an interview. She was startled when asked if she'd like to be on welfare. "I don't need anything like that," she replied. My parents might be sick and lame, she added to herself, but I'm not.

The social worker nodded. "Then there's the allowance for dependent children, which you should apply for as soon as possible. You'll need a copy of your family register, your resident card, a certificate of income, your personal seal, and the application form. There are a number of other benefits available to someone in your position, so don't hesitate to consult the social welfare officer." Takiko bowed her head repeatedly and left the office.

Meanwhile, Takiko wasn't the only one at Midori Nursery who'd decided to transfer to a public day-care center, and the nursery, which relied solely on its fees, seemed headed for a financial crisis. Apparently a number of people transferred to public day care in March every year, but the vacancies had always been quickly filled before. This turnover was perhaps only to be expected at a private center like Midori Nursery, which accepted infants from six weeks on, since the public centers generally wouldn't take children under eight months, or four at the very earliest, and even then only in April when the fiscal year began, unless there were very exceptional cir-

cumstances. This year, however, there were an unusual number of applicants for transfers, including several whose children
had been at Midori Nursery for one or even two years.

Though Takiko couldn't follow all the details of the nursery's
finances, she could appreciate that if the numbers dropped too
far they'd be left with vacancies they couldn't fill quickly
enough and would have to almost double the charge to the
remaining parents—which would simply not be feasible.

An emergency general meeting was called and lasted until
ten o'clock at night.

"This is getting us nowhere," a mother who served on the
committee finally said. "We'll just have to ask everyone who
wants to quit to speak up, one by one."

It had been an emotional meeting from the start, and after
two hours and a great deal of talk it had moved no closer to
practical matters. The staff grimly resisted any suggestion of a
pay cut; in fact, they said, they would have liked to request
an increase, however small, plus paid leave to attend training
courses. The parents only sighed and repeated that they could
never agree to higher fees. "Even now it's costing us as much
as our rent," said a mother. "If the fees went up no one could
afford to keep their children here—and if we could, we might
just as well hire ourselves a baby-sitter."

"We're not a baby farm," said a staff member. "As you
know, we aim to become fully licensed and eventually develop
a quality of day care that isn't available at the existing public
nurseries. Isn't that what we've all been working for?"

As proposed by the committee member who had run out
of patience, those who wanted to go elsewhere were made to
stand up one by one and explain their decision. This seemed
largely a way of relieving the others' feelings, the real question

being: What sort of person would abandon us at a time like this?

Each of the transferees stumbled through an account of his or her circumstances. The man whose wife was chronically ill in the hospital was among them.

"Believe me, it's very painful to have to leave, with so many things still to be done, but the economic factor is a big one. And to tell the truth, the time and effort involved have become too much for me. I realize I'm being selfish, but I'd like to think I've done my share over the past two years. Look at it this way: the effort to build up a facility like this into a licensed nursery and the effort to improve the existing public nurseries and adapt them to parents' real needs are actually two sides of the same coin. I mean to go on working just as hard for those goals after transferring."

Several people applauded when he'd finished speaking. Their faces, and the faces of those who didn't applaud, were flushed.

All the transferees had much the same thing to say. Though bewildered as to why she too had to defend herself when she had no reasons apart from the financial one, Takiko said simply, "I can't afford the fees." Nobody applauded, but nobody pressed her further.

Unable to find words, one mother who had served for two years on the committee shrank from the many sharp looks and broke down in tears. "I just can't go on like this, it's killing me. I have to have a break. I can't take it any more."

No one spoke while she wept.

The emergency meeting did nothing to change the number of people who wanted to leave. Two others in Akira's Dandelion group were being transferred. Kazuya Yoshikawa, who had enrolled on the same day, was apparently staying on at Midori Nursery.

In mid-March Takiko received a letter from the welfare office notifying her of Akira's admission to the municipal nursery and a postcard advising her that her application for a dependent child allowance had been approved. The amount was unexpectedly small. The nursery fees had been waived.

By now Takiko felt no particular emotion toward the parents at Midori Nursery, nor in response to these notices. She was neither disappointed nor overjoyed. Her mother and father, however, were very interested in this new turn of events. The child allowance was a modest amount that Akira's birth had brought in. Her mother rubbed cheeks with him, over his protests, and said, "Isn't Akira-chan clever!"

On the first day of April, Takiko started him at the municipal nursery, which was within walking distance of home. The welfare officer also visited at the beginning of the month.

There was a single young cherry tree in the municipal nursery's narrow yard, and it was coming into blossom when Takiko began her daily trips with Akira on her back.

The nursery was housed in a sunny concrete building. The room where Akira spent the day was wallpapered with a pattern of animals. He was still the same friendly baby in these new surroundings; he didn't even act shy with the new helpers. There were nearly a hundred children at the nursery, ranging up to kindergarten age. Takiko felt uneasy when she saw the bigger ones playing in the yard, as if she'd been forced to look at something unpleasant. What she saw in them was the length of time that lay ahead of her. Her baby couldn't escape those unforeseeably long years, turning three, turning six—growing, in other words. Takiko had never before thought of Akira, or herself as his mother, in those terms. She didn't want it. Then what did she want? Her mind went blank.

Nevertheless, the days went steadily by without sparing them. The color of young leaves caught the eye everywhere in the city. Takiko went on walking wherever the mood took her—it was more like a pleasant stroll than work—her spirits lifting at the sight of the leaves' fresh color. Akira was supposed to have the operation at this time of year. But when she went nervously for a consultation at the hospital and explained that it would take her a little longer to raise the money, they put it off to July so readily it was almost a letdown. In his present condition, they said, there was no particular hurry. As she left the university hospital, the vivid young gingko leaves enfolded her in their brightness. She half closed her eyes. She had the feeling that her whole body was taking on the transparent color of their play of light.

Still unable to sell off her cosmetics, Takiko enjoyed her daily strolls. She also continued, with Akira, to spend an occasional night at Kawano's apartment. While she didn't want to be a burden in any way to Kawano, who was younger, it was always she who sought his body first, and she who attempted greedily to bury herself in pleasure as if in a great hole she was digging with all her might. But she also felt she could stop seeing Kawano at any time and not regret a thing.

Her thoughts far from her job, she was again walking along the street she had come to know well, having visited it many times, in the old and elegant residential section of central Tokyo. The young leaves on this street seemed especially dazzling. She stopped outside Misawa Gardens, and there discovered a sheet of paper pasted up on the concrete block wall.

It was a small notice. On it was written "Staff Wanted

Urgently." Beneath these words was added "Male only, age 20 to 25."

Takiko gazed intrigued at the notice, her mouth open. After glancing around she went in through the gate of Misawa Gardens, her mouth still open.

There was nobody in the yard. She peered into the greenhouse on her left. It contained a seething, swirling mass of every shade of green. The hot air and the smell of leaves made it difficult to distinguish shapes.

"Excuse me," she called out into the green interior. There was no sign of anybody there.

"Excuse me," she called again, loudly. A deep voice made some reply from down at the far end. Startled, she fell silent. A rustling in the greenery drew rapidly closer.

"Oh, it's you." The leaves of the nearest palm swayed and a short man in a black T-shirt emerged before her. His tanned face and the bright gleam of his eyes gave him a very youthful look, but his receding hairline suggested he couldn't be so very young.

The man smiled, squinting up at Takiko who stood framed in the light from the doorway. "I've seen you before. Looking through the gate, weren't you? Are you interested in this kind of thing?"

Takiko nodded without thinking and then hastened to explain: "I'm not sure. I've never worked in a greenhouse. But I often feel like coming over and having a look. I'm healthy and really quite strong, and I think this might be just the job for me. I'd like to apply." She bowed her head deeply, then went on, choosing her words carefully now. "I've just seen the notice outside. Does it have to be a man? I'm dressed up for my job right now, but actually I love getting muddy and climbing trees. Would the work really be too hard for me?"

Laughing, the man motioned Takiko ahead as she stood in the doorway, and came outside. "I wouldn't say that, but it would be pretty tough for a woman. What do you do now?"

"I sell cosmetics. But I'm hopeless. I can't sell a thing." She held up the sample case that she was carrying. He burst out laughing.

"I see. Well, you can't expect to do much business, can you, when you're always goofing off around here?" Laughing, he settled himself on a garden rock.

"Oh, no, I'm not trying to get out of working. I'd never make any money if I did," Takiko said eagerly. Already, she couldn't tear herself away from the greenhouse.

"That's true enough." The man became serious. "But it's turned out to be heavy going? And so you'd like to try puttering about with plants for a change? But I reckon you'll find the work's harder. We can't afford to pay much, either."

"No. But I don't mind, as long as I can work here." Takiko gave him a hard look as she asked, "What are the hours like?"

"Now just a moment. You do realize what sort of work it is?"

"Not exactly. What would I have to do?"

"Deliveries. It's delivery work. You'd be hauling around a lot of big tubs, collecting them and bringing them back, or going out and watering the plants. . . . You don't understand, do you? You know the potted plants in restaurants and offices? Most of them are hired from places like this. But since no one bothers to take care of the poor things, they're always getting sick and dying. So we go out and look after them, and after a while we put in replacements and bring the old ones back here to perk them up. We treat them, see, taking plenty of time. Now do you understand?"

Takiko nodded. Her smile made the man relax his stern expression. "That's the main part of our work these days," he went on. "We used to handle garden plants, but in a location like this the business didn't do so well. Though we still have clients in the neighborhood. . . . There were a lot of gardeners in this area once. A long time ago. Business was good in the old days, but not any more. Our proper greenhouses are up at the mountain. We grow the plants there, and bring them down here when they reach a certain size. Kind of like a busload of youngsters coming to Tokyo to find jobs."

As she laughed at the man's words, Takiko took a fresh look around at the ornamental plants. Now that she'd heard his explanation, the ones set down outside did seem to be a lackluster shade of green—perhaps they'd just been brought back from offices. The man then told her the hours and the monthly wage, and asked her age. "I'm nearly twenty-two," she answered. Her birthday was in June.

The question suddenly reminded her of Akira's father. It was almost two years now since he'd asked her age. Nearly twenty-two. Not much different from when he'd asked. Yet she found it strange now to think of how she'd burst out laughing. Why had it made her laugh? This time she'd answered without giving it a thought, and her answer hadn't caused any amusement.

Staring at her heavily made-up face, the man said, "Uh-huh. But surely there must be any number of decent jobs for someone your age? Hawking cosmetics is a job for middle-aged matrons, isn't it?"

"When you've got a child, age doesn't have much to do with it. It's not as if I'm good with the abacus or anything." Her face reddened as she spoke.

"A child?"

"Yes. . . ."

"You've got a child?"

Takiko's face grew redder at the surprise in the man's voice. "But he's still a baby. . . ."

"Well, well. I guess it's nothing to be surprised at. People get married young these days."

"Um . . ." Unable to go on, she hung her head.

"What? I'm sure it won't make any difference. Anyway, I can't make the decision on the spot, but I'll have a talk with the boss. He's my old man, in fact. Could you bring us a simple résumé? I wonder if you'd mind starting off on a temporary basis, till we see how it goes?"

"That's fine with me. I'll bring my résumé tomorrow, then. Please do consider me. I'd love to work here." She brought her feet together neatly and bowed politely.

As soon as she reached home after collecting Akira that evening, she sat down at Atsushi's desk and wrote out her résumé on paper also borrowed from her brother. Résumés were no trouble—she had already written dozens. She set down her family background exactly, while recalling the man's words. Her parents, her brother, and her baby.

Next day, she first went to the ward office and, though perhaps it wasn't necessary, obtained a copy of her family register, then put it into the envelope with her résumé and headed for Misawa Gardens. It was the first time she'd been there in the morning.

A small truck loaded with tubs of trees was parked outside

the gate. Two men were unloading, one on the truck and one on the ground: the man she'd met the day before and another of about thirty, in a navy zippered jacket, with a bony face and body.

When Takiko called to them, they both turned at once and stared in her direction. There was no expression in their eyes.

Starting to feel a little apprehensive, Takiko told them she'd brought the résumé she'd been asked for yesterday. The man she'd met nodded, still without expression, and stripping off his muddy work gloves and wiping the sweat from his face he took the envelope that Takiko held out and put it in the back pocket of his trousers. He was breathing hard, his chest heaving.

"I'll pass it on to the boss later. But it'll be two or three days before we can give you an answer. Either way, you'll hear from us by phone." He put his work gloves on again, then suddenly smiled at her. "I see you're not wearing makeup today. Sure does make a difference. But don't get your hopes up about the job."

"No. Well, I'd be really grateful if you'd consider me."

She bowed, then as she raised her head she happened to meet the eyes of the man in the back of the truck. She bowed hurriedly to him, smiling. The man, who might soon be working with her, quickly turned his head away. As she left, Takiko thought he wouldn't be an easy person to work with. If he hadn't been there she might have asked to stay and watch for a while.

Two days went by, then three, and still there was no word from Misawa Gardens. Or at least her mother, who was in all day, said there hadn't been any calls for her.

On the fourth day, Takiko went to Misawa Gardens again. Neither the owner's son nor the other man was there. There was no one in sight. Hesitantly, she pressed the button on the intercom outside the house she took to be the owner's. She wore no makeup again that day. She did have her sample case with her, though, and in the few moments before the front door opened she hid it behind the shrubbery. She mustn't risk what so often happened on the job: she would be observed through the peephole and her business suspected, and then the homeowner would pretend to be out.

The door opened. A boy of about ten and a girl of five or six who looked like his sister came out.

"Who are you?" the boy demanded, though in polite terms.

When Takiko asked if there was anyone at home who knew about Misawa Gardens, the children clattered off inside without replying.

After she'd been kept waiting a while, a small old man came to the door. This was clearly the owner. The muscles of one side of his face were contorted.

"You must be Odaka-san." The old man's words were hard to catch. "You don't want to be temporary, is that it?"

Not quite sure she'd understood him, Takiko asked what he meant.

"Temporary won't suit you, will it? Then I'm afraid you'll just have to forget about working here," the old man said.

Startled, Takiko protested, "Oh no, of course I don't mind. You mean I can have the job?"

"Yes. You were supposed to have been contacted. Hadn't you heard?"

"No, but anyway, that's wonderful. Thank you very much."

She bowed her head with almost excessive politeness, still more surprised than overjoyed. She didn't stop to worry over the fact that the message hadn't reached her.

Since they hadn't thought of hiring a woman, apparently the decision had not been easy. However, as the job involved constant visits to coffee shops, cafeterias, and offices, they had begun to think that a woman's touch might not be a bad thing and decided to give Takiko a try, while also hiring a permanent worker as they'd originally intended. While the old man was explaining this, his son arrived back from somewhere. Takiko thanked him too.

"It's not really a job to be all that grateful for, you know. Still, if it works out we might be able to take you on permanently. Try it for a while, anyhow, and see what you think. Would you like to get started tomorrow?"

Still smiling, Takiko nodded like a child.

He went on to give her detailed instructions on what to wear and the gear she'd need to provide herself, such as cheap cotton work gloves. He told her to be there by eight-thirty, then added, "Was that your mother who answered the phone yesterday? Her voice was just like yours."

"Was it? . . ." Takiko couldn't help sounding a little wary.

"That's right, couldn't tell you apart on the phone. Make sure she knows all about us, now. We don't want to go giving her surprises—and besides, there's nothing to hide, is there?"

"No."

"Even if it's not the sort of job you can be proud of . . . How's your baby? Getting on okay?"

Takiko nodded.

"How do you manage in the daytime?"

"I've got him in day care."

The little girl ran out of the house just then, wailing "Daddy, Daddy," and flung herself against the man's body.

"Have you two kids been fighting again?" he grumbled with one hand on his daughter's head, then turned to Takiko and said, "Well, anyway, that's it for today. I'll show you the job tomorrow."

"Yes. I hope I'll do well here."

The man disappeared into the house, the little girl pulling him by the hand, while Takiko still had her head lowered in a bow. The old man had been letting his son do the talking while he stood aside, smoking a cigarette and surveying the plants outside; now he too withdrew with a slight bow.

Takiko went out and retrieved her sample case from behind the shrubbery, then looked over the greenhouse and the rows of potted plants that surrounded it as if she were seeing them for the first time. These were the things she'd be seeing and touching every day. She had a sense that the many-shaped leaves, the many shades of green, were rustling closer to her as she stood there. They gave her a strong impression of being moved by some emotion—not a tranquil one, she was sure. She felt both fond and afraid.

The other man she'd seen wasn't anywhere in sight that day.

Takiko went straight from there to the branch office of the cosmetics company, where she returned the sample case she'd had on loan and canceled her contract, then hurried on to Akira's nursery. As she arrived he was being given an afternoon snack in a high chair. When he spotted his mother's face peeking in through the window in the door, he burst into extravagant wails. A startled helper in a pink apron came out into the corridor and asked, "What's the matter?"

Takiko told her that she had finally found a new job. "And since I don't have anything else to do today, I've come to pick him up."

"Please don't just turn up whenever you feel like it—you'll only unsettle him. You should at least have phoned first." At the end of this lecture the helper conceded that as Akira had already seen his mother's face and was now upset they would let her take him just this once. Warning Takiko to be more careful in the future, she brought him out to her. He promptly stopped crying and beamed.

At this new, impersonally large nursery, Takiko was often scolded and made to feel small. She missed the notebook, too, in which Midori Nursery had kept a detailed record of Akira's day. She had to content herself with the new environment, however.

That evening Takiko also told her mother about Misawa Gardens.

Next day, she started the new job. The days felt longer than they had before. But the early-morning start meant that she finished in the late afternoon, and these hours fitted in nicely with Akira's at the nursery.

The job kept her in a whirl. She never seemed to catch up, though she could have sworn she was giving it all of her considerable strength. For the first couple of weeks, all she was able to do when she arrived home was sprawl on the futon she'd left out, her body one great mass of aches. She couldn't get started on making dinner or washing the diapers. Yet she wasn't at all anxious about the job. She liked the idea of her body gradually growing stronger, her arms thicker; but she was impatient with her muscles: Couldn't they get past this pain any faster?

Misawa Gardens had a staff of seven: the company president, his son, who was managing director, three permanent employees, the man they'd just hired, and herself. As two of the staff were at "the mountain" on the outskirts of Tokyo, Takiko worked alongside the younger Misawa, the man called Kambayashi whom she'd once seen unloading the truck, and the new man. It was the new man, twenty-five-year-old Sasaki, who became her regular partner. Sasaki had remained at college until, when he couldn't re-enroll for a ninth year, he was forced to think about finding a job. He had heard about Misawa Gardens from another student and decided to take the job because it would allow him to go on studying music on his own at night. When Takiko sounded surprised at this, he laughed apologetically. "I mean popular music. I write pop songs and enter them in competitions. Maybe one of these days . . ."

Sasaki was easygoing and kind, and she was glad to have him as a partner. She laughed a lot on the job. As they became friends she took to teasing him and falling about laughing at her own jokes.

Every morning they loaded the small truck with tubs of plants and made a run around the city, consulting their checklist. First Takiko would open the door of the client's office or shop and give Misawa Gardens' name, then they would both set to work replacing the plants. If there were just two or three tubs to go, Sasaki carried them by himself. Where the plants only had to be watered, on the other hand, Takiko did it while he stayed in the truck. Since many of their customers used the tubs as ashtrays, this work could take an unexpectedly long time.

They had to cover at least ten places each day—dark basement coffeehouses, fancy bakeries, small securities companies, hotel lobbies, architects' offices, beauty salons, banks.

The route changed daily and they never seemed to see the same faces twice. As they ran around the city in the truck, Takiko was overwhelmed by its endlessness. In every seemingly deserted building she entered, there would always be a number of people at work behind whatever door she opened. There were people in every coffeehouse, and crowds of people in every bank. People counting money, people talking, people eating, people bending over charts and diagrams. And none of them paused to watch her: if the normally motionless leaves of the indoor plants shook, that was Takiko on the move. It seemed to her that it was the potted plants in her hands that were speeding freely about the city. The streets appeared to her only as corridors for plants. Rubber plants hurtled along them, and dracaenas and silk cotton trees, ground rattans and coco palms. Green things whose very simplicity and lack of emotion struck her as harsh. Day by day, Takiko felt herself taking on the simplicity of their greenness.

While her days were occupied with the potted plants the sunshine was turning summery, and the June rains were almost upon them by the time she noticed. The color of the greenery on street corners, too, was growing heavier.

Perspiration filmed her forehead as they loaded the truck first thing each morning. By noon the red T-shirt that was practically her uniform these days would be sweat-stained— though the patches were small compared to Sasaki's.

"If it's like this now, what *are* we going to do in the summer?" Taking off his soaked T-shirt as soon as they arrived back at Misawa Gardens for lunch, Sasaki appealed jokingly to Kambayashi, who was sitting outside the greenhouse, bare-chested himself, munching a sandwich.

Although she saw Kambayashi nearly every day, Takiko hardly ever spoke with him. The man always seemed bitter about something. Perhaps it was this manner of his that had made him appear physically unimpressive at first. As the temperatures rose, however, and he stripped to the waist more often, Takiko had to change her mind about that. His body displayed a healthy strength and strikingly classic lines. Though he must be nearly ten years older than Sasaki, it was Kambayashi's body whose health and youth were exhilarating to see. Yet above it his lifeless face always wore an aged look that seemed deliberate. All the same, it wasn't as if he was cold to Takiko. He taught her the trees' names and characteristics when she asked. And it was he who had given her first aid when she hurt herself slightly loading the truck. Kambayashi seemed, moreover, to be in a special position at Misawa Gardens. Before she realized it, Takiko had ceased to think of this taciturn man as such a difficult type to get along with.

He answered Sasaki, with a smile, "You'll be used to the heat by then."

"Not the way *I* sweat. It's wiping me out. I guess really the job's easier in the winter?" Sasaki was mopping his face with his T-shirt.

"Well, in the winter, central heating dries out the plants, so the servicing's easier in the summer, I'd say. We have to do more replacements in the winter, too."

"Oh. Then I'd better spread my wings while I can." Sasaki spread his arms and turned his face, laughing, to the clouded sky.

"Besides," Takiko said, looking from one to the other, "it's nicer in the summer. I wouldn't mind the winter if it was *really* cold. But I'd rather have the summer than halfway cold weather. Wouldn't you?"

When Kambayashi's eyes met hers he gave a slight nod. She smiled back, vaguely pleased. Sasaki said, "Yeah, children like the summer. Anyway, I'm off to find some air conditioning. How about you, Taki-chan? Let's go somewhere cool and have chilled noodles."

"Hmm . . . No thanks, I think I'll buy some sandwiches and eat them here. Don't be too long."

"Pity. I was planning to treat you."

"Really?"

"Uh-huh. It's too late now, though. Next time, okay? See you." Sasaki pulled his sweaty T-shirt on again and strolled off alone.

Takiko ran out to pick up some lunch. Most days she bought a carton of milk and something from a nearby bakery. Now that she had company in the lunch hour, she looked forward to it the same way she did as a child.

When she returned with her paper bag, Kambayashi was still sitting with his lunch on his knee, smoking a cigarette.

"Oh, Kambayashi-san, were you waiting for me?" She sat down beside him.

"No. Just thought I'd give you this. Want it?" Kambayashi said morosely. He'd left a pork cutlet sandwich.

"You don't mind? It looks delicious. Here, have my curry pie instead."

"I don't want it."

"Oh? But it's delicious too," Takiko murmured regretfully, and started on the pie at once.

Kambayashi watched in silence as she ate, kicking off her sneakers and sticking out her bare feet, until suddenly he asked, "Looks like you can manage the job, doesn't it?"

After swallowing her mouthful, she answered, "Yes, I hope they'll keep me on."

"You should be safe for a good while."

"No one can say what's going to happen years from now anyway, can they?"

Takiko smiled at him and took another big mouthful. A fly was resting its wings on Kambayashi's smooth shoulder. Unaware of it, he was looking away at a yellow butterfly circling a coco palm that had come back from a client that morning. Its yellow was vivid among the green.

"Do you think that far ahead too, Taki-chan?"

"A little. But there's so much you can't know that it seems better not to think about it at all. It's scary, thinking ahead. Who knows, I might drop dead any minute now, if something were to happen."

"What do you mean, 'something'?"

The fly on Kambayashi's shoulder moved onto the cutlet sandwich. His hand shooed it off. It flew away in the direction of the yellow butterfly.

"I mean, I might choke on this pie, or be bitten by a poisonous spider, or a plane might crash right here, or there might be a big earthquake."

Kambayashi started to laugh.

"Don't you ever think like that, Kambayashi-san? Or is it different somehow when you've got a wife and child?"

"No, not much different. I think ahead, though—can't avoid it. But you, Taki-chan—what was the story when you had your baby? What was it all about?"

The laughter was already gone from his face. Takiko stiffened at the suddenness of this question. Although it was natural enough that Kambayashi should know about her background, she hadn't expected him to take a special interest. What's more, since she'd had Akira no one outside her home had ever asked her a direct question about the fact. The complete lack of questions had disconcerted her at first. The circumstances of Akira's birth had become something of which only her mother and father could speak, and by now Takiko had grown accustomed to it being vaguely acknowledged without anyone inquiring directly.

Was he only asking because he had no manners? Takiko was more anxious than put out. "What was the story? I'm still not sure, but I don't regret it, or anything like that."

Kambayashi nodded silently. Takiko continued, choosing her words. She was fearful of the words she spoke. It seemed impossible to convey accurately her feelings since giving birth to Akira, but she didn't want to say anything that would betray them. Her hands were cold.

"Of course, I'm not jumping for joy either. I've finally realized how tough it's going to be. That's been kind of disappointing, and I do get discouraged. Because you just can't get away from a child. I sometimes think I've accidentally gone and crippled myself for life. But still, I suppose I am glad, all the same. Or maybe I'm just making the best of it since there's no turning back now. It's changed all kinds of things, somehow. . . . But what's it to you, anyway, Kambayashi-san?"

Takiko's struggle to express how she felt, and her frustration at the clumsiness of her efforts, turned without warning to anger as Kambayashi simply sat there listening in silence. Depending on how he answered, she was angry enough to give him a good slap on the cheek.

Kambayashi reddened under her hard stare, and said, laughing, "What's it to me? I just thought I'd ask."

"And? Are you satisfied?" Takiko was still glaring at him. He nodded, then handed her the cutlet sandwich.

"Have this too."

She accepted the sandwich and bit into it fiercely. After watching her, Kambayashi murmured, "My son's ten, but he can barely talk. All he can say is 'Momma' and 'wee-wee,' things like that."

"Why?" Takiko couldn't help sounding startled. But she stumbled on the answer at once and asked again, "Is he, um, retarded?"

"That's right. And it seemed to me just now that what you're saying is what I've been thinking myself. Though they may be two completely different things."

Kambayashi gazed at the coco palm where the yellow butterfly had been fluttering a few moments ago. The butterfly had moved over to a Washingtonia.

Takiko didn't know what to say to him next. She was ashamed of her agitation compared to his calm. She hadn't known anything about him. In fact she had simply assumed that he was one of those fathers who couldn't possibly guess the resistance she must feel to talking about Akira; one of those fathers who innocently projected their hopes into the future with blithe assurance, with joy even, unaware that their own children's possibilities remained unclouded only because they were still so very young. She had talked to Kambayashi in a tone that implied as much. She had been assuming that every child who didn't have to be called illegitimate must be blessed with a father and mother and perfect health. Why, then, had he not objected but actually agreed with her?

His child. A ten-year-old who was growing up an infant. Takiko didn't know any retarded children, she had only caught sight of them occasionally on trains or in a park. The children she had glimpsed in passing had struck her as, yes, different. Something unusual about a child's appearance or behavior would catch her eye, and then she would realize that he or she wasn't doing it on purpose, that this was how the child was normally, and she would hurriedly look away in embarrassment at her mistake. The children were generally not alone. Once, on the train, she'd noticed a girl—probably a younger sister—with a tall retarded boy. The bags they carried suggested they were both on the way home from school. The girl, in her early teens, never looked away from her brother. She wasn't talking or smiling, simply gazing as if she couldn't take her eyes off his face, which had an air of vaguely enjoying something.

Takiko couldn't help trying to imagine Kambayashi's expression as he played games and exchanged looks and smiles with his child. Nothing came clearly to mind—nothing but light. Why should that be? She would have liked to ask Kambayashi, but was unable to put the question into words.

While Takiko was reflecting silently, Sasaki came back. Kambayashi got up. Relaxing at last, she hurried to finish her lunch.

"You're not *still* eating? Here, I'll spray your feet—it feels great," Sasaki said, picking up a rubber hose. First he sprayed his own legs, arms, and head, then directed the jet at Takiko's toes.

Catching the midday light, the water flashed and dazzled.

THE MOUNTAIN

In June, Takiko turned twenty-two. On her birthday her mother said, "It's your twenty-second today, isn't it? How's it feel? Are you past the age of wanting to celebrate your birthday?"

On the point of agreeing, Takiko changed her mind and answered, "No, I am glad, actually."

"Hm . . . Yes, you've got a good ways to go yet. But I

can tell you," said her mother half jokingly, "sooner or later it gets to be the day you hate most."

"I wonder."

Takiko wasn't so sure. If she was pleased about her twenty-second, she had a feeling that the same would be true of any birthday. She no longer felt the thrill they'd given her as a child, and the sense of expectancy also had faded. It was no longer a special day. The day that Akira was born would be far harder to forget. Yet this newly conferred figure of twenty-two did give her a tangible sense of time passing, days going by. It wasn't especially welcome, nor was it especially unwelcome; it just had a nice solid feel.

Since she'd learned of the ten years that Kambayashi had spent as the father of a boy with Down's syndrome, time that had been different from anything he had known before, Takiko had had a distinct feeling that she now existed in that kind of time too. And she wanted to go on feeling this way. This intention even made her proud. It was as if Kambayashi's presence had given her, for the first time, words for her having and raising Akira. Kambayashi had accorded to her own child a weight equal to his retarded child's. Of this she could feel sure.

She wanted to catch every word from him that she could. She waited eagerly each day for time alone with him, and when it finally came she tried, eagerly and openly now, to find out every little detail of his life as a father. She didn't want to know what Kambayashi was like as a person. He was a father who had come to shun any other identity. To be able to talk with such a father was enough—in fact it was a stroke of luck.

Kambayashi responded with fatherly words whenever Takiko

prompted him. In this role he told her about the day-to-day life of the child and his mother. He spoke in a self-mocking tone, while also seeming to choose, for Takiko's sake, to tell of the pain that having a special child made inevitable in many ways; at the same time there was an unmistakable glow of childish pleasure in his face as she showed surprise or sighed at his words.

Gradually, Takiko began to rib him a little. "But you don't mind, do you?" she interjected. "You look very happy, you know."

Then Kambayashi's face took on such a disgruntled look it was funny. "It wouldn't make any difference if I did mind," he said defensively. "Anyhow, I don't really know any other kids. So, okay, I take more interest in him than anything else. What can I do?"

Takiko hastened to assure him, "Of course, it's the same for me. I'm ridiculously happy every time I see Akira's face. Really, so happy I feel like a fool." He gave a relieved smile.

"Yes, I know, it's as if my son's dopiness rubs off on me. Because when I'm with him nothing else seems to matter. I get so carried away I don't know what's come over me, and I end up like him. You see, he doesn't get bored, and he doesn't try to get away with things. He always shows exactly what he feels. So you can't hold back yourself, can you?" Already, Kambayashi's face had regained its look of pleasure.

Though Takiko couldn't imagine herself in Kambayashi's place in any practical sense—spending ten years with a child whose condition was untreatable, apparently due to a chromosomal abnormality—she felt she could do without further explanations as long as she was studying his face. It was satisfying, but something also filled her with a greed for more.

She saw herself walking around with a big belly, herself in labor making her way to the hospital early one midsummer morning, herself doing this and that since Akira's birth—all superimposed on Kambayashi's face. These images of herself bothered her and even aroused a kind of anger in her.

Takiko blamed her lingering discontent on the lack of time: there was never enough for a good long talk.

It was true that she didn't have much time to meet and talk with Kambayashi. They'd be lucky to have one lunch hour per week alone together when Sasaki ate out and Misawa wasn't around. Each day she was in suspense over what Sasaki was planning to do for lunch. Secretly overjoyed when he said, "I think I'll eat out today," she would arrive back at Misawa Gardens as if she hadn't a moment to lose—only to discover that because of that day's schedule Kambayashi was nowhere to be found. Extreme disappointment would bring tears to her eyes. Wishing she'd gone with Sasaki, she would wait alone for Kambayashi until the afternoon's work started.

Almost before she knew it, the rainy season had set in, bringing day after day of steamy heat and drizzle.

On delivery rounds Takiko had to wear a large, ill-fitting black raincoat. The moment she put it on she would be dripping with sweat. Lunch was eaten either in the back of the truck or in the greenhouse, where it was no cooler with the coat off. And she had still fewer opportunities to talk alone with Kambayashi.

Nevertheless, everything was going very smoothly for Takiko at this time. Akira had begun to crawl freely about the house and could no longer be kept shut up in the storeroom, even when her father was at home. Akira's presence made itself clearly felt all through the house. There was no denying he belonged there; that he should disappear from the house was unthinkable now. He turned his smiling face to her father and tried to climb onto his knee. And her father only tried occasionally now to fend him off.

Takiko was made newly aware of her attachment to Akira. Even the sight of his grizzling, tearful face brought a flush of joy. She would always think of Kambayashi then. If only he could see. She wanted to tell him: I've decided to do everything I can, too, and beyond that not to give it another thought. Look how I'm smiling, how happy I am.

But once she set foot outside the house, and left Akira at the nursery, Takiko couldn't afford to think like this. Would she get to see Kambayashi that day? Never mind if they couldn't talk, as long as she could catch his eye. To see Kambayashi's face was to try out her feelings for Akira. Takiko was seeking Kambayashi's approval of her smiling face, and even of Akira's.

All she wanted was time to spend with Kambayashi; surely that wasn't so unreasonable? Despite her high spirits while she was with Akira, however, Takiko found herself constantly on edge during the day.

At about that time she had news of Akira's father, Hiroshi Maeda. An envelope arrived from one of her old office colleagues. The one-page note inside said, without apologies, "I'd forgotten all about giving you this, but it turned up again when I was tidying my desk, so I'm passing it on." Enclosed was a letter from Hiroshi Maeda. It must have reached the office sometime late last year. Opening it, she found a receipt issued by Maeda's department and made out to the company. She'd been supposed to receive this paper from Maeda at his window and file it at the office.

In a letter accompanying it Maeda had written, "As I resigned suddenly and cleared out my desk in a hurry, several items I should have dealt with have since come to my attention, and this receipt is one of them. I'd like to set things straight in the department's records. What you do with it at the company's end is up to you." There'd been no need to address the letter to her personally for a business matter like this, she thought, but then she realized that as far as Maeda knew she was still working in the company's accounts section. He'd probably felt more comfortable sending it directly to her rather than to another member of the staff. What surprised her more, though, was the fact that Maeda still remembered her name. There was nothing else at all personal in the letter. She couldn't even find Maeda's address on it; he'd written the name of the government department instead.

The letter must have been mailed over six months ago. She noted it was postmarked October 20 at a Tokyo post office in his department's district. Could he have been summoned back from the country to deal with unfinished work? Or did it mean that he'd returned to Tokyo for good? October 20: that was about when she'd started Akira in day care at Midori Nursery. He'd been just two months old; it was also then that he'd developed the hernia. Takiko had quit the office four months earlier, and Maeda had quit his job and gone home to the country a further six months before that.

Yes, that was right, she confirmed to herself. Her memory hadn't become hazy at all. She could recall these things readily, as if turning the pages of an album. But these memories existed only for Akira's sake. If it weren't for Akira, that period of time a year ago would most likely have extended flatly on into the present, as Maeda still assumed it did. It suddenly struck her as odd that the memories she attached to certain dates had meaning only for her, unknown to anyone else. Yet these memories had grown distant; they aroused no special feelings. She didn't suppose she would ever forget Maeda's name, and seeing Akira would always remind her of small traits of his. Every unfamiliar trait she noticed in Akira she had to put down to Maeda. But that was all it amounted to. Akira had already begun to look at the world through his own eyes, put food into his own mouth, and move his own body about. It wasn't Maeda doing this, nor Takiko.

After some hesitation, she placed Maeda's letter between the pages of Akira's Midori Nursery notebook. She could always throw it away. But if she did so right now she might never have another reminder of Maeda. There, she thought, now I can safely forget his name.

She could only conclude that the man Maeda meant nothing to her any more. They were very unlikely ever to meet again; it didn't seem likely that Akira would ever meet him either. He was far too distant a figure to mean anything to her as Akira's father. She should have been content simply to rejoice in having gained Akira's existence, which was immeasurably important to her, from the one small impetus that was Maeda.

Yet after she was made newly aware of her distance from Maeda, she seemed to become terribly unsteady. All her movements were so awkward that it was a wonder she didn't drop and break the plant tubs she delivered.

She longed to see Kambayashi's face and hear his voice talking about his child.

Once a month, Kambayashi made a trip to "the mountain," where Misawa Gardens had its main greenhouses. Sometimes he went alone; sometimes Misawa accompanied him. Although two of the staff were based out there, apparently the work they did needed to be checked. Another purpose of these trips was to return badly damaged plants that were on their last legs and bring back vigorous young seedlings. Although the place was known to everyone at Misawa Gardens as "the mountain," strictly speaking it was a hill lying just this side of the actual mountains.* On its sunny slopes Misawa Gardens had four greenhouses where, Takiko understood, they raised larger trees for garden and roadside use, and also flowering plant seedlings for bulk demand.

Late one afternoon when they'd finished work for the day, Misawa remarked to Takiko, "We're planning to build a proper house on the site, and then the boss will live out there—kind of in retirement. But he seems to think it's too much trouble, so nothing much is happening. It's a nice place, though. Once we've got the big house built we can invite all of you, and your families too, to come and visit."

Kambayashi was due to make another trip to the mountain the following week. Takiko suddenly had an idea. It was nearly two weeks since she'd last run into Kambayashi.

"How would it be, then, if I went next week when Kambayashi-san goes? I'd give up a day's wages. Please, just this once? I'd really like to see the mountain for myself. I've been dying to go for ages. I'm sure it'll help me take better care of the plants once I've seen where they were brought up. What if we count it as my summer vacation? I wouldn't get in Kambayashi-san's way."

Takiko was prepared to go on pleading until Misawa gave

---

*As a colloquial term, *yama* (mountain) can refer to a piece of privately owned wooded land that may not be truly mountainous.

in and agreed to this "vacation" of hers—which, however, he did with surprising ease. Perhaps he resigned himself to it because his own casual remark had brought on this sudden interest in the mountain.

"Well, I suppose it might be good for morale. Come to think of it, you and Sasaki are the only ones who don't know the place. I'd better let him go up there once next month too, to be fair. Think you can manage the job on your own for a day or so? You could get Kambayashi to lend a hand for half a day. Well, there's no telling until you try. So we'll have you go this month, Taki-chan, and Sasaki next month. All right?"

Sasaki, who happened to be nearby, nodded without much enthusiasm. Beside herself with glee, which she restrained with difficulty, Takiko thanked Misawa and called over to Sasaki: "Isn't it wonderful? I've been longing to go to the mountain. It'd be better still if we could go together. But they're planning to build us a vacation home one of these days—won't that be great?"

"Yeah. And while you're at it, how about a place by the sea? It's the beach for me," Sasaki said as he swung first one arm then the other in circles.

"Yes, a beach house wouldn't be a bad idea, would it?"

"Give me a break, you two. So now you want *two* holiday homes? Please remember that Misawa Gardens is just a dinky little company." The managing director wore an exaggerated frown.

"Oh, come on, think big. You ought to be considering an overseas branch, at least." Takiko caught Sasaki's eye and burst out laughing.

"Just listen to you," Misawa said, starting to laugh himself. "The moment you get to go to the mountain you're talking like a partner in the firm. Your picnic's a week away yet, so don't get too excited. Do some work."

The trip was to be on the Friday of the following week. As if belatedly noticing that Takiko was the one member of the opposite sex among them, Misawa suddenly added that Kambayashi usually stayed the night in a small hut they used as a toolshed. The round trip could be made in a day, however, and when he'd discussed it with Kambayashi they could probably arrange for her to return home that night, but he wasn't sure; if she would wait a little while he'd let her know.

Takiko was at a loss as to how to spend the seven days—a whole week—until her unexpected "vacation." It seemed a brittle thing of glass that she had to protect with her hands. Could she keep it intact for seven days? Would she really be so lucky?

Her mother agreed to pick up Akira from the nursery on the Friday evening. When Takiko raised the subject, apologizing seriously and stiffly for having to ask this favor, her mother answered with such alacrity it seemed to be just the thing she'd been waiting for. "Of course, dear, anytime you like. It's silly to try and do everything yourself. You've made it this far, you should give yourself a break."

Takiko almost took issue in spite of herself. It was the word "break" that she resented. A break was the last thing she wanted—when she was trying to feel Akira's weight more firmly and clearly. To accept unflinchingly the restrictions on her freedom which, now that she'd found them at last in the shape of Akira, seemed not merely restrictions but bonds with other people.

And this from her mother who'd been so set on an abortion,

who wouldn't tell anyone about Akira's birth, who could calmly recommend putting him up for adoption. Her mother who had torn up the posters for the Midori Nursery bazaar rather than risk offending the neighbors. She couldn't see herself ever being allowed to forget these things, though she didn't want to dwell on them either; after all, her mother had her own encumbrances (among them, her father and Takiko herself) and she hadn't let them go. And the same might perhaps be said of her father. When she thought of her parents in this light, Takiko would have liked to wipe away all these recent memories. But that wasn't allowed. She ought not to forget, no matter how painful her refusal—to her mother and to herself.

In the end she just muttered "Thanks" and didn't argue at all.

Her mother laughed good-humoredly and said, "You needn't worry about Akira-chan."

Anyway, Takiko had to remind herself, the important thing now was to go to the mountain with Kambayashi; to have one full day at his side so that there'd never be any doubt of Akira's weight again, and no more regrets even if it proved to be her last opportunity. In the meantime she didn't want to hear or see a thing. To get safely through seven days was all that mattered. There must be no quarrels, or accidents, or illnesses.

Saturday, a half holiday, and Sunday went by uneventfully. The drizzling rain continued.

When work resumed on Monday nothing had changed at Misawa Gardens. Sasaki was still uninterested in Takiko's "vacation," and the subject didn't even come up. There was no chance to see Kambayashi that day, but they did meet the next morning. Though there wasn't any reason to be surprised by this, Takiko tensed and turned momentarily pale when she caught sight of him.

"Good morning," Kambayashi said with a smile.

Takiko returned a loud "Good morning, Kambayashi-san," her heart pounding. She waited for him to mention the mountain, but he went off into the greenhouse. Hadn't he heard about it from Misawa yet? Her disappointment lasted all day.

She didn't get to talk with Kambayashi the next day, or the day after that, and meanwhile nobody else mentioned the mountain either.

By Thursday morning she was beginning to think the offer might never have been taken any farther. Had she simply misunderstood? But she couldn't bring herself to clear up the doubt. All she had to do was speak to Misawa, she knew, but she couldn't do it. If I haven't been told anything by the end of the day it'll mean I'm not going to the mountain with Kambayashi tomorrow, she decided. It'll just be business as usual. She was unable to smile adequately at any of Sasaki's jokes that morning.

When they returned to Misawa Gardens at lunchtime, Misawa was there—which was unusual at that hour—standing in the rain with Kambayashi and looking at a tub of *Rhapis excelsa*. Takiko froze at the sight of them. It wasn't safe to assume they'd been waiting to discuss tomorrow's trip.

Misawa came over, smiling, to the cab of the truck.

"Hi there."

Kambayashi followed; he too wore a casual smile.

"The weather doesn't look too good for tomorrow," Misawa said. "It's a pity to miss the view, but there's sure to be another chance. . . . Anyhow, I've just been talking to Kambayashi.

Be here at eight o'clock. That'll do, won't it?" He turned to Kambayashi, who nodded. "It takes a good three hours from here, so don't be late."

Takiko's mouth hung open as she nodded vigorously.

Misawa went on to explain that Kambayashi would stay overnight as usual, and that there was a place in town where Takiko could stay if she could make baby-sitting arrangements. Of course she was free to go home instead, but she'd be pretty late getting back. It was up to her to decide which would make it easier to come to work the next day.

As Takiko wavered, Kambayashi said, "The folks at the mountain have offered to put you up. So why not take your time?"

"What about you, Kambayashi-san?" she asked in a small voice.

"Me? The mountain, same as always. But I'll have dinner at the house, so really you needn't feel shy."

"I see. I'll stay, then," Takiko said finally. Why not, if it meant she could have Saturday as well with Kambayashi? Where she stayed was irrelevant.

Once they'd given her all the necessary instructions Kambayashi and Misawa went off together into the house, which doubled as the office. Takiko breathed freely at last, then smiled to herself.

Sasaki, who'd left the driver's seat and was smoking at the rear of the truck, invited her to lunch.

"Great," she said, "let's go. I'll have chilled noodles."

She gave up trying to hide how pleased she was over lunch and back at work later. Her face was flushed, she laughed at every little thing, struggled to carry the biggest tubs by herself, and burst into song in the truck. Sasaki was disgusted. "What's

got into you? Is an overnight trip such a big deal? Incredible!
You won't catch me going anywhere if there's work involved."

By the end of the afternoon her high spirits had tired her
out, and she began to feel a headache coming on.

Keeping an eye on the time—now there were twelve hours
to go, now there were ten—she picked Akira up from the
nursery, raced home, efficiently disposed of her chores, had
dinner and a bath with Akira, then settled down in the storeroom to organize her gear for the mountain. Akira didn't get
sick, and her mother's condition was unchanged. Her father
did nothing to bar her way either. Nothing untoward happened. However, she couldn't relax yet—not until she was out
of the house tomorrow.

That night she had some cold saké and went to bed early.

Next morning, giving herself more than enough time, she
was on her way by seven. Akira, left with his grandmother,
sent up a howl behind her back. He was to go to the nursery
at eight. She would have liked to drop him there herself before
she set off for the mountain, but as it had turned out she
couldn't manage even this much. With the decision to stay
the night as well she would be putting her mother to far more
trouble than she'd originally intended, but she couldn't stop
to worry about it. She ran down the alley, not looking back
even when Akira cried.

Her pulse had been racing since she woke up, rather as
though she were in the middle of an unpleasant dream. The
rain was still falling quietly.

She stayed anxious all the way there on the train.

When she spotted Kambayashi beside the truck outside Misawa Gardens, she couldn't overcome her anxiety quickly
enough to smile. He had on the navy blue sports shirt he

always wore, and his slightly squinting face was smiling. He somehow gave the impression that his clothes didn't fit, but this was usual too.

"You're early, Taki-chan."

When he spoke she came to herself at last and answered casually, "What's the time?"

"Twenty to. I'm just about to load that." He pointed to a tub of *Rhapis excelsa*.

"You're very early yourself, aren't you, Kambayashi-san?" The racing of her heart was under control now. All that had happened was that here was the father of a child, a good ten years older than herself; he was real and not an illusion. And though it hadn't been a year yet, Takiko herself was the mother of another child.

"Not espccially."

"Really? You're always this early? That must be tough on you."

Takiko's voice was gay as she stood under her umbrella watching him carry the *Rhapis excelsa* tub.

"I live nearby. It doesn't take five minutes on my bike."

"Oh? I never knew that."

The load consisted only of the *Rhapis excelsa* and a fern palm. The truck departed through the rain.

The streets were nearly empty, and they were in the suburbs in under an hour. The opposite lanes were congested with traffic heading for the city center.

On the way there Takiko was so intent on talking with Kambayashi that she almost forgot about the mountain. Every remark of his, no matter how trivial, gave her spirits a lift. Best of all, he showed no sign of being uncomfortable alone with her. She felt quite triumphant at being able to share this brief respite, both of them lowering the guard they maintained because of their children. He was the first person with whom she didn't have to be on guard, or force herself to forget what was special about her child, or have any misgivings in talking about this specialness.

She would have liked to tell Kambayashi what she was feeling, but, finding herself content to sit back and listen, she let her own words go unsaid.

The route was familiar to Kambayashi. He took the trouble to teach her the names of rivers they saw from the windows, and point out hiking trails, an old castle site in a town they passed through, and so on. He reminisced about the difficulties they'd had back when the greenhouses were first built at the mountain. By the time they arrived Takiko had also gleaned some inside information about his job at Misawa Gardens: it was not the first place he had worked, he had been a busy salesman with a large corporation until the birth of his child ten years ago. The younger Misawa had been a colleague and drinking companion of his at that job, and when he returned to the family business he invited Kambayashi to join him.

During a long red light at the turnoff for the mountain, Kambayashi said with some surprise, as if he suddenly remembered to ask, "Why were you so interested in coming up to the mountain, anyway, Taki-chan? You were dead set on it, weren't you? It's not bad, of course, but it's nothing to get excited about. Hope you won't be disappointed."

"I won't be," she replied, laughing. "As long as I could go somewhere, I didn't really care where. Though I've never liked company trips, and school trips, and that kind of thing. Besides, it's fun being with you, Kambayashi-san."

Kambayashi was taken aback. "Hey, what's with the flattery all of a sudden?

"But it's true," Takiko said with a carefree laugh. He looked so flustered he might have been about to cry.

Once off the main road the truck swayed and jolted. The road grew steadily worse.

They pressed on along the deserted country road between blue-green fields that stretched away on either side without any sign of a house. Market-garden plots of summer vegetables undulated gently across the hilly land. While the light rain had misted over the far distance and concealed the view of mountains, the blue-green of the fields and roadside grass was tinting the fine raindrops with a brightness that seemed to lend a chill to the air and even dazzled Takiko.

"Doesn't it look pretty?" she murmured impulsively. Kambayashi looked askance.

"Around here? Not enough to notice. Though maybe if we could see the mountains."

"No, really, it is pretty. Doesn't it feel kind of like we're underwater? Clear green water. Everything's so crisp and bright."

"Does it look that way to you? I'm not keen on this drizzly kind of rain, myself."

"Mm. And everything's so green. Ah, I'm so glad I came."

Kambayashi laughed. "You're a funny old thing, Taki-chan. But you may be right—there's something to be said for a misty day like this. Yes, summer's on the way."

"Wasn't it like this last time you came?"

"It wasn't so stifling. The weather was better then, anyway. But even if it had been raining, it's always fresher in May—there isn't that smell of grass."

"I like the way the grass smells. I'm glad I came in the rainy season."

"You'd find something to be glad about whenever you came, wouldn't you? Lucky you." Kambayashi gave another laugh that showed a silver-capped tooth. His mouth looked astonishingly large when he opened it to laugh, and his features lost their normal reserve. This big mouth of his was such a funny sight that Takiko started to laugh too.

The road forked, one branch climbing gradually uphill. The truck took this route.

As before there were vegetable gardens on both sides of the road, but behind them dark stands of cedar closed in, giving a true sense of the mountains. Takiko was gazing up the road ahead and thinking that it wasn't so odd that Misawa Gardens called their property "the mountain," when Kambayashi stuck his right arm out the window and said, "That's it. See? Those are our greenhouses."

With a start she turned to look in the direction he was pointing. Sure enough, in a break among the cedars, several big unnatural objects were visible, gleaming silver.

A private access road took them in a wide detour around the vegetable plots. They emerged from the cedar grove and drove on uphill past the backs of the greenhouses, then suddenly the view ahead opened out. They were at the top of the low hill. Except for the faintly greenish mist of rain, nothing seemed to interrupt her field of view off to the right. Takiko had a feeling that they'd wound up in some strange place not connected to the earth's surface.

"It's no good, you can't see a thing today. Not even the road we just came along down there," Kambayashi complained as he pulled up slowly in front of the greenhouses.

There were four of these in a row backing onto the forest of cedars and scrub. One was as tall as a two-story house. Two men emerged from it before Kambayashi had stopped the truck and sounded the horn.

"You made good time today," one of them, a small but muscular man in his late fifties, called to Kambayashi in the cab.

"Well, come on in." The hut to which the men led them through the rain was a tentlike lean-to of plastic sheeting at the entrance to the greenhouse from which they had appeared. Inside there were several chairs of different types obviously picked up from junk heaps, a table consisting of plywood on concrete blocks, and a green tarpaulin floor cluttered with tools. It was a curiously comfortable place, though, once they were settled in. A naked light bulb dangled overhead, and there was even an electric hot plate. Saké bottles lay scattered around. What Takiko liked best about it was that she could keep her eyes on the deep, almost oppressive greenery inside the greenhouse.

There Kambayashi introduced her to the two men. The tall younger man told Takiko bashfully that his name was Akimoto. The older man added that she and Akimoto were the same age. His name was Kido, and it was at his house that she was to stay the night. On being told this Takiko hastily improved on her greeting.

The truck had to be unloaded first, but because of the rain and because Takiko's presence made this a special occasion they postponed the work until after lunch.

"We've heard a lot about you, so we've been looking forward to meeting you. Akimoto here has been fidgeting all morning."

Akimoto blushed violently at Kido's words. Takiko, blushing herself, said, "I hope I'm not being a nuisance."

For lunch, Kido's wife had prepared rice balls for everyone. All fifteen were gone in no time. Takiko had three and Akimoto put away five. They were very good. Normally, the men said, they each brought their own lunch; Akimoto was in fact married and had a child who was a year old. When she heard this Takiko stared. She hadn't known anyone until now who was a father at her age.

Afterward, over cups of tea, Kambayashi got down to discussing the work schedule with Kido. Akimoto began to watch an antiquated portable TV he produced from under the table. The news was on. Takiko also watched the screen while her attention wandered.

It was hot inside the cramped hut. She felt the hot air that crept out through the square opening from the greenhouse on her face and body. The outer entrance had no door either. There was a wooden rod laid across the threshold, which hadn't stopped the rainwater coming in and wetting the tarpaulin. Through this opening could be seen the pale green mist that made one feel remote to look at it, while the opposite doorway yielded glimpses of a world of swirling, vivid, deep green. This windless, rainless world in which massed green plants bred silently in hot air gradually drew and held Takiko's eyes.

After a while, the men got to their feet.

"No use roaming around in this rain. What a bore for you, Takiko-san. And after coming all that way too," Kido said, glancing back as she rose to join them.

Kambayashi also turned to her. "Still, I guess there's no point in hanging around here, so you might as well come with us. We're not especially busy today, anyway."

"Thanks. If there's anything I can do to help, just let me know."

Takiko shrank as all three pairs of eyes stared at her.

The hours till evening didn't drag at all, however. Kambayashi wore the one spare raincoat and Takiko carried her umbrella as she toured around.

First, they unloaded the *Rhapis excelsa* and the fern palm from the truck and carried them into the greenhouse on the far left. Inside there were neat rows of tubs containing medium-sized ornamental plants. The house was longer than it had looked from the outside, and Takiko was reluctant to venture into its tunnel-like interior. She did make a timid tour on her own, though, unable to resist setting foot in this frightening plant realm. She was soon in a swelter brought on by the heat and the frenzied profusion of greenery.

When they'd finished shifting the load, Kambayashi and the others moved on to the next greenhouse. She hurried after them.

This one was for flowers. A multicolored array of tropical blooms—purple and pink, yellow and blue-green—were set out in small white pots in the same orderly rows. The men began transferring number-five pots of bougainvillea onto wooden trays. Apparently this was part of a shipment due to be sent out that day. Takiko made another tour on her own, but unlike the ornamental plant house this one had a lightness and gaiety about it. It must have held over a thousand flowerpots. She'd never seen such quantities of flowers. As even the tallest plants were barely knee-high, walking among the little flowers had a kind of fairy-tale charm.

While Kambayashi and the others went on with their work, she tried the two remaining greenhouses. One contained more rows of medium-sized ornamentals in tubs. And the last of the four, the big one with the plastic lean-to at the door, also housed ornamental plants. But when she tried going in, its size took her breath away once again. Without fear now, she gaped at the tropical trees that towered above her to several times her height. Trees like gigantic umbrella sedges. Trees whose trunks were hidden by their three-foot-long palmate leaves, which suggested the word "jungle." Coco palms and Washingtonias (the only shapes she recognized). Trees that bore dense clusters of banana-like leaves and heavy-looking banana-like bunches of crimson flowers. Yet in fact she could count those that reached all the way to the greenhouse's plastic ceiling, while beneath them the many tubs of six-foot trees interleaved their varied foliage, barely leaving room for an aisle. It was like a spot where the jungle cleared a little, Takiko thought, letting in the light and bringing welcome relief to someone walking through its midst; and she sighed again and again, overwhelmed by the tropical trees' sheer vigor.

When she had inspected all four greenhouses, Takiko again felt an almost insupportable joy. Since no one seemed to mind if she didn't give Kambayashi and the others a hand with the work, she decided to do as she pleased and went back for several more looks, each time marveling anew at the overwhelming plants.

She remembered that they called this place "the mountain"—appropriately enough, she felt. It was a special place, and a strange one. It wouldn't allow her to keep her thoughts on anything. The flow of the plant sap seemed to roar in her ears.

She rolled up her jeans and walked around outdoors in her sandals. The soft drops of rain felt pleasantly cold on her bare legs, which were glowing from the greenhouse heat. Wet blades of grass tickled her ankles. As she ran about through the weeds and grass she was smiling to herself.

In the rain, she suddenly remembered the ten-year-old Down's syndrome boy whom she knew only from Kambayashi's description. A distant image of herself also came to mind, walking sleepily to the nursery every morning with Akira on her back and a tote bag in each hand containing diapers, changes of clothing, and towels. "Who could that be," she asked half aloud, "and what's she doing there?" It was as if she herself had turned into the biggest plant in the greenhouses. "And who can this be here?"

The outdoor work was evidently over for the day once the mountain's truck had been loaded with bougainvillea, geraniums, and *Euphorbia milii*, and Kambayashi had selected two dozen tubs of ornamental plants to take back to town. Akimoto went off to deliver the shipment. He was due back around six, and would take the truck directly to Kido's house. Kambayashi and Kido then sat down to go over sheets of figures in the hut. Reassured by their presence, Takiko stayed in the jungle which opened out at the back of the hut. She never tired of seeing that deluge of green.

When Kambayashi looked in to say, "Let's call it a day," it was after four.

"If the weather were better," he added, to neither her nor Kido in particular, "we could've gone for a drive for a couple of hours, but we wouldn't see a thing in this. I guess we'd better go straight to the house."

"Right. And it might still clear up tomorrow. This is a day for drinking. Are you a good drinker, Taki-chan?"

Takiko shook her head. "Not that I don't enjoy it, but . . ."

She asked Kido, "It must take a lot to get the three of you drunk?"

"There's no stopping the two from the mountain once they get going," Kambayashi answered instead. "They're like a couple of mountain bandits."

"But what about you, Kambayashi-san?"

"Me . . ."

This time Kido answered. "I'm afraid he can't take much alcohol. Can you?"

"Oh yes, I can. That's why I'm forced to join the bandits every time I come up here, even though they know I don't like drinking bouts. I've had enough of it. But they tell me it's an important mountain ceremony, these mountain folk. Watch out, Taki-chan, it's you they'll be after tonight."

Kido laughed delightedly.

They left the greenhouses, with Kido riding in the back of the truck that had brought Kambayashi and Takiko.

The truck returned down the road through the fields that they had traveled over in the morning, and in a quarter of an hour entered a small town on a branch line of a private railroad. Kido's house, on the edge of town, was an old two-story place with nothing remarkable about it. A drab but spacious house, it stood looking rather isolated in the middle of a large lot with no wall or gate.

Along with the others, Takiko washed her feet and her hands and face at an outdoor faucet. She became aware of a fat woman who must be Mrs. Kido standing on the veranda, holding a towel. She looked about the same age as Takiko's mother, though perhaps the plumpness of her face took a few years off her true age.

"Hey, this is the famous Taki-chan from Misawa Gardens."

As Kido had got in first before she could introduce herself, Takiko bowed sheepishly.

Mrs. Kido told her how much she'd been looking forward to meeting her, with a smile that suggested she meant it, then urged her to come in quickly.

Beer was brought out as soon as the three of them were seated in the eight-mat room which gave onto the veranda. While explaining that she hadn't expected them quite so soon but would bring snacks later to go with it, Mrs. Kido joined the guests and poured herself a glass instead of returning to the kitchen. The cold beer felt good after the green swelter of the hothouses, which still lingered in Takiko's body. She drank two glasses in a row.

Mrs. Kido was clearly curious about Akira, and until Kido sent her off impatiently to get the snacks ready she kept coming back to the subject of children. "I couldn't have one of my own, you see. I cried my heart out when I knew. We have an adopted daughter, a lovely girl, but it's not the same thing, after all. I'm sure it's a hard life for you, but when he's your own, I expect that compensates. Is he a lively little fellow? Has he turned one yet? And everything's been going well? How nice."

Unable to forget that Kambayashi was within earshot, Takiko couldn't relax even when Mrs. Kido disappeared into the kitchen. Kambayashi himself was lying on the tatami, completely at home, his eyes on the screen of a large color television over in the corner.

Kido joined her next. He fetched a bottle of shochu from beside the TV set, brought clean glasses and ice, and pressed Takiko to have some of the strong stuff. He talked about Akimoto's marriage, told stories of drinking bouts in which Kambayashi and Misawa sometimes figured, how he came to know the company president, and so on—none of which was of very great interest to Takiko.

By the time his wife called to them to say that the bath was ready, darkness had descended at last outside, where the rain was still falling. At Kido and Kambayashi's insistence, Takiko took the first bath. It was a relief to be alone. It occurred to her that she might not be able to get away from the Kidos' company until she and Kambayashi went home in the truck the next day. She mustn't be dissatisfied with what she had. But she felt listless with disappointment. She undressed slowly, stepped onto the tiles and removed the bright blue plastic panels that covered the bathtub. She used one to stir the water, but found it still too hot. She ran the cold tap, filled a washbowl from the spot where it cooled the tub, and began pouring water over herself. She didn't feel like either washing properly or getting into the bath. She just went on pouring hot water over her body.

Why couldn't she stay up at the hut on the mountain too? As she doused her sweaty hair, the fact that she couldn't struck her as strange. Because Kambayashi and Takiko would be a man and a woman together. Because everyone had that idea fixed in their heads. What if she told them it wouldn't be like that? Maybe she could still persuade them to let her stay at the mountain? It wouldn't be like that. No matter how long she might spend alone with Kambayashi, they would never be on those terms. She could be sure of that; in fact, that was why she wanted the time alone with him. How could people think otherwise, when all that passed between them was entirely remote from what "man and woman" implied? However, this was clearly not a point that would go down well with the people around them.

When she came out into the changing area, there was a dark blue cotton robe patterned with yellow sunflowers beside the basket that held her clothes. It seemed not to have been worn for a long time; perhaps it belonged to the Kidos' adopted daughter. After putting it on and smoothing her wet hair with the palms of her hands, she returned to the parlor.

"Ah, that looks good on you. She's quite a beauty, isn't she, this Taki-chan?" Kido, a little flushed with drink, commented jovially at the sight of her.

Shrinking with embarrassment, Takiko sat down at a distance from both Kido and Kambayashi.

"Oh, that is cute," Mrs. Kido exclaimed, coming into the room. "It fits you perfectly, doesn't it?"

"Thanks for the loan." Takiko bowed her head.

"That's all right, no need to be shy in our house. Funny, though, I was just thinking the other day that we'd never have any use for that yukata again."

Takiko glanced in Kambayashi's direction. He was taking in her appearance with a vague look on his face. When their eyes met he managed an unfocused smile, like someone woken from a nap. For a moment Takiko felt an acute sadness.

Kambayashi and Kido took quick baths after her. As they rejoined her in the parlor—Kambayashi dressed to go back to the mountain, Kido in his yukata—Akimoto drove up in the truck from making the deliveries.

Chopped, lightly broiled bonito with grated radish, stewed chicken giblets, chilled tofu squares, and other dishes were set out on the table. Then Mrs. Kido joined them and the party began. Kido and Akimoto replenished each other's glasses with shochu and Mrs. Kido kept pace while urging Kambayashi and Takiko to drink up. Though she hadn't gotten over her sense of disappointment, Takiko decided to forget her usual limit and accept a refill. Kambayashi was also drinking, little by little, and occasionally adding some remark to Kido's and Akimoto's conversation.

Mrs. Kido may have been the strongest drinker of them all. She talked and laughed so much and so loudly that it certainly seemed that way. She made Takiko laugh frequently as well and saved her from being bored. The men turned and smiled and spoke to Takiko from time to time, as if remembering she was there, then went straight back to their own conversation. Just when Mrs. Kido appeared to have joined in she would lean toward Takiko again, woman to woman, complaining about Kido or repeating what she'd said earlier about learning of her infertility when she was young.

As the men's conversation was turning to Kido's uncle, an expert boar hunter who had nevertheless died in a careless accident, Takiko stood up and made her way to the toilet. After managing there somehow—though very unsteady on her feet— she returned to the parlor and sprawled on the tatami, unable to last any longer.

"Oh dear, are you all right, Taki-chan?" Mrs. Kido looked around. Takiko put her hand to her hot cheek and gave a small nod.

"I just need to lie down for a bit. I'm so sleepy . . ."

She closed her eyes. In her sudden stupor the men's voices sounded soft and oddly close. She could hear Kambayashi's among them—or a voice that registered vaguely as his. Her whole body melted and flowed into drunkenness. It was a comforting sensation, like that after shedding tears.

"Guess that's why I can't ever seem to settle down myself. In my grandad's day they hunted walrus up there with the Gilyaks and the Yakuts. I reckon that was all over by my father's time, though. I was only three when we left, so I don't remember a thing. Wouldn't mind going back for a look at the place, you know."

As she took in what this voice was saying, Takiko thought she must already be asleep. It was the last thing she thought.

She woke abruptly from a deep, dreamless sleep, suddenly aware of how uncomfortable she was. As she opened her eyes, she sat up anxiously, roused by a sense of something being wrong. Kambayashi was sitting smoking some distance away. She glanced around in confusion before she remembered what she was doing there.

Kido and Akimoto were sprawled asleep where they'd been sitting. There was hardly any food left on the table, the ashtray was piled high with butts, and a half-gallon shochu bottle lay empty at Kido's side. She must have been asleep for quite a while.

"Kambayashi-san . . ."

He'd been watching her expressionlessly, but now, as if prompted by her murmur, he said in a low voice, "You're awake, are you? It's the middle of the night."

"Everyone's asleep, then?"

"They've had as much as they can hold."

With a glance at the forms of Kido and Akimoto, Kambayashi stretched and gave a huge yawn.

"Wow, that's some mouth." Takiko chuckled, feeling as

though the sight had cleared her head. Shutting it in a hurry, Kambayashi smiled.

"It's that big, eh?"

"Oh yes, I've never seen such a big mouth."

"Really?"

"She's right, you know, it amazed *me* at first," Mrs. Kido broke in, sticking her head out of the kitchen and startling Takiko. "My, you did have a good sleep, Taki-chan. He was asleep too, you know, till just now. And now those two are out. Well, good riddance, eh?" she said to Takiko, adding, "I've put out your futon upstairs, so why don't you turn in? This oddball here insists on going back to the mountain to sleep. I've been trying to tell him he needn't bother when he can stay here."

"It's no bother. It's just that I sleep better there." Kambayashi hung his head a little as if apologizing to them both.

"Well, suit yourself. I'm going up to bed." Mrs. Kido went back into the kitchen. A window banged shut, the light went out, and footsteps echoed up the stairs from the passageway on the far side of the house.

While she was listening distractedly to Mrs. Kido's footsteps overhead, Takiko stiffened as she remembered the man's voice she'd heard while half asleep. A chill ran through her.

"Say . . ."

Her voice came out strangely. Kambayashi glanced over at her while sighing lightly.

"Say, was that you, Kambayashi-san, talking about walruses and things?"

"That's right. I didn't think you were still awake then." Kambayashi lit a new cigarette.

"I was asleep, but I could sort of hear. What were you

saying? Do you come from someplace like that—where there are walruses?"

"I only heard about them from my grandfather. And he was talking about the old days."

"But still, you come from somewhere like that? Where it's freezing cold?" Takiko persisted, almost frowning.

"Well, yes. But why? Are you from Hokkaido yourself, Taki-chan?" Kambayashi asked in turn, puzzled by her intense interest. A little embarrassed, Takiko smiled and shook her head.

"No, it's nothing like that. It's just that I once saw a boat that went there, when I was a child, and my father scared me by saying that it was much, much colder where that boat was going."

"That's scary?"

"It scared me. Because I couldn't even begin to imagine it. All I could think of at the time was something like the palace of the Snow Queen—which is still how I think of it, actually. That's why it scared me. Perhaps it scared my father, too. I bet it did, and you know why? Because something made him want to go there." Takiko stared at Kambayashi, letting this thought sink in.

"Hm . . . Yes, it's strange, isn't it? I guess there's something about the cold that makes you want to get in deeper, to see what it's like. You'd think you'd want to come out of the cold and take it easy." Kambayashi recrossed his legs and sighed.

"But my father did come down here. And you, Kambayashi-san, you're here. Why?" As she spoke, Takiko pictured a world without green, a world of white snowfields.

"In my grandfather's day, I don't think people had much choice. If you wanted to get anywhere you probably had to go north. There must be a lot of mixed blood in my body. Ainu, and Gilyak, and—"

"Gilyak?"

"They're a minority who live only in Siberia now. Kind of like Lapps."

Takiko, very impressed, nodded over and over.

"I don't know all that much about them myself, of course. But . . . I sometimes look at my boy and think, if we'd had a life of hunting reindeer and catching salmon he'd have managed, in his own way. It's a dream of mine. You've got to have one, you know. Stupid dream, isn't it?"

"Oh, no. I long to live like they do. . . ." She thought of telling Kambayashi of how she had made up the story that Akira's father was one of them, and opened her mouth to go on; but when it came to the point, she was too embarrassed after all.

Kambayashi laughed softly at the words she'd left dangling. "You long to, eh? Well, that about says it for me too. Aren't you sleepy? I'm kind of groggy. Can't seem to sober up. I went and drank some of that beer as well, before you woke up. Well, see you tomorrow. Don't hurry over in the morning."

Though Takiko wasn't happy about this abrupt ending of their conversation, since she couldn't keep him from leaving, she sat and watched his departing back.

When Kambayashi had slid the glass doors of the veranda shut behind him, the house was silent. Kido and Akimoto were out completely. She didn't think she'd be able to sleep, even if she went upstairs to bed. The faraway world—like the land of the Snow Queen—of which Kambayashi had just spoken had left her head achingly clear. She picked up a bottle of shochu that stood beside the table, poured some into a nearby glass, and took a drink.

Outside, the truck's engine revved. When he gets back to the mountain, she wondered, will he go straight off to sleep? She followed the sound of the engine. The truck was slowly turning in front of the house. So he knew a much, much colder place—the place that had existed only in her fantasies. How had she come to meet him? She felt another chill, and huddled smaller.

The sound of the truck stopped. She waited, but it didn't restart.

Takiko went on sipping her shochu without taking very much notice of the engine's silence. She couldn't get over her surprise at having found Kambayashi in her fantasy snow scene. Pleased as she was, there was something almost fearful about the discovery, as if she were being watched by an invisible presence. She couldn't stop trembling at her discovery of something that shouldn't have existed.

Kambayashi's truck was still quiet. There was no sound of the rain outside either. All she could hear, like a sediment in the silence, was a muffled sound, as of passing cars on the far-off road.

Takiko suddenly woke from her reverie and realized that the truck hadn't started up again. It couldn't have just vanished in the misty rain with Kambayashi aboard. She got up, hurried onto the veranda, and opened the doors. It was still raining. The haze reflected the light from the house and prevented her seeing even a short distance.

She stepped unhesitatingly into the sandals she'd discarded in front of the veranda, and after closing the glass doors began to run through the rain, shielding her head with the yukata's wide sleeve. The drops, small and not cold to the touch, made the air oppressively close.

The rain still held a faint light when she was quite far from Kido's house. Though she had no sense of direction in this new place she ran hard, straight ahead.

Mud splattered up to her cheeks from a large puddle that she must have landed in. The yukata's hem was heavy. Takiko came to a halt and looked around. She made out a large black bulk in the mist off to her right. She ran on toward it.

The truck was now a heavy, cold mass sunk into the rain. It was the old familiar truck with a green canvas cover on the back. One of its rear wheels was in a ditch.

Takiko put one foot on the cab step and peered through the window. Kambayashi wasn't there. She went around to the rear and peered under the canvas. There he was, sprawled asleep on one of the packing blankets.

Relieved, Takiko climbed into the back herself while she decided what to do. The truck bed would be pitch-dark if she let the flap of the heavy cover drop, so she held it open with one hand and gazed at the black shadow that was all she could see of Kambayashi's body, while with the other she wiped her wet face and tucked the muddy hem of her yukata up around her thighs.

It was a quiet, cozy place. After a while she began to feel her rain-soaked body glow with warmth. I want to sleep nestled close to that body, Takiko thought as she gazed at him. Like a child in its father's arms. Perhaps Kambayashi won't know if I do it while he's asleep.

Taking care to keep the mud and the wet sleeve of her

yukata away from him, Takiko lay down in the darkness with her hand and her cheek against Kambayashi's back.

He moved his shoulder a little, but gave no sign of waking.

For some time Takiko lay absolutely still, feeling with her whole body the warmth from Kambayashi's back. His warm, broad back. Many emotions lived in the heartbeat and breathing of this single body, grief and joy melting together. She could feel all too surely the heat of Kambayashi's body holding onto life, and couldn't rid her mind of a scene in which that body was surrounded by an endless frozen plain that contained all the moisture of the earth and sky. What a tiny black dot a solitary figure was, running here and there in its midst. Yet at the same time Takiko was remembering thc flood of green she'd seen that day in the hothouses. What was rapidly rising in her own body, she felt, was that excess of green.

She put her left cheek where her right had been against Kambayashi's back. Then she tentatively rubbed her nose and pressed her lips against it. Her lips felt cold to her. Gingerly reaching out her hand she touched Kambayashi's shoulder, touched the arm that lay along his side. The tips of her fingers, too, were cold. In this man's body, larger than hers and hotly alive wherever she touched it, Takiko couldn't help being aware of a sadness that it seemed would never escape it now.

Kambayashi's body shifted again. Takiko withdrew her hand and huddled up as if to hide herself behind his back.

He groaned in his sleep and tried to roll over toward that side. She moved fast to get out of the way, but she didn't make it in time and his arm landed on her face. His sweat-dampened palm covered her lips. It smelled faintly of earth. She held her breath and watched to see what he would do next. With another slight groan he changed the position of his hand. It shifted over her eyes. But without pausing this time the hot hand crept over her nose, cheeks, and hair. As it came through her hair to her earlobe, his body stiffened for an instant. Not knowing what to do, in desperation Takiko hugged his body to her and buried her face in his chest.

"Who's there?" Kambayashi whispered, gasping with fright. Takiko didn't answer. She too was so frightened she couldn't speak.

A little time went by as neither moved or spoke.

His hand on her head slowly moved on. It came to her neck and stopped on her shoulder.

She heard him whisper again. "Taki-chan?"

Driven by fear, she groped to find Kambayashi's lips and pressed hers to them. The tears seething inside her were on the point of spilling over. When his hands had reassured him that it was Takiko, Kambayashi relaxed.

His lips, covered by hers, didn't move. They were dry. Takiko shifted her face to one side and, after touching her lips to his cheek, buried her face against his neck. His heartbeat was pulsing there also.

Kambayashi didn't try to push her away. He was vaguely stroking her head.

She would have liked to lie dead still under his hand but, nearly suffocating, she raised her face and took a shaky breath.

Kambayashi's hand stopped. Afraid, she tried again to lie dead. His arms hugged her tight. The beating in his chest carried directly to hers. His breath was hot, and misted on contact with the air. It was as if their two bodies had turned into the wildly swirling green.

Kambayashi kissed her forehead, kissed her cheek, palm,

neck, shoulder, felt for her breasts, pushed away the yukata with both hands, pressed his face against her bare breasts, and sucked her nipple. With tears in her eyes, Takiko wrapped her body around his.

Their two bodies rolled over and over, tangled together. Takiko wished hers would split apart, split in two and melt irretrievably into the rain and earth.

Kambayashi embraced her tightly again and again, now pressing her breast, now caressing her face, stroking her thigh, letting out a breath. She ran her hands over his body with rough energy. They felt the places hidden by each other's underwear. Their desire was plain there. By now their underwear seemed merely in the way to Takiko. But Kambayashi retained it, on his body and hers.

At length, he raised himself from where he lay breathing deeply with his face against her belly, hugged her head to his chest and whispered, "You've got to go back now."

At once Takiko clung to him with all her strength. "No, no, make love with me, you have to make love with me." Her voice was tearful, yet as she spoke she felt that what she'd blurted out wasn't what she meant.

"No, we mustn't." Kambayashi's voice didn't seem to be his either. Takiko could say nothing more. Nothing but sadness remained. Her tears flowed.

Only when he had pulled her to him many times, moaning, then clinging trembling to her just as he was about to let her go, could Kambayashi move away from his own desire. His body resounded with a cry of grief.

"Go, now."

With this he lifted the canvas and Takiko climbed down, weeping aloud, and started to run through the rain.

FACES

Dark, dense leaves were rippling below. Above them spread a heat-hazed sky where pigeons circled.

This was the view from the tenth-floor window of the university hospital. The woods behind the hospital almost hid the steeply climbing main road, appearing to merge with the wood that belonged to the shrine on its other side. At certain times of day, if she looked very carefully into the woods as though parting the heavy foliage, she could just make out the tiny figures of babies and their mothers. They were far away, too far to hear their voices, dots so faint it was strange that she could spot them at all. Babies on their mothers' backs. Babies in strollers. But Takiko could see each one clearly. It was there that she had walked last July, very pregnant, and looked up at a canopy of leaves that shone transparently in the midsummer sun. She'd been grateful for the thick grove's blue shadows after panting along hot roads. The roof of the nursery she'd visited that day remained invisible among the rippling leaves, however, no matter how persistently she held her breath and stared.

It was July, and high summer. Akira had had the operation on his inguinal hernia as scheduled and was in the children's surgical ward. It was a short stay, only six days. Takiko took some time off work, before and after a weekend, to be at his bedside for the six days, sleeping at the hospital. The surgery was so simple that there was almost no need for concern. All the same, it had been painful enough—blindingly painful— to watch Akira's small body as he spent the night with an empty stomach, then in the morning received several injections followed by a general anesthetic and was wheeled in a deep sleep to the operating room. A couple stood beside Takiko in the linoleum-floored corridor, watching their child go to another operating room. The corridor was dark, only the floor gleaming faintly at their feet—or so it appeared to Takiko. Beside her the sick child's mother sobbed, a low, dreamlike sound drained of all strength. Her husband was supporting her. They were a well-dressed young couple, not yet thirty, who might have caught Takiko's eye in the street, though she would have glanced quickly away.

"Look, it's going to be all right. Take it easy. All we have to do is wait calmly till she comes out." Every time her husband spoke to her, half scolding and half comforting, the child's mother shook her head and sobbed again. "Come on, let's wait in the ward. Okay?"

Holding each other, the couple went into the elevator and retreated to a ward on another floor. Takiko was left with no one beside her. She could scarcely expect Kambayashi to be there. She waited for the elevator to come back and returned to Akira's room.

For several hours, until Akira arrived back in the ward, she could think of nothing to do except stand at the window and gaze at what could be seen from there.

The bed assigned to Akira was by the window of the four-bed room. The child in the bed opposite, a boy of six or seven who was in for a long stay, was watching his personal color TV with the grandmother who looked after him. The other two beds were occupied by a girl a little bigger than Akira and a newborn infant less than a month old, whose mothers were deep in conversation at the sink in the corner where they were washing something. They were discussing the evidently very urgent surgery that the infant had undergone the day before. She had an artificial anus like a small red push button on one side of her swollen abdomen. It was this that had drawn Takiko's eyes the previous evening once she had settled into the ward with Akira. Noticing that she was being observed as she carefully wiped the infant's body with gauze, the mother had put on a smile and explained what the object was. Then she had asked what Akira was in for. Takiko had been ashamed to answer with such a minor ailment. Sure enough, a look of disappointment had come to the mother's slightly flushed cheeks, but still she cheerfully admired Akira's obvious good health. The older boy knew exactly how many days in the hospital a diagnosis meant, and he gave Akira a scornful look as he stood holding the rails of his bed, laughing happily. "The last kid in that bed had a hernia too. I'm not gonna remember this one's name, 'cause he'll be gone in a few days anyhow. He better not make any noise if he knows what's good for him."

The boy's grandmother scolded him and apologized with a bow to Takiko, who couldn't help feeling increasingly ashamed of Akira's healthy body with the glow of the blazing sunshine outside the hospital still on his skin.

The boy was kind only to the girl in the next bed. She had been in the hospital nearly a month already, awaiting a major operation. It was taking a long time to build up her strength, her mother said, and she too glanced enviously at Akira.

Though Takiko had spent just one night in the ward, as she gazed out the window and waited for Akira to come back from the operating room, she began to have a sense of remoteness. Was it really only yesterday that she'd been out there, soaked with sweat in that world where smells and sounds clashed under the burning sky, shuttling back and forth to the nursery and running around in Misawa Gardens' truck? When was it that she had caught her breath every time she raised her eyes to the glare of the midsummer sun, sadly aware of her body which would not forget the embrace with Kambayashi in the darkness? A different kind of time quietly filled the small room on the tenth floor. Yet even as she was thinking this, her body recalled the feel of Kambayashi's deep breaths with a sear of pain.

The green woods that filled the view below, rustling heavily.

The dull spread of sky. The blocks of old houses beyond the trees, interrupted here and there by an office building. And in the far distance the tall silhouettes of skyscrapers, clustered like a stand of forest trees. Everything she could see from the window seemed numbed by the sky's heat. The tenth-floor room, though, was more than adequately air-conditioned.

There were no mountain shadows on the skyline. No pale blue mountains or glinting horse-shaped traces of snow. These weren't vineyards of flashing white-backed leaves rustling beneath her gaze. And she wasn't standing on a mountainside where the grapevines crept upward like a giant creature. But she felt as though she was—that she stood in the place she'd pictured so often from her mother's stories of home. She sensed the cold, crystalline hardness of its quartz. As if she were trapped inside a crystal. A hexagonal crystal of rock quartz. A girl in the mountains surrounded more bountifully by grapes and quartz and sky than anyone else on earth. Beautiful things that trapped her in solitude. How fondly she would remember the girl she'd been.

The world below is clearly visible from the mountain slope, stretching away beyond the rustling vine leaves. All too clearly and minutely visible. The world where people live. Countless grains of light glitter as if every surface had been sprinkled with quartz dust. There are houses, roads, adults, children down there. They look like toys, but they aren't toys at all. A world that appears even more distant than the blue peaks floating on the skyline. But it is this world that she wants more than anything to watch, when she could look away and spare herself this slowly welling sadness. When she needn't know how alone she is.

The girl on the mountainside can't take her eyes off the

glittering world below, although she is about to burst into tears. If only she could leave the mountains. But there's no place for her away from these slopes, no other place where she is herself. Whenever the tears threaten to brim over, the barefoot girl breaks into a run; she knows her way about the steep slopes. Faster, faster. Something in the girl's body echoes like the howl of an animal among the mountains. It sweeps down to the vineyards as a gust of wind. The girl races on and on. When she has run till her body is empty, she stops abruptly and lets her gaze return again to the distant, delicately sparkling world below. Rivers trace silver lines. The sea is in sight. As her eyes follow the coastline, drifting ice appears and expands into a world of white. There's something running freely over that white expanse, its heartbeat reverberating. She can see Kambayashi's face, his cares forgotten, his big mouth open in a shout of laughter—a Gilyak of another age.

It was one month to the day since Takiko had been to Misawa Gardens' "mountain." When she thought back, she found it surprising how substantial the time had been.

She had groped blindly in the intense light of her own body. She had put the emotions and scenes inside her into words directed as endlessly as prayer toward the unseen Kambayashi. There were curses and lacerating words among them. How could she blot out that night from this body? For a month she had screamed the same question.

That night, Takiko had run on weeping through the rain, stumbling and falling many times.

When she came to a standstill in the light from Kido's house, she realized that she looked like she'd been swimming through muddy water. She wished she could simply go away and never come back, but she couldn't bring herself to plunge into the dark rain again. She peered in through the glass doors. The light left on in the room filled it with glaring brightness. Kido and Akimoto were obviously sound asleep. Rubbing her brimming eyes, she moved away from the doors and had another look at her yukata. She could hardly go inside like that. With a sigh, she stripped it off. She began by rinsing the mud from her body at the faucet. The water dashed pleasurably against her naked skin. As she scrubbed roughly at her face, she let out one last sob as if to say "That's enough."

She washed the yukata, wrung it out thoroughly and went into the house with it, naked but for her pants. She turned off the parlor light and went straight upstairs. The sliding doors were open between the two upstairs rooms, and Mrs. Kido was asleep in the next one with her leg bent up at the knee. Takiko hung the yukata over the windowsill, wrapped herself in the flannel sheet and lay down. Then, painfully aware of her body still whirling in unison with Kambayashi's deep breaths, she went to sleep.

A fine drizzle was still falling next morning. Takiko was the last to wake up. The yukata she had left to dry on the windowsill was gone. She put on the sweaty-smelling T-shirt and jeans she'd worn the day before and went downstairs, where Kido and his wife, Akimoto, and Kambayashi were sitting at the breakfast table. She hurried to the toilet, stopping on the way back to wash her face. Thanks to a good sleep it showed no trace of the night before. Her cheeks glowed and her eyes were clear and wide-awake. Whatever happens no one must ever find out, she reminded herself as she studied her reflection. With Kambayashi, for the first time Takiko had known a man to control his desire. Through the painful struggle to control it, she had also realized desire's outright power for the first time. The realization made itself felt as a deep sexual pleasure such as she had never experienced before.

Having prepared herself, Takiko returned to the parlor. She looked at Kambayashi with a smile and said, "Good morning. So you didn't go back to the mountain after all?"

His face reddening, Kambayashi grinned back self-consciously. Sensing his uneasiness, she had difficulty breathing.

"That's right," Mrs. Kido put in unconcernedly, to Takiko's relief. "Gave us all a surprise when we got up this morning. It was Akimoto who noticed the truck first. Our friend here was still sleeping peacefully inside. Talk about easygoing! And that was when we heard about all the trouble you had with the truck last night, Taki-chan. You'd have thought he'd have woken up the men, even if it took a kick or two, instead of making a poor weak girl lend a hand. He's such a slob. Getting you covered in mud. We ladies deserve better treatment."

Mrs. Kido included the other two men in her indignant look and burst out laughing. While Takiko was doubling up in a show of helpless laughter, her eyes darted to Kambayashi's face. It appeared to be in a cold sweat as he apologized with what struck her as exaggerated gestures. If there hadn't been other people watching, she thought she might have cried out with pain herself. At the same time, it was a relief not to have had to do the lying.

Kido was hungover and feeling low. Akimoto and Kambayashi went outside together and hauled the truck out of the ditch.

"Looks like the rain might let up soon," Kambayashi said when he came in. Takiko had started alone on a late breakfast. "The sky's getting lighter. Hope it'll clear up a bit before we go home. I would've liked to show you the view from the mountain."

"I hope it does clear up. I really do." Takiko looked Kambayashi in the face for the first time that morning. He smiled and nodded slowly. She returned the smile. She had a sense that Kambayashi's child and wife, whom she hadn't met, were right there smiling gently with them. Was Akira smiling right now too, as he played with a helper or stared cross-eyed at the nursery's pet birds? Kambayashi, she couldn't help noticing, was not at all ashamed of the desire that he'd let touch Takiko in spite of himself. He had a child who didn't know enough to be ashamed of sexual desire. He had to keep a careful watch on the boy's sexual nature to make up for his lack of worldly knowledge.

After taking the morning off they set out for the mountain in the two trucks, Kido and Akimoto riding in one and Takiko and Kambayashi in the other. There should have been any number of words to speak to him during the short time they were alone together, but Takiko was unable to say anything. Her heart racing, she braced herself to stop her body being pulled imperceptibly toward Kambayashi's. He too was silent.

It was still raining at the mountain as well. Kambayashi and the others began to load tubs destined for the greenhouse in Tokyo. Takiko made another tour of the four greenhouses. Her head reeling from the steady heat and the swirling green, she repeated under her breath, "But I don't understand. I'm afraid. Please let me understand. I don't." She was afraid of the sexual pleasure which still enveloped her so overpoweringly that she couldn't even recognize it.

Since there seemed no point in waiting for the rain to lift, it was decided that before Kambayashi and Takiko headed back to Tokyo they would all have lunch at a place about an hour's drive from the mountain, a ranch-style park and restaurant that served "Genghis Khan barbecues." This time they paired off with Akimoto and Takiko in one truck, Kambayashi and Kido in the other. As Akimoto wasn't much of a talker, Takiko chatted away about a silly mistake she'd made on a sixth-grade trip, things the passing landscape reminded her of, and the like. She laughed, and sang what she could remember of songs she'd learned on the class trip. She wanted to be alone.

The ranch restaurant was doing a slow trade. Outside it was even colder than the mountain, and the heavy mist that lay over the ranch meant they wouldn't get to see any cows or horses after all. They made do with eating as much as they could. It was the first time Takiko had had the barbecued mutton dish, and although the taste made little impression she concentrated entirely on eating.

It was about one o'clock by the time she and Kambayashi started for home. "Come again in August, you can swim in the river—and stay longer next time," Kido and Akimoto urged her as they saw them off. The three hours they would spend alone on the way to Tokyo would be the last such opportunity; she couldn't count on ever having another chance once they'd arrived back. If she said nothing now it would mean nothing had happened last night, and she could never feel the warmth of Kambayashi's body or his heartbeat or his breath again. She mustn't want his body. This she had been made to realize since last night. Yet her own body would surely shatter in pieces if she meekly obeyed. She would settle for any kind of connection. Couldn't that connection be about to begin?

She continued racking her brain for the words to say to him.

Perhaps observing her silence, Kambayashi made light conversation about Kido's and Akimoto's families. Takiko listened attentively, showing more interest than necessary, but the words weren't registering. Before long Kambayashi also fell silent.

The truck went on running smoothly, never veering even slightly from its route.

The three hours were slipping away. The look-alike housing developments were already far behind them, suburban railway stations with their small shopping centers passed by, the patches of brush and gardens with trees grew sparse, the houses crowded together, taller buildings began to stand out, and before she knew it the truck was well inside the metropolitan area. While the sky was dark as ever, the rain seemed to have stopped. She felt a comforting letdown as if, one way or another, she was home. The inorganic, flimsy texture of the roads and buildings and taxis and people was agreeably familiar.

How many minutes now to Misawa Gardens? Takiko felt the city's familiarity hit her like a blow. The joy of the night before, like a dream, or a rainbow, was fading before her eyes. A rainbow. She wanted something more certain than that.

The truck was approaching a corner she recognized.

Sensing despair in her voice the instant she spoke, she cried to the silent Kambayashi, "Stop! Stop the truck!"

He nodded, slowed, and pulled over to the curb. "I've stopped. What's wrong?"

Still she couldn't find words. What appeal could she make, and how? That rainbow was in sight. And yet Kambayashi was there beside her, so near, and so very casual.

". . . I don't like this."

She was barely able to murmur it. Kambayashi remained

silent for a while, then with a sudden attempt at a smile he told her, "Ten years ago . . . my wife took it hard. She cried and screamed that she wanted to die. Even now, I've got to keep an eye on her all the time. I'm arranging to take over at the mountain when Kido-san retires. Once our boy grows up somehow, the Misawas have promised him a job, as long as it's at the mountain. You will stay at Misawa Gardens, won't you, Taki-chan?"

She nodded uncertainly. She was unable to cling to Kambayashi or appeal to him in any way. After studying her face for some time, he restarted the truck.

Takiko was brought back to exactly the same routine as before.

Akira still yelled early each morning, and soiled his diapers, and rested his weight in her arms, while her mother still couldn't quite give up the idea of separating them, and upset herself trying to persuade Takiko that it was only common sense and would make her life and Akira's easier. And her father meanwhile was as aggrieved as ever: everything had turned out wrong except his son Atsushi—no, even Atsushi was sure to be a disappointment—and when he took a good look at his rotting shack of a house he found it taken over by the young woman who was supposed to be his daughter and a baby whose very crying radiated vitality. The sight of these two creatures drove him to hurl the violence of his emotions, indistinguishable from hate, against them. And all the while he cursed his wretched job which only wore him out but which he had little hope of quitting.

When Takiko came home from the mountain, she found despair plainly visible in her father and mother. And she felt something identical in herself. It appalled her to think that this despair might be the only thing that she could be sure of. Was that it? Was that possible? The pleasure that Akira, Kambayashi, and even Misawa Gardens had given her at first had been so many rainbows that faded from the sky after rain. Nothing was left. Or almost nothing: each time the rainbow reappeared, a hard quartz crystal of despair grew inside her—a cold, jagged crystal that would never mold itself to a human body.

You're wrong, she wanted to cry out in protest to herself, even if the quartz edges of despair ripped her throat. No, it can't be true. That wasn't just a rainbow. It's still shining. I can't see a thing without that light, can't do anything, can't breathe.

As she went on reporting for work at Misawa Gardens and seeking out the figure of Kambayashi without even being able to touch his arm, she felt a gradual chill come over her. Just to touch his chest would have been enough. Why couldn't she even do that? Why wasn't it allowed? She had never been so baffled. If only she could believe that Kambayashi disliked her. He wanted her too, she could tell he did. Then why didn't he do as he liked with her? As Hiroshi Maeda and her other men friends had done. But it was surely because he would not act this way, being Kambayashi, that she felt such despair when she saw they could never be together as man and woman.

There were several times over the next few weeks when she had to have lunch alone with Kambayashi. He talked about his child more intimately and easily than ever before, no longer struggling to hide his joy in being a father. His child's delight when he bought him a baseball uniform. How funny he looked posing away in it. The other children and parents at the special school he attended, and various other scenes. All these things

Kambayashi had learned and received from his child. Kambayashi lived in this state of joy. It was Kambayashi.

At such times Takiko could watch his face and listen to his voice excitedly enough. And before she knew it she was eagerly telling him of her life with Akira. How he'd started hauling himself up on furniture. How she'd panicked when he helped himself to the red from Atsushi's watercolors and she'd thought he had a mouthful of blood. How he loved the flush toilet and was always wanting to paddle in it.

Kambayashi would become simply a father with whom she could talk unreservedly about her child, and she a mother who had no one else to confide in. Their talks satisfied her more than ever.

But as the end of the lunch hour approached she would begin to feel the crystal inside her. It made her tremulous and dizzy. She wanted to touch Kambayashi's body, to bury her face in his neck.

She had to withdraw into herself, her head lowered and body hunched with the effort.

"But," she had burst out once, chilled and shivering, "but . . . somehow it's not enough."

"You're too young to be talking like that." Kambayashi had laughed and passed it off as a joke.

Being reminded she was young increased her hopelessness. She was even beginning to hate Kambayashi. Just because his child had Down's syndrome, did he have to be so satisfied with himself?

Her father had accused her of the same thing a few days earlier: You're mighty pleased with yourself just because you've had an illegitimate child. So now you think you can push everybody around, huh?

She couldn't let this pass, it was so far from the truth that it galled her. "What do you mean by that? What are you getting at?" she yelled back, and as they both lost control she was struck by her father for what was, when she came to think of it, the first time in a long while. She had unknowingly grown thoughtless and abrupt around the house. And Akira, absorbing her mood, had become a nervous and fretful baby.

As she bent double with pain from a kick in the stomach, Takiko flung an armful of the diapers she'd just finished washing at her father's face as she screamed, in tears, "Damn you, you—I hate you!" Her father struck her wet cheek. She scratched his face, and he caught her arm and shoved her backward. She screamed and cried as if wrenched open. All the while she was aware of Kambayashi's eyes, which only made her cry louder. "Huh," her father snorted, "what do *you* know? You're just a kid. Stop crying, damn it. When are you going to quit living in a dream world?"

Takiko couldn't stop. She was sobbing incoherently, "Dad, Dad." Kambayashi watched her in the distance: the Kambayashi who'd assured her that her pain as the mother of Akira was the same as his own.

The date of Akira's operation was drawing near as the days and weeks passed in this way. There was no reason to postpone it. With a small advance on her wages from Misawa Gardens she should be able to afford the surgery and hospital costs. Her mother hadn't forgotten the date either. "You're going to be rid of this at last," she said to Akira, taking a long farewell look at the swelling which these days was present more often than not, distending his scrotum to nearly the size of an adult's fist. "And the sooner the better, eh? In the days before they could operate," she told Takiko, "I don't suppose it would have killed him, but the other kids would have given him a terrible time, poor boy. He'll get enough of that as it is."

Takiko muttered in reply, "He won't remember a thing about it, will he? Maybe I should take a photo to remind him."

"What a thing to say—even as a joke! Your own child!"

Takiko reluctantly took Akira in the carrier for a preliminary examination at the university hospital. His having to go into the hospital was an unwelcome setback at a time when she should have been watching and appealing to Kambayashi. Kambayashi wasn't in the street, or in the waiting room, or in the examination room, nor was there any reason he should be. Takiko couldn't help scowling at her surroundings. And this too she was reporting to Kambayashi.

After the examination was over, as she'd taken the rest of the day off from Misawa Gardens she gave Kawano a call for the first time in almost three months. It was a little before noon, and he was at home.

Takiko reached his apartment in under half an hour. He let her in without much of a welcome, having only just got up, and began to make coffee.

As soon as Akira was out of the carrier he began to protest because he'd missed his morning snack at the nursery. "Ma, ma, ma," he yelled at the top of his voice. Explaining to Kawano that he was due to have surgery, Takiko prepared his bottle at the sink in the corner. Nodding a little in reply, Kawano put on some music with a light, bouncy rhythm amid the yells.

He didn't seem to have changed much. As she gave Akira the bottle she looked around Kawano's single room and felt at ease. The stereo and records took up most of the available space, but it was an airy room all the same. When Akira was quiet, Kawano turned the record down. Sipping his coffee, he told Takiko it was a jazz arrangement of a Spanish tune. He made a habit of playing records while she was there, and also of giving her simple explanations. The breeze through the room was pleasant on her sweaty body.

"I wish I had this place."

A year ago she had dreamed—though she hadn't thought it a dream—that she and the coming baby would live in a room exactly like this. She had been in no doubt at all. That dream had been the one thing sustaining her then.

"Don't make me nervous. I don't want to wind up homeless," Kawano said with a smile. Takiko smiled too.

"Why does it make you nervous?"

"If you put your mind to it, Odaka-san, a wimp like me would end up saying, 'Okay, it's all yours.'"

"No, you wouldn't. Not even you, Kawano-san."

Akira had fallen asleep in her arms before he finished the bottle. Outside the window, she could see the drab sunless garden that belonged to the landlord. The ferns that had found their niche there were thriving. The apartment was quiet inside and out. A cicada was singing in the distance.

After putting Akira down on a nearby cushion, Takiko drank her cup of coffee, which was not quite cold.

"Getting big, isn't he?" Kawano said as he selected the next record. "Last time he could barely sit up, now he looks ready to walk any minute."

"He'll be one next month. He's got his lower front teeth, you know."

"One, huh? He'll soon be walking, and talking, and showing intelligence. It's all still to come for him."

"Right . . ."

Takiko drank the last of her coffee and slid over to Kawano's side. He looked around and gave her a sighing smile, then, saying "Well," he got up and drew the curtains. She waited for him pensively.

"It's odd, you don't seem quite yourself today, Odaka-san," he whispered as, once he'd closed the curtains and taken off his pants, he came back in his underwear and put his arms around her from behind.

"I'm the same as always," Takiko whispered as she leaned back against him. "Wait, I'll take these off."

She unbuttoned her jeans and, lifting her hips, shed them along with her underpants. Then she sat up and took off her T-shirt. Kawano, now naked himself, buried his face against her breasts. Holding tight to his back she touched her lips to his sweat-scented hair.

They tangled roughly and sweatily on the tatami. Takiko first closed her eyes, then stared at the ceiling, breathed in, breathed out. The strength drained unexpectedly from her body. She shut her eyes. She felt trapped inside a purple quartz crystal, and as she clung to Kawano's body for support, she couldn't hold back her tears. The sadness had come over her with a startling suddenness.

"What's wrong? Gee, you gave me a shock. Has something happened?" Kawano peered into her face, then relaxed his body and stroked her back.

"Sorry. Just . . . look at us. Anyone would think you were older than me." She was wiping her tears and sobbing as she spoke.

"It's always been like that." Kawano pouted, then smiled.

"Is that right?" As she was studying Kawano's face she wanted to weep again, and she did. He stayed silently stroking her head. Distantly, in her mind's eye, she could see herself running around outside the mountain's greenhouses. She could see her small self holding hands with her father, watching the ferry about to leave harbor. She could see the tree shining by the window of the hospital where Akira was born. She could see the dazzling summer sky as she set out for the hospital in the early morning. She could see her mother entertaining Akira. And Kambayashi's big mouth smiling.

The cicada continued to sing, the breeze from the window blew over her naked body. In a corner of the room Akira was still asleep, his arms and legs outspread. When she opened her eyes, Kawano was there, naked like herself. It was very peaceful.

"Kawano-san, have you heard of Down's syndrome?" She moved away from him to lie face down on the tatami.

He shook his head and lowered his eyes to his chest, which was streaming with large drops of sweat.

Takiko told him what she'd learned from Kambayashi about his child with Down's syndrome, and how the father worked with her. She told him how much she enjoyed talking with this father and how she'd even come to enjoy the struggle she was having raising Akira.

"You're in love with this guy?" Kawano murmured. He had a look of innocent surprise. Takiko nodded hesitantly.

"But I can't tell him that. He feels it shouldn't be said." She heard the sound of her voice appealing to Kambayashi in the back of the truck. Her face contorted and she scowled at Kawano.

"You must really be in love with him."

"Mm . . ." She was almost in tears again.

"I see."

With a sigh, he gazed in a vague way at Takiko's naked body. She too looked at her breasts which were wet with sweat.

"But, I'm not really sure. Maybe, maybe it's just that I'm afraid of Akira. Yes, I am. Because I can't see myself ever being able to give up everything for Akira's sake, like he's done for his child. But that's what Akira's telling me to do—give up, give up."

She pressed her tearful face against Kawano's chest. For a moment he trembled as if in fear, then he held her firmly. "Why think of yourself and him in the same way? They're two completely different things."

She gave many quick nods of her head, and pressed her lips against his before he could go on.

They threw themselves into receiving and releasing each other's desire in a rush of sweat. Takiko heard her own resonate with his as she moved her body violently. For the first time she felt she didn't want to lose this shared desire of theirs.

By the time they separated, Akira was awake, babbling to himself and playing with the curtains which were swaying in the breeze.

As Kawano hastily pulled on his trousers after checking his watch and pointing out that he had to leave for the coffee shop at two-thirty, she couldn't resist saying, with a blush, "Thank you, Kawano-san."

He gave her a scowling look as he replied, "Well, don't just sit there. Hurry up and get ready."

She hurriedly found her underwear.

Akira was laughing at their movements around the room.

"All right? . . . Shall we go?" Kawano asked, when she was dressed and had Akira on her back. She nodded.

"But . . . is it okay if I come again, after Akira's operation?"

"Suit yourself. You don't have to keep asking me all the time," Kawano answered irritably with his face averted.

Akira had the operation on the Saturday of the following week.

When he returned to the ward four and a half hours after going into the operating room, he was white-faced and still unconscious. He looked tiny on the bed, lying neatly on his back. Takiko, hardly daring to breathe, kept her eyes fixed on this corpselike, tiny body. She simply stared without another thought or sensation.

It was evening when the anesthetic wore off. He opened his eyes a fraction at the sound of an infant's crying in the next bed and recognized Takiko's face. She didn't manage to smile immediately. She caught her breath with fear. He was still pale. Perhaps his body was partly numb, for instead of trying to prop himself up with his hands as he usually did when he woke, he lay still and let out a weak voice.

"Maa, maa, baa . . ."

The incision didn't seem to be hurting him. She released a long breath.

It was mealtime, and the ward was bustling. The meals for patients and the relatives attending to them had to be picked up from the delivery cart in the corridor. When Takiko moved away from the bed Akira started to cry for the first time.

His dinner was a thin rice gruel with scrambled egg. Putting off feeding it to him until later, she quickly prepared his formula. She lowered the railing and sat on the bed, taking him on her lap. She was afraid the incision might be painful, but Akira remained indifferent to it and only cried lustily for the bottle in her hand.

Outside the hospital there was still an hour till dinnertime.

The heat-filled midsummer sky shone dully in the window. She had never lived ten floors above the city before. Her eyes kept straying to the expanse of sky in which not a single building or power line was visible from the bed. It wasn't a flat plane: its white was thicker in places, while in others there were glimpses of hazy blue. These shades changed subtly as she watched. The calm, elusive changes, different from any on the ground, set up a stirring inside her like the sound of the wind. It was as if her body were turning transparent; it was not unlike sadness, but it was quite entrancing too, leaving her as rapt as one who has taken leave of the earth. She recalled its surface fondly.

Would Kambayashi be holding his child right now, his big mouth laughing? Would Kawano be listening to a record at his part-time job? What about the mothers who were in the maternity hospital a year ago? What was making them sad or happy now? The fathers and mothers at Midori Nursery: she could see their smiles and their faces streaked with tears. Would Mrs. Kido still be telling every young woman she met about her longing for a child? What was Hiroshi Maeda seeing and feeling now?

When he'd finished the bottle, Akira began to breathe evenly in sleep. Takiko set him down on the bed and ate her dinner on the bedside table, her eyes on the window.

The boy in the far bed was howling, "No-o-o, Granny, you're too fussy, I want Mom . . ."

The infant's mother was breastfeeding and watching the older boy.

The little girl, who wasn't as tall as Akira, was taking a stroll around her bed holding her mother's hand. She had started to walk while in the hospital, Takiko had learned.

When she'd hurried through her dinner and returned her tray and Akira's, with its contents untouched, to the delivery cart, she moved the bedside chair over to the window and gazed out at the sky again. Little by little it was taking on the tints of evening.

Takiko felt herself at rest for the first time since she'd gone home from the hospital with newborn Akira. She could only be thankful that she had another four whole days alone with him, idle time with nothing to do but look after him. Here, as in the maternity hospital, she and Akira were just a mother and child, a pair who didn't even need names.

Once the sky was dark, for a short time the pediatric surgery ward rang with the voices of children playing with the doctor on duty. The boy from their room raced screeching up and down the corridor.

When her eyes met Takiko's, his grandmother smiled wryly and said, "No use telling a six-year-old to be quiet, is it? The doctor says it's probably better than letting him get too nervous, which is kind of him, but still . . . He does listen to his mother, mind you. But she has to have a rest now and then. And there's another little one at home."

"Hey, hey, don't get carried away or you'll burst your good-luck charm." The doctor's voice echoed after the boy as he came tumbling red-faced through the door.

"Beat it! I'm sick of this thing, it gets in my way!" the boy squealed back, shoving his pajama pants down and tugging at the plastic bag taped to his lower abdomen. The bag, which appeared to be connected somewhere internally by a clear tube, contained a pool of dark liquid.

"Doctor! Doctor!" his grandmother shrieked.

"Now what are you up to, sonny?" The doctor rushed in

from the corridor, his white coat flapping open, and picked the boy up lightly with both hands.

"Huh? Nothin'. Come and play some more, you gotta play with me," the boy said ingratiatingly without letting go of his plastic bag.

Small children, mothers, and doctors who'd come out of the other rooms were laughing in the corridor.

Akira stayed asleep, his face peaceful.

Takiko went into the corridor herself and wandered down it. The intensive care center was dim and hushed, in complete contrast to the cheerful din of the rest of the ward. A child was sleeping in an oxygen tent. The shadow she could see must be its mother.

Next door was the nurses' station, and at the end of the corridor there was a smoking area with a sofa. Here Takiko had had to wait on arrival with Akira the previous day. The feeble *Dracaena warneckii* and the spotted loosestrife inevitably reminded her of her job. A couple—clearly parents—were sitting on the sofa.

Back in the room, following the others' lead, Takiko dragged a cot out of the equipment room, set it up beside her patient's bed, and drew the surrounding curtains. Bedtime was eight o'clock.

Her time in the tranquil, secluded ward continued. Every day she washed diapers and did the rest of the laundry, hung it out on the rooftop clotheslines, prepared bottles for Akira and fed him his meals, took his temperature, gazed out the window or took strolls in the corridor with him in her arms— he was his usual lively self since the day after the surgery—or took catnaps with him on his bed. She had forgotten the sound of her own voice; she had forgotten her face and her body.

Now and then a ray of light slanted in like a sunbeam through trees, bringing memories of herself in the outside world, and with them pain. Whenever this happened she went over to the window and gazed wide-eyed at the sky, the greenness of the woods that frothed at the foot of the building, and the rows of roofs that glared in the midsummer heat. She was drawn there by a haunting sense that these things were her body. She would gaze at its expanse, its brilliance. The sound of voices crying pulsated out there like a rainbow. Heartbeats reverberated, and desire. She wondered at the rainbow's resonance. Then she would turn back to the roomful of sick children and let out the breath she'd been holding. Her fear of the voice that told her to give up seemed to have melted away.

Even without her crying aloud in anguish, the world outside rang endlessly with vast cries. Takiko turned to the children and the adults in the room and gazed at the child she had borne and was raising.

As Akira was recovering well, the doctors barely paused at his bed, even during the professor's weekly teaching rounds. She watched the interns cluster to examine the children in the other beds while she amused Akira, who kept on wanting to get down, with toys on loan from the hospital.

The girl who had just turned one had apparently gained weight and would at last be having surgery in a week's time. Her mother's glad voice rang out.

The boy seemed to have made a little progress and then relapsed. He could be heard abusing the doctors: "I thought you said I could go home in the summer? You liars!"

When the group moved away from the boy's bed, the young doctor who was his bedtime playmate stayed behind to whisper, "Hey, you be good and stay in bed, you hear? I'll be back later. And I've still got the score sheet." Half hiding his face under the blanket, the boy seemed to have nodded wordlessly in reply.

The group on their rounds finally reached Akira's bed; by the time the professor had glanced at Akira's incision and nodded, they were already on their way to the infant's bed next door. Takiko relaxed and raised her head to see the same young doctor and another, equally young and a familiar face also, leaning on the railing of Akira's bed and smiling down at him. These two had performed the actual operation, but Takiko's only direct contact with them had been when they explained the procedure, and even then they had been depressingly businesslike. At other times they paid still less attention to Takiko and Akira, almost as if they were deliberately ignoring them.

She braced herself involuntarily. Was there something not quite satisfactory?

"Really, he's the image of my son," murmured the doctor who had whispered to the boy. "It's kind of spooky, like he's right here."

"Aha. So this is what yours looks like? He's very cute, isn't he?"

"Isn't he?" The doctor's faint sigh was quickly followed by a blush as he seemed to remember Takiko's presence and fled to the next bed. The other doctor also moved on hastily without having spoken to Takiko at all.

As they left her, Takiko blushed too, touched and embarrassed by the doctor's unexpectedly fatherly words. She glowed hotly. What was this dazzling sight she'd just seen? Something made her take another look at Akira's body, which had been given a new radiance in her eyes.

The next day, Wednesday, the newborn infant who had

received an artificial anus was discharged. Her mother, flushed as usual, explained that she would come back in a year or so when she was stronger, for a second operation which would make the prosthesis unnecessary. She bowed her way out of the room as if reluctant to part from it rather than its occupants, and went away with the infant in her arms.

Akira was due to leave the following day. Atsushi, on summer vacation, was to come and meet them in order to carry the bags. Takiko had phoned her mother to confirm that they'd be leaving as scheduled and had been told, "I'll send Atchan along then, since he's only loafing around. All right?" She remembered how a year ago she'd upset her mother by trying to insist on going home from the maternity hospital unaccompanied.

"That'd be a big help. Are you sure he won't mind?" she asked. She heard her mother speaking to Atsushi, who must have been beside the phone, and Atsushi promptly agreeing.

She was completely accustomed by now to hospital life. She simply forgot herself and spent the time absentmindedly, without boredom. Their approaching departure caused her no joy and no regret. The place was too remote from the midsummer heat outside for her even to remember what it was like. Each day had a dreamlike simplicity: all she had to do was function automatically as a mother and care for her child. Every conversation she overheard was about children's illnesses. She heard terms like "cancer," "brain tumor," "occlusion of the bile duct." As she washed diapers and hung them out on the roof, walked the corridors, and bathed with other women in the ward's bathroom, she was fascinated by the attending parents who took these terms upon themselves over the heads of their children.

The newborn's bed was occupied that same afternoon by a new patient, a boy of about two. His parents deposited a pile of luggage and began busily unpacking it all around the bed. A big thermos, toys, picture books, a bedside lamp, a stack of bath towels, the child's and his mother's clothes, an alarm clock, a calendar, tumblers. The neighboring bed grew more and more cheerful before Takiko's eyes. Watching dreamily as she shared a nap with Akira, she wondered at anyone being so well-prepared.

Even so, something seemed to have been left out, for the mother was complaining to the father, who replied just as irritably and rushed off down the corridor.

The child looked tanned and healthy, his body still glowing from the sunshine outside. A nurse who'd come for a look at the new arrival said smilingly, "You're from out of town, aren't you?"

The mother nodded shortly and mentioned a town in the next prefecture that Takiko hadn't heard of.

"I thought so. I can tell by your complexions. I expect it's all that fresh air that makes the difference."

The mother, still unsmiling, was looking at her child and the area around the bed.

A doctor joined them and made a brief preoperative examination—apparently for an inguinal hernia like Akira's.

"You're sure he has a hernia? I can't see any problem." He sounded bored.

"Of course he has a hernia. We were told to come for the operation. That's why we're here," the mother snapped, her high-pitched voice ringing through the quiet ward.

Taking no interest in the new patient, the older boy was building, knocking down, and rebuilding a tall tower of blocks on his bed. There was no sign of his grandmother; perhaps she was in the laundry room.

The girl was asleep, her cheek resting against a soft toy. Her mother was meticulously folding clean laundry. Now that she'd lost the company of the woman she had always talked to she was impassive, paying no attention to the new patient and his mother.

After a while the doctor and nurse went away and a sleepy stillness returned to the room. Takiko dozed off again. Though afternoon was the official visiting time, formal visitors were rare in this ward. In Takiko's room the little girl's father had visited once on Sunday, and that was all. It was, in fact, the quietest, most luxurious time of the day.

In the middle of her nap, someone tapped Takiko on the shoulder. When she dreamily opened her eyes, there was Kambayashi's face glistening with sweat.

She sat up with a start and looked again, blinking hard, then got down from the bed. In her confusion she had trouble fitting her feet into her slippers. When she looked up from her feet, there was a man's face, unmistakably Kambayashi's. He was wearing a smile that looked as if he were still squinting in the blazing sun outside. Takiko gazed at his face with wide eyes and open mouth. Ah, yes, she told herself with a sharp pang of familiarity—forgetting to wonder what he was doing there—this is what Kambayashi looks like, this is his face. There he was before her eyes. Once he had wiped the sweat from his forehead and looked self-consciously around the room, he turned back to Takiko with a wry smile.

"Hey, I didn't mean to give you such a surprise. How is he? Everything okay?"

"Yes, we're leaving tomorrow." After she'd answered

vaguely, her heart sped up as if she'd only just realized that she was face to face with Kambayashi himself.

"Really? But you won't be coming back to work right away, will you?" He lowered his voice so as not to disturb the people around them and studied Akira's sleeping face.

"They say he'll have to rest at home for four or five days. But I can't take that much time off. I'm going to ask my brother and my mother to keep an eye on him since they're at home, and I'll come to work in about two days." She kept her eyes on Kambayashi's profile. He was smiling at the sight of Akira sleeping with his mouth gaping slightly. That smile was almost crushing her. She had to open her mouth and draw a deep breath.

"There's no need to rush back. Not if you're going to be there permanently. I'll mention it to Misawa myself. He's very like you, isn't he, Taki-chan? Especially around the mouth. Isn't he sweet?"

Takiko looked down at Akira and smiled. The lump in her chest seemed to flow away in a clear shining stream that wasn't tears.

She turned to Kambayashi again. "What's up? You really did give me a surprise."

"I'm here to visit you two, of course. I was on a job nearby and I remembered this was the hospital and thought I'd just drop in. Knowing you, I figured you'd be getting bored. Everyone's been worrying."

"Have they? Thank you," Takiko murmured, and glanced around at the window. The cloudless blue was intensely bright. "The view from here's great. Want to take a look?"

Kambayashi was evidently ill at ease wearing his earthy-smelling work clothes in the quiet hospital room. Stooping his shoulders, he moved meekly from the bedside to the window and gazed out. Takiko stood beside him, her eyes on the spread of summer sky and the ground beneath it. The pungent smell of his sweat reached her. She surveyed the view from the window eagerly.

"You can see for miles, can't you?"

She nodded. She would have liked to tell Kambayashi what the view meant to her.

A single pigeon was flying a little below window level.

"This is great. It must help take your mind off things."

She nodded again, smiling. "I've spent the whole time looking out. It's kind of like being up in the mountains."

"Hm, it is, isn't it? That reminds me, bring your boy next time you come up to the mountain. Kido-san's been saying they'd love you to come again, too. Seems his wife's taken a liking to you. There's Akimoto's kid, and I'll bring mine along, and we'll have a barbecue or something—make a party of it."

Kambayashi spoke while gazing at the sky. Takiko stared in spite of herself at the side of his face, looked around at Akira asleep in the bed, then turned back to the window and, pressing her forehead to the glass, looked at the dazzling expanse outside.

"I'd like that too."

"Besides, you didn't get to see a thing last time. . . . Right. Well, then, I'm off. I'll tell everyone you're doing fine." Kambayashi's face as he moved away from the window seemed faintly flushed.

"You're going already?"

"Can't stay, I've got work to do."

"Oh . . . Thanks for coming. I'm glad about the mountain. I was afraid they wouldn't let me go again," Takiko said as she saw him to the door.

"Nonsense. Everyone'd be disappointed if you didn't go up there." Kambayashi spoke rapidly, his eyes on Takiko's face. She smiled and nodded vigorously. He nodded in return as if caught up in her enthusiasm, then placed a hand on the back of his neck, opened his big mouth and started to laugh.

"Well, I'll be going." He went away still laughing. His departing back was hunched and awkward as if in physical pain.

She went over to the window again and contemplated her own heartbeats and her own unuttered cries ringing out beyond it. She had to narrow her eyes in the midsummer light.

It was after eleven o'clock when Atsushi finally showed up the next day. Having packed, dressed Akira, and settled the bill, Takiko was sitting on Akira's bed with nothing to do but keep him entertained while she waited.

Akira was repeatedly grasping the railing and pulling himself up, letting go and plumping down heavily with a grimace, then getting to his feet again.

"You needn't be afraid. There's nothing to be afraid of."

Takiko was amusing herself watching his movements. He seemed less worried by the incision than by a fear of standing on his own legs. From his point of view, that would be an unaccountable, impossible event. It must also be a very compelling one, however, for laughing and crying by turns he went on doggedly trying to do without support until he was upright for a count of three, and then five.

When Atsushi came up to the bed, Takiko burst out excitedly: "Look! He can stand! Show Uncle, Akira. Go on, do it one more time."

Akira sat stolidly on the bed and laughed, looking back and forth at their faces.

"What, you're not going to do it now that Uncle's here to see?" Takiko pouted in disappointment.

"Silly, why not let him take his time at home? Come on, let's go. You're ready, aren't you?" Atsushi said briskly.

He took the two large carrier bags; Takiko took Akira, and bowed her head to the others in the room as they went out into the corridor.

"It's mighty hot outside. You'd be better off staying here."

Atsushi's face certainly looked as though he'd had all the heat he could stand. Takiko noticed the big patch of sweat staining the back of his short-sleeved shirt.

"You do look hot. It's kind of scary."

Retrieving their sandals from the shoe locker at the end of the corridor, they took the elevator down. The lobby was still bustling with the morning's outpatients. Atsushi held the heavy glass door open for her at the entrance. Takiko glowered at the summer sunlight whose dazzle filled her view, then plunged out into it.

Holding her breath, she descended the gently sloping drive-way under the scorching sun. The gate gave onto a bus route, a broad, steep street. The strong summer light seemed grad-ually to loosen the stiffness of her body, grown completely accustomed to air conditioning.

Takiko stopped when she reached the road, rearranged Akira in her arms, and looked around at as much of the hot sky as she could see from there. Her body was in the midst of mid-summer. After taking a deep breath, she started down the slope.